Praise for the a
Nicky and Noah

"Joe Cosentino has a unique and fabulous gift. His writing is flawless, and his use of farce, along with his convoluted plot-lines, will have you guessing until the very last page, which makes his books a joy to read. His books are worth their weight in gold, and if you haven't discovered them yet you are in for a rare treat." — *Divine Magazine*

"a combination of Laurel and Hardy mixed with Hitchcock and *Murder She Wrote*...Loaded with puns and one-liners...Right to the end, you are kept guessing, and the conclusion still has a surprise in store for you." — *Optimumm Book Reviews*

"adventure, mystery, and romance with every page....Funny, clever, and sweet....I can't find anything not to love about this series....This read had me laughing and falling in love....Nicky and Noah are my favorite gay couple." — *Urban Book Reviews*

"For fans of Joe Cosentino's hilarious mysteries, this is another vintage story with more cheeky asides and sub plots right left and centre....The story is fast paced, funny and sassy. The writing is very witty with lots of tongue-in-cheek humour....Highly recommended." — *Boy Meets Boy Reviews*

"This delightfully sudsy, colorful cast of characters would rival that of any daytime soap opera, and the character exchanges are rife with sass, wit and cagey sarcasm....As the pages turn quickly, the author keeps us hanging until the startling end." — *Edge Media Network*

# Books by Joe Cosentino

<u>The Nicky and Noah Comedy Mystery Series:</u>
*Drama Queen*
*Drama Muscle*
*Drama Cruise*
*Drama Luau*
*Drama Detective*
*Drama Fraternity* (coming soon)
*Drama Castle* (coming soon)
*Drama Dance* (coming soon)

<u>The Cozzi Cove series (NineStar Press):</u>
*Cozzi Cove: Bouncing Back*
*Cozzi Cove: Moving Forward*
*Cozzi Cove: Stepping Out*
*Cozzi Cove: New Beginnings*

<u>The Dreamspinner Press novellas:</u>
*In My Heart: An Infatuation & A Shooting Star*
*The Naked Prince and Other Tales from Fairyland*
Bobby and Paolo Holiday Stories: *A Home for the Holidays* and *The Perfect Gift*

<u>The Jana Lane Mysteries:</u>
*Paper Doll*
*Porcelain Doll* (The Wild Rose Press)
*Satin Doll* (The Wild Rose Press)
*China Doll* (The Wild Rose Press)
*Rag Doll* (The Wild Rose Press)

# Drama
# Muscle

A NICKY AND NOAH MYSTERY

## Joe Cosentino

Cover art by Jesús Da Silva
Nicky & Noah Logo by Holly McCabe
Cover and interior design by Fred Wolinsky

★

To Fred for everything,
and to everyone who inhabits the
world of bodybuilding as a
participant or spectator.

# Cast of Characters

**THEATRE PROFESSORS AT TREEMEADOW COLLEGE:**

Nicky Abbondanza
*Professor of Play Directing*

Noah Oliver
*Professor of Acting*

Martin Anderson
*Professor of Theatre Management/ Theatre Department Head*

**THEATRE OFFICE ASSISTANT:**

Shayla Johnson

**THEATRE STUDENT:**

Jimmy Saline

**BODYBUILDING PROFESSORS:**

Brick Strong
*Department Head of Bodybuilding*

Van Granite
*Professor of Bodybuilding*

Cheryl Stryker
*Professor of Bodybuilding*

Edwin Pyuun
*Dean of Physical Education*

**BODYBUILDING STUDENTS:**

Rodney Towers (*Zeus*)

Maria Ruiz (*Athena*)

Tim and Kim Sim (*Hercules and Adonis*)

Jonathan Toner (*Achilles*)

Mack Heath (*Ganymede*)

Jillian Flowers (*Aphrodite*)

**GYM FACILITIES MANAGER:**

Tony Piccolo

**HUMAN RESOURCES:**

Micky Minor

**ADMISSIONS:**

Abigail Strong

**CAFETERIA:**

Sue Heath

**HEALTH-FOOD STORE CLERK:**

Carob

**DETECTIVE:**

Jose Manuello

**NOAH'S PARENTS:**

Bonnie and Scott Oliver

**MARTIN'S HUSBAND:**

Ruben Markinson

**WE'LL NEVER TELL:**

Dick Danghammer
*Police Officer*

Marvin Meekbottom
*Undertaker*

# Chapter One

As the ethereal sound of horns parted the heavenly clouds, the young gods and goddesses appeared in a ray of white light. Standing as strong as the stone columns behind them, the deities displayed stunning muscles, colossal beauty, and mammoth ambition housed in the smallest and most seductive of white garments. Lightning flashed as they formed a resilient line and each struck their first flawless pose. Zeus was dark-skinned and as powerful as thunder. Ganymede at his side had skin of white porcelain and a clever stare. Hercules and Adonis were the perfect blend of masculine vigor and physical splendor. Athena was a gorgeous, olive-skinned warrior, and Aphrodite a lovely, fair-skinned temptress. Achilles watched them all, vowing to be victorious in the end.

"Good work, everyone!"

That was me, Nicky Abbondanza, Professor of Directing at Treemeadow College, a white-stone Edwardian-style private college in the quaint and picturesque village of Treemeadow in the equally quaint and picturesque state of Vermont. As inscribed on the two bronze statues at the college's entrance, the college's name comes from its founders, Harold Tree and Jacob Meadow. Tree and Meadow were madly wealthy, madly generous, and madly in love. The old gents would no doubt be proud to know that Noah Oliver (Professor of Acting) and I have become a current generation couple at Treemeadow College. That's not to say Noah and I look anything like our college's founders. We aren't made of bronze for one. We wear dress shirts, slacks, and blazers in the fall season rather than heavy dark suits. Also, the Treemeadows were small, thin, scholarly types. Noah and I are both tall. I am of the dark hair, long sideburns, Roman nose, pumped body (thanks to the gym on campus) variety. Oh, there's one other small thing. Well, it's not really small. To the delight or horror of my past boyfriends, I have a nine-and-a-quarter-inch penis—flaccid. Luckily, Noah is delighted and totally open (pardon the pun) to new adventures. Noah has luxurious curly-blond hair, batting blue eyes, and the warmest heart in New England. His body is firm and smooth, but not toned as he never goes near the gym—until now!

Each year the top students in the Bodybuilding Department compete in a contest to be named the Top Toned Tan Trojan at Treemeadow (Try saying that three times fast). Actually, the real name is Treemeadow's Annual Bodybuilding Competition. The winner receives an enormous gold cup, and more importantly, the year's college tuition free. Given the rising cost of tuition at Treemeadow, this is no lightweight matter (pardon the pun again).

Bodybuilding Department Head Professor Brick Strong asked my Theatre Department Head, Martin Anderson, if Noah and I could use our theatrical expertise to add a dramatic flair to this year's bodybuilding competition. Since I was not directing a play that semester, Martin agreed to give Noah and me release time, thereby changing our mantra from "Let's put on a show" to "I'm gonna pump you up." That led to Noah and me hauling lighting, smoke, sound, and set equipment, along with a number of skimpy Greek period costumes, from the Theatre Department building to the Physical Education building. The plan was that I, as a directing professor, would direct the production, and Noah, as an acting professor, would work with the student-athletes on stage presence for their individual poses.

"Okay everyone, Professor Oliver will take it from here." I stepped aside and leaned against the gym wall.

Noah flicked back his gorgeous blond locks and took my place in front of the students like a new king taking the throne after a revolution. Sounding delectably butch, he said, "Let's take a little time to discuss each of your characters. The Greek period was a—"

"That's the period we've selected for the competition in terms of characters, set, and costumes," I said.

Noah smiled in my direction.

I think Noah and I are the perfect couple. "Rodney, we know that your character, Zeus, was the father of gods and men—" Rodney Towers was tall, dark, and massive with muscle. "—which is why your toga has a thunderbolt on it," I said.

Noah stiffened.

"I'm always happy to help," I said.

"So I see."

"But Professor Oliver is totally in charge now. So everyone, please listen to Professor Oliver," I said.

"Thank you." Focusing back on Zeus, rather Rodney, Noah said, "The Greek gods in mythology were part god and part human—"

"Which is why I selected this motif for the competition. You all have human emotion, but your strength and powers are supernatural."

"Right," said Noah with a tight jaw.

I folded my arms across my chest. "Professor Oliver is really good at working on character development, so pay close attention to him."

Noah took in a deep breath. "And the Greek gods were quite amorous—"

"With both sexes," I said. "Zeus and Ganymede were just one pair of famous lovers who influenced the arts."

"Excuse me, everyone." Noah put a hand on my shoulder and ushered me to a corner of the gym. "Nicky, I appreciate your help, but—"

I put my arm around Noah. "You don't need to thank me. I love you, and I am *always* here to help you."

"Well can you please...*stop*?"

"Did I say something wrong?" I asked dumbfounded.

"I would like to be able to finish a sentence! Will you let me do that?"

"Of course."

"Thank you."

"I won't say another word," I said as we walked back to the students.

"Promise?" Noah whispered in my ear.

"Of course." I looked at my watch. "You should move the rehearsal along, since there's lots more to do."

Noah opened his mouth to say something, but Rodney Towers interrupted. "Professor, I was thinking about what Professor Abbondanza mentioned."

Noah sighed. "Which of the numerous things said by Professor Abbondanza are you referring to, Rodney?"

"The thing about Zeus and Ganymede getting it on." Rodney looked as if someone had held his nose and poured vinegar into his mouth.

Noah tried to speak again, and Maria Ruiz (our Athena) interrupted. "Homophobe anyone?" Maria stood nose to nose with Rodney. "What's wrong with you, Rodney?" She pointed to the twins at the other end of the line. "Tim and Kim are playing Hercules and Adonis. Everyone knows they were a couple. You don't hear them complaining."

"Um now that you like mention it, Kim would rather, you know, play another part," said Tim.

"Um so would Tim," added Kim.

Posed with their hands on their hips, the twins looked like an advertisement for *The King and I* in double vision.

Let me explain. Kim and Tim Sim (Try saying that three times fast), as identical twins, can read each other's minds. I could never read my brother's mind when we were kids. That's why I had to read his diary, listen in on his phone conversations, and bug his book bag.

The muscles on Rodney's massive back curled as if snarling. "Let me make myself clear, Maria. I'm not happy playing Zeus, because I don't want any part of an *unnatural* lifestyle."

Maria shot him dagger eyes. "And pumping iron three hours a day and spray-painting our bodies is *natural*?"

"Maria knows all about being *natural*. Don't you, Maria?"

said compact Jonathan Toner (Achilles) with a smirk on his pimply face.

"Shut up, Jonathan," replied Maria as if swatting a pesky fly.

Rodney said to his workout partner, "Maria, don't rag on me because I believe in the Bible."

"Then you better get to work in the fields, 'cause you're a slave, honey," Maria answered with a wave of her muscular arm and snap of her strong fingers.

"Kiss my muscular black ass."

"Kiss my muscular Latina ass."

Noah said, like a referee at an A.D.D. Little League game, "Okay, let's talk about your character, Maria. Athena was the goddess of wisdom, courage, and justice. As you think about your poses —"

"Try to incorporate those feelings into your performance," I said.

"Right," Noah added with narrowed eyes in my direction.

I mimed buttoning my lips and rested my back against the wall.

Noah continued, "And Jonathan, Achilles was shot in the heel, the only weak part of his body."

"Hence the term 'Achilles heel,'" I added, then placed my hand over my big mouth.

Jonathan flexed his small, high-peaked biceps. "There's no part of *me* that's weak."

"Except your brain," said Maria.

Waving his stubby finger under her square jaw, Jonathan said, "Careful, Maria. You don't want to piss *me* off."

Like a substitute teacher on the last day of school, Noah tried to keep control. Noticing Mack Heath (Ganymede) standing quietly, Noah said, "Let's talk about Mack's character."

Middle weight, fair, perfectly proportioned, and amazingly cut, Mack said, "Didn't Ganymede represent youth and beauty?"

"Correct!" I said then covered my mouth with both

hands.

Jillian Flowers (our Aphrodite), a raving blonde beauty, gazed at Mack with lust in her violet eyes. "You um totally are like Ganymede, Mack."

Mack's cheeks grew flushed. "Thanks."

"For what?" Jillian asked.

"You just said I'm like Ganymede."

Jillian said, "Um isn't that like who you are, you know, playing?"

Poor Jillian. Last year, while working out, a barbell accidentally fell on Jillian's head, leaving her with poor short-term memory.

"Let's talk about your character, Jillian," said Noah, clearly hoping to get things back on track. "Aphrodite is the goddess of beauty —"

"And love," I added, then hid my face underneath my blazer.

Jillian batted her long lashes at Mack, then rested her strong hand on his mountainous shoulder. "Did um Aphrodite and Ganymede ever like, you know, hook up?"

"No, they didn't, Jillian." Mack slid his shoulder out of her clutches.

"Who didn't what?" asked Jillian in confusion.

"Aphrodite and Ganymede were never a couple," Mack explained, then walked away.

Jillian responded, "Who said they were?"

"Tim is like getting, you know, bored," said Kim.

"Kim um wants to like get back to, you know, rehearsing," added Tim.

Having lost his patience, Jonathan walked past each of his classmates with a smirk on his pockmarked face, like a carnival sharpshooter wiping out a row of rubber duckies. "Jillian, Mack isn't into you. Mack isn't into anybody, except Mack. Tim and Kim, you don't need this competition. Stay home and wait for Daddy Big Bucks Sim to kick the chop suey. Maria, you don't want to tick me off, and you know why. Rodney, join the twentieth century."

Before World War Muscle broke out, Noah said, "All

right, everyone. Let's make a circle on the gym floor to do a theatre exercise called Tug of War."

After the mime exercise, Noah decided to work on individual posing routines. He asked Rodney and Maria to come on stage, and the rest of the students to take a twenty minute break.

I said to Noah, "Great idea to work with them two at a time. I'll help you — "

Noah walked me into a corridor off the gym. "Nicky?"

"Yes?"

He looked at me with soft blue eyes and rested his arms around my shoulders. "Do you love me?"

"I love you more than life itself."

His soft, warm lips met mine. "If you want to keep your life and love, go get a snack and come back in twenty minutes." Noah kissed me. "Make that thirty."

I entered the snack bar in the Student Union building and found Jonathan and the unhappy Sim twins changed into their street clothes and sitting at a booth near the door. I joined the three young men as Helga served them their usual two pounds of (thankfully cooked) hamburger — each. Helga's real name is Sarah Peterson, but since she is a full-figured German woman with blonde hair worn in side braids, the students all call her Helga.

After Helga banged down the plates, then left for "a cigarette break," I said, "I'm looking forward to the competition, guys."

"Um so are we," Tim and Kim said, then downed their hamburger meat like cavemen.

Jonathan picked at his meat, then picked at a pimple. "Tim, are you meeting with your...advisor after rehearsal?"

"Why would Tim be like meeting with, you know, Professor Granite so like late?" asked Kim.

"Maybe to talk about Professor Granite's vote in the competition." Jonathan poured the salt from the salt shaker into the pepper shaker then added with a sneer, "Will you be meeting with Professor Stryker after the rehearsal, Kim, to talk about *her* vote?"

"Kim doesn't like meet with his, you know, advisor at like night either," said Tim.

I laughed. "Only theatre faculty are crazy enough to be on campus this late at night."

Pushing away his half-eaten plate, Jonathan said, "Since you two guys are free after rehearsal, let's hang."

"We don't think so," said Tim.

Jonathan sneered. "You may want to rethink that, guys."

Putting my size-ten foot in my mouth, I said, "Jonathan, it sounds like you are threatening them."

As if reincarnating Eddie Haskell, Jonathan said with a sweet smile, "I would never threaten one of my classmates, Professor." He turned to the twins. "Right, guys?"

The twins nodded and continued ravaging their meat.

Tired of the smell of red meat and testosterone, I excused myself and walked over to the counter to purchase a cup of tea from a student aide. After checking my watch and realizing I still had some time to kill (or Noah would kill *me*), I sat down at a booth to drink my tea. I heard familiar voices behind me and realized they belonged to Mack and Jillian, who were, by the smell of it, devouring enormous turkey breasts.

Jillian asked between bites, "Um do you like mind, you know, sitting with me, Mack?"

"No."

Just as I was about to find another booth, Jillian asked, "How do you like think um rehearsals are, you know, going?"

I listened like a priest in a confessional with a gay porn star.

Ever the diplomat, Mack answered while chewing, "Professor Oliver has a lot of patience."

Jillian giggled. "Especially with Professor Abbondanza."

I realized that if I moved slightly—balancing on one hip and contorting my body in a right angle—I could see their reflection in the mirror, but they couldn't see me.

"Mack, you like looked really um good up there. You are like incredibly toned."

"Thanks, Jillian."

"Mack, you like looked really um good up there. You are like incredibly toned," Jillian repeated.

Mack responded gently, "You already said that, Jillian."

She smacked her pale forehead. "Um sorry."

"No problem," said Mack.

*They say love is better the second time around.*

Jillian continued in adoration. "You um look even better than Tony Piccolo's silly old pictures of his son. You're, you know, a sure like bet to win the, you know, competition, Mack."

He rested his perfect arms on the table. "According to Jonathan Toner, Professor Strong favors *you* to win."

Jillian rolled her eyes as if high tide. "Don't like listen to anything *Jonathan* says. I, you know, think Professor Strong will vote for *you* to win."

"I hope this doesn't upset you, Jillian," said Mack. "Jonathan is telling everyone that you and Professor Strong are...*hooking up.*"

Laughing, Jillian fidgeted with the flower design on her T-shirt. "That's like crazy. Professor Strong is, you know, an old man. He was like once married to Professor Stryker. He um must be like over thirty-five."

*Heaven forbid!*

"If I was like going to make a play for like a professor, it, you know, would be like that hot theatre professor."

*I always liked Jillian.*

"Um Professor Oliver. But he's like obviously, you know, partnered with um Professor Abbondanza. They must like have an um father/son kind of, you know, relationship."

*I'm only five years older than Noah! Well, seven. But who's counting?*

Having finished her meal, Jillian pressed her firm breasts against Mack's pectoral muscles. "I have my um eyes, you know, on a *younger* man."

Mack asked, "Who?"

"Who like what?" asked Jillian.

"You just said you have your eyes on a young man."

"Oh." Jillian pressed her sculpted thighs (housed in pink short-shorts) against his. "I um think you like know who it is."

Blushing, Mack took her hand in his. "I'm flattered, really." After a long swallow of his saliva, he said, "I don't feel that way about you. I'm sorry, but I never will."

Jillian looked like a beagle left out in the snow. "Is it um because of the like memory thing?"

"No." Mack pushed away his empty plate.

"No like what?"

"You asked me if I'm not interested in you because of your short-term memory lapses from the barbell accident. I said that isn't it."

"So if it's...um not that...what's like wrong with me, Mack?" she asked with tears brimming in her almond-shaped eyes.

"You're terrific. It's me."

"Are you like gay?" she asked, disappointed.

*That woke me up!*

After a long exhale, Mack said, "The truth is I'm not attracted to anybody. It's been that way for as long as I can remember."

*Poor kid. He just hasn't met the right man yet.*

Mack shrugged his massive shoulders. "Maybe I'm asexual." His perfectly sculpted body tensed like an accordion. "Jonathan is the only one I've told...besides you."

"Told what?" Jillian asked in oblivion.

Mack repeated, "I've only told Jonathan that I think I'm asexual."

Her button nose crinkled. "You um think you're like asexual, and you told *that* creep?"

He nodded. "Jonathan wanted to fix me up with some girl in his acting class." Mack laughed pathetically. "He was going to charge her money to date me. Crazy, huh?"

From the look on Jillian's face, I could tell she wasn't thinking the idea was all that far-fetched. She took his hand and placed it on her lap. "Mack, um if there is like ever anything that I can, you know, do to like help you sort this out, I am like *totally* available."

★

By the time I got back to the gym, Rodney and Maria were taking their break, and Noah was working with the Sim twins and Jonathan Toner. I started over to help Noah.

"Hey, Professor!" A man of about sixty years old, wearing sweat clothes laden with the college logo, motioned me over to an alcove at a corner of the gym. I walked over to the short, emaciated man. He sat at a desk surrounded by washing machines, dryers, and athletic equipment. As I stood next to him and looked up at the bulletin board above his desk, I was mesmerized by pictures of a stunning young bodybuilder in briefs executing various competitive poses. In the last picture, the young man, rightfully so, held a huge winning cup.

"That's my son, Robbie," the man said. "He won Treemeadow's Bodybuilding Competition eighteen years ago."

"I can see why." I couldn't stop looking at the photographs of the young bodybuilder with his perfectly proportioned body, rippling muscles, handsome face, and warm smile. "Where is he now?" *Don't worry, Noah, I'm just looking.*

"Robbie lives in Florida with his wife and two kids. He's a lawyer."

I smiled at the man who seemed to have as many memories as gray hairs on his head. "I'm Nicky Abbondanza from the Theatre Department."

"I know." He shook my hand firmly. "Tony Piccolo. I heard you was coming to help us out with the competition."

I sat on the edge of his desk, and Tony and I were eye to eye. "What do you do here?"

He chuckled. "Everything, launder the kids' clothes so they stay fresh, clean off the weight equipment so the kids don't get sick, restock the supplies so they have all they need, and bring them snacks when they get hungry."

I took in Tony's tired, warm eyes. "That's a lot to do."

He nodded like his head was loose. "I like the kids, Professor. They remind me of Robbie when he was their age. They keep me feeling young."

I was again unable to stop looking at Robbie's pictures on the bulletin board. "I'm not surprised your son did well."

"He was the best bodybuilder ever at Treemeadow College."

*No argument here.*

"And that's saying something." Tony stood next to me and put his wrinkled hand on my shoulder. "They're all terrific kids, Professor. While other students are drinking, drugging, and having orgies, these kids are exercising to stay healthy and fit. I love each one of them as if they was my own." The dark circles under Tony's hazel eyes deepened. "That's why I called you over here." He said as if a secret, "Listen, don't pay no mind to their bickering and complaining. It's all a part of growing up. Even my Robbie complained here and there when he was their age. But deep down, these kids are the best, and they'll come through in the competition."

Shaking his veined hand again, I said, "I wish we had someone like you in the Theatre Department."

"I'm fine right where I am, Professor. My wife died many years ago. Robbie moved away. These kids are my family."

I took a last gaze at the mesmerizing Robbie. "Seems Treemeadow was lucky to have Robbie."

I heard Noah and Jonathan Toner arguing. *My sweet Noah who never loses his temper?*

Tony pointed to Jonathan. "Even that one. He's a little instigator and out for himself, but he don't mean no harm to nobody."

I walked over as Jonathan asked Noah, "Professor, is my posing routine last because the bodybuilding professors told you to feature Tim, Kim, and Jillian before *me*?" He added like a child whose brother received a larger lollipop, "Or am I last in the lineup due to your obvious bias against me?"

Noah replied as if counting to ten, "Jonathan, your

posing routine is last because Achilles is the heel in Greek mythology."

Having none of it, Jonathan rose on his tippy-toes to make eye contact with Noah's chin. "Is that the same reason why I'm *last* in the opening lineup?"

Noah took a deep breath in an unsuccessful effort to calm down. "Actually, Jonathan, it *is* the reason you are last. And for the record, I have no bias against you."

Flailing his arms in Noah's face like a crossing guard at a highway intersection, Jonathan shouted, "If you have no bias against me, Professor Oliver, how do you explain the D grade I got for my monologue presentation in Acting class?"

Noah clasped his hands behind his back, no doubt to keep himself from strangling the young bodybuilder. "I *explained* that by reminding you that during your class monologue performance you forgot your lines, broke character, swore, and spoke so softly you could not be heard past the first row in the lab theatre."

Jonathan responded like a preschool teacher explaining snack time to her charges, "I want to be an action-film star, not a theatre actor. In movies they have microphones for volume, and they do retakes when actors forget lines. Don't you *know* that, Professor?"

"I know a great deal about movies, Jonathan, including that you lack the discipline to be cast in one," replied Noah, obviously at the end of his long rope.

Jonathan looked like a bull in a closet full of red capes. "You'll regret that, Professor."

Hearing all the shouting, Rodney, Maria, Mack, and Jillian came back from their breaks. Rodney said, towering over Jonathan, "Cool down, dude."

Jonathan turned on Rodney. "Or what, Rodney? The Lord will turn me into stone, and I'll resemble *you*?"

Maria stood between Jonathan and Rodney. "Enough, you guys!"

With his green eyes shooting venom like gamma rays, Jonathan said, "Right, Maria, *we're* guys. You were a guy too—when you were Mario and had a dick instead of a slit."

Maria lunged for Jonathan. Rodney held Maria's arms behind her back as Mack pinned Jonathan's hands behind his back.

"I'll take care of you later, Toner," said Maria as she shrugged away Rodney's hold and walked off her anger.

Jonathan screamed, "Let me go, Mack!"

Mack whispered in Jonathan's ear, "You need to calm down for your own good, Jonathan. You don't want to get thrown out of the competition."

Jonathan wiggled in Mack's hold like a wild horse at a rodeo. "I don't buy your good-guy act, Mack."

"Leave Mack like alone!" Jillian said with a no-nonsense look.

"You can defend him from here to Barbell-Brain Land and Mack still won't get it up for you, Jillian," replied Jonathan with his saliva and venom spraying onto Jillian's confused face.

"Um defend like who?" asked Jillian.

Having had enough of the drama (pardon the pun), I said, "All right, everybody. Rehearsal is over for today. Let's work out and regroup *with calmer heads* tomorrow night."

I grabbed Noah by the arm and led him to the door.

"Why didn't you defend me to Jonathan, Nicky?"

"You told me not to say anything at rehearsal."

"I didn't mean if I'm being attacked!"

"Noah, you better go home and cool down."

His beautiful shoulders softened. "Sorry, Nicky. I shouldn't have let Jonathan get to me."

I looked into his baby-blue eyes. "Noah, that kid is toxic. Don't be so hard on yourself."

Noah replied with an adorable smile, "When I'm hard, I'm not by myself."

"Even though my mouth was fatter than a televangelist's wallet tonight?"

"Your fat mouth is perfect for me, Nicky."

We shared a quick but tender kiss.

Noah patted my ample crotch. "And it seems I won't be *by myself* tonight."

24

After another kiss, I opened the door for Noah, and he asked, "Aren't you coming with me?"

"Definitely," I replied grinning from ear to ear, "but I want to do my workout first."

"That's my cue to exit," Noah responded with a wave of his hand.

"You should try working out sometime, Noah. It's good for you. Not that I'm complaining. I love your body." I squeezed his bulbous butt.

He kissed the cleft in my chin. "I get enough work out at home."

I ran my fingers through his blond, curly locks. "You can do squats tonight."

We shared a knowing laugh. Noah left and I popped some vitamins into my mouth (for extra energy), chased them down with water from the cooler, then made my way to the men's locker room, where I was greeted by the familiar smell of sweat, cologne, and sperm. I changed into my sweat clothes, stretched my thirty-five-year-old muscles then headed for the weight room.

At the universal gym, I began pushing and pulling on a torture device for the back and shoulders. Though they were facing away from me, I could overhear Rodney Towers (on a pecs machine) and Maria Ruiz (on a thigh machine) as they worked out.

"Is what that fool Jonathan said about you true?" Rodney asked as he adjusted the pin on his machine upward to Never Never Land.

Defensive, Maria said, "What if it is?"

"If it's true, it's against God."

Maria snapped her legs together on the machine and adjusted her sweatpants. "Who made you God's spokesman?"

"It's right there in the Bible."

*What is this, the Spanish Inquisition?*

Her dark eyes ripped into his. "Rodney, do me a favor and stuff your two thousand-year-old book of fairy tales where the sun don't shine." She rose and began to leave. "I have better things to do than argue with a fool."

Following her, Rodney called out, "You'll burn in Hell for that, Maria."

Having worked my back and shoulders to rebellion, I guzzled some water from the water cooler (and threw in some more vitamins for good measure). Next, I moved over to the free-weights area, where I worked the same two body parts with free weights until I collapsed from exhaustion after the third rep.

My shoulders screamed in agony and warned my giggling pectoral muscles that they would be on the hot seat at my next workout session. On my way to the cardio room for the last phase of my workout, my bladder sounded the alarm, so I decided on a quick pit stop.

As I entered the locker room I heard giggling and moaning coming from the adjoining shower area. Feeling like a voyeur, I ducked behind a locker and snuck a peek. *Where's a bag of popcorn when you need it?*

Kneeling on a bench between the shower stalls, Jonathan Toner was on all fours with Tim Sim standing in front of him and Tim's twin brother, Kim Sim, planted behind him. Tim massaged and squeezed Jonathan's small but potent back muscles while Jonathan stroked Tim's bulbous pectoral muscles and rippling six-pack abs. The stereotype was certainly not true in this case as Jonathan took Tim's substantial tool in his mouth and hungrily licked, slurped, sucked, and joyously gagged on it. At the same time, Kim rubbed Jonathan's small, tight bottom and shapely, rock-hard thighs while Kim's identical tool plunged inside Jonathan again and again, gaining traction and intensity with each thrust. Looking like a pig on a spit, Jonathan squirmed and squealed in delight, begging for more. Finally, the threesome exploded like Hiroshima. Then Tim wiped himself with a towel, Jonathan rinsed his mouth at the sink, and Kim threw his condom into the garbage.

The three young bodybuilders moved to the locker area to get dressed. I darted over to the other side of the locker, but they still spotted me.

"Hello, boys," I said as I leaned into the locker and banged my elbow against it.

"Hi, Professor," the three boys said in unison as they walked by me.

"I just had a great workout, but I really need to use the urinal. That happens when you drink a lot of water, and you should drink a lot of water. Water is very good for you." *I'm babbling like a brook.*

I relieved myself at the urinal in the shower room then left through the locker-room door. The minute I hit the hallway, I realized I had dropped my college ID card. Not wanting to be stopped by Security, I backtracked into the locker room unseen by the three bodybuilding students. Luckily I spotted my card next to a locker. As I bent down and reached for it, from my vantage point the three boys couldn't see me, but I could see them.

Putting on red briefs, Jonathan said, "That was just what I needed to calm me down. Let's plan a return engagement."

*I'll skip the second showing.*

Tim and Kim Sim opened their lockers and slipped into identical blue boxers and button-down blue shirts and slacks. "Um, we don't think so, Jonathan."

Jonathan put on a green and blue polo shirt and jeans, then slammed his locker shut. "What's up, guys?"

*Not much anymore.*

When the twins didn't respond, Jonathan said in a huff, "You can go back to kissing Professor Stryker's ass, Tim. And you can suck Professor Granite's dick, Kim. I'll still beat both of you in the competition."

Kim joined his brother in putting on black loafers, then said like an accountant at an audit, "Jonathan, our father is like very um old world. If he like found out...about us, he would, you know, cut us off."

After slipping on his sneakers, Jonathan put his arms around the twins. "Be that as it may, you boys both *did* what we just...*did.* And since you will be coming into a lot of money soon, I think it's only right that you two share the wealth with your favorite classmate."

Kim's eyes bulged out of his head like torpedoes as he said to his brother, "I like *know* Jonathan is trying to, you know, blackmail us, Tim!"

Jonathan squeezed their powerful shoulders. "Let's just say I'm asking you to spread the wealth a little by donating to my charity."

*Seems like they already donated.*

"The Get Me to Hollywood to Audition for Action Movies Charity," Jonathan added.

"And if we don't like *donate* to your *charity*?" asked the twins with four piercing eyes aimed at Jonathan.

Jonathan responded with a sagacious wink, "Then I'll just have to pay sick Poppy a little visit, and tell him *all* about the titillating time I just had with his twinky twins."

*Try saying that three times fast.*

Pulling out of Jonathan's grasp, Tim said in shock, "Jonathan, even you um wouldn't like do something like that!" Tim added to his brother, "Kim, didn't I like just say that?"

Jonathan scratched his small washboard abs. "Oh, you'd be surprised the things that I would do, Sim. I'll see you tomorrow, guys...to collect the first donation."

Jonathan walked out of the locker room. The Sim twins seethed in anger, engaged in a silent argument.

Realizing that Noah would be worried if I didn't get home soon, I started my delayed cardio exercises on a stationary bicycle in the spinning room. After fifteen minutes, my legs went on strike. So I limped to the next room, deciding to finish my workout with ten minutes on the elliptical machine. As I mounted the last torture device of the evening, I noticed a green and blue polo shirt hanging over the side of a running machine at the other end of the room. Upon investigating, I found it was Jonathan Toner—and he had no pulse.

# Chapter Two

After Detective Manuello interviewed me for two hours at the gym about finding Jonathan Toner, he finally let me go home — with my promise to return the next morning.

Images of Jonathan Toner's lifeless body hanging over the running machine kept me from getting much sleep that night. I purred like a kitten when Noah served us breakfast (blueberry buckwheat pancakes with pecans and vitamins for me) in our four-poster bed on the second floor of our Victorian-style home (owned by the college). Noah jumped back into bed next to me and rested his gorgeous blond locks on my shoulder. I kissed his head and he kissed my neck in return. As we ate, we watched the trees outside our window wave at us with hands the colors of pumpkin, amaranth, crimson, and goldenrod that reflected in the nearby lake.

"I'm not a fan of Jonathan Toner's, but I'm sorry to see him dead," Noah said, unleashing his amazing strawberry scent.

"You may be the only one," I replied, kissing his cheek, then licking off the blueberry stain.

Noah's blue eyes doubled in size. "Do tell!"

"As you know Jonathan spilled the beans about Maria's sexual-reassignment surgery. *And* after their threesome in the shower room, Jonathan threatened to out Tim and Kim Sim to homophobic papa Sim," I said, drinking my orange juice.

Wiping the juice off the cleft in my chin, then kissing it, Noah replied, "It sounds like the bodybuilding students are bigger drama queens than our theatre students."

"Tell me about it." I put my arm around Noah's shapely

shoulders.

Noah rested his back on the carved oak headboard. "With Jonathan obviously not able to compete, who do you think will win the competition?"

"According to Jonathan, the three bodybuilding professors, who will also serve as judges for the competition, support Jillian Flowers, and Tim and Kim Sim." I nuzzled my nose into Noah's neck. "I tell you who I'd pick?"

"Obviously not me since I hate working out."

I kissed his smooth neck. "I'd vote for the son of the old guy who is the gym caretaker. He sure looks striking in his old pictures."

Noah's eyes turned into slits. "Where can I find him?"

Laughing, I replied, "In Florida, married with kids, and probably weighing three hundred pounds."

Noah finished his orange juice, then squeezed my biceps. "You know, Nicky, all this talk about bodybuilders and sex in the showers has me thinking."

I said tongue firmly in cheek (Noah's), "Thinking about what, Noah?"

Noah took my hands and pulled me off the bed. "Oh, I don't know. Maybe about the need for us to check out *our* shower." He ran his long index finger down my chest and stopped at my groin. "To see if it still works."

My penis hardened. "Looks like it still works." I cupped Noah's growing bulge. "And wouldn't you know, yours works too!"

We stripped off our undies and raced into the bathroom, past the clawfoot tub and into the shower stall. Once our bodies were lathered with strawberry soap, Noah and I kissed as our organs engaged in a loving duel. Noah sank to his knees and caressed what he fondly calls "Mr. Mushroom." Unable to wait a moment longer, he took all nine-and-a-quarter inches into his eager mouth, and sucked until his jaw, and my groin, ached with pleasure and eventual release. I knelt down and returned the favor as Noah rubbed his warm hands against my long sideburns and pulled on my hair at just the right moment. Then Noah wrapped his arms around my back and clasped his legs around my hips. I took a condom from inside a large crack in the tiles (thanks, Victorians) and entered him, thrusting like a rodeo rider, until we blissfully ended our early morning refreshment.

A half hour later, Noah and I (wearing dress shirts, chinos, and blazers), stood in the Bodybuilding Department office in front of the department office assistant's desk. We looked at one another in surprise as the gray-haired, elderly woman behind the desk snored loudly, perched over her computer monitor. Professor Van Granite, who was much younger than the office assistant (and me), noticed our confusion.

"Mary has worked in the Physical Education building for fifty-five years," said Granite. He winked at me. "That's twenty years older than you, Nicky!"

"Why doesn't she retire?" I asked.

Granite responded, "Because she gets insomnia at home, and at Mary's age, she needs her sleep." He nudged my side. "Most older people do." Then he hooked his muscular arm with Noah's and stood behind me. "Age before beauty, Professor Abbondanza."

*Luckily for Van Granite, Mary's snoring drowned out my response.*

Department Head Brick Strong's windowless office in the Bodybuilding section of the Physical Education building reminded me of the custodian's office in my grade school. Professor Strong's rickety desk sat between a large drain pipe and an overflowing trash can.

The middle-aged ex-military man ran his thick fingers through his crew cut as he invited each of his guests to sit on rusty metal folding chairs assembled around his desk like cannons surrounding a target. Brick sat behind his desk on an old black chair perched on four squeaky wheels. Clockwise around Professor Strong sat Professor of Bodybuilding Cheryl Stryker, Professor of Bodybuilding Van Granite, my handsome Noah, yours truly, and Detective Manuello.

Though the Bodybuilding faculty wore sweat clothes, the bulges and curves of their formidable muscles were visible through the thick fabric.

Granite cased Noah's body like a photocopy machine, until I caught Granite's eye and he looked away—at my crotch. Then he checked himself out in the mirror on the wall. Obviously liking what he saw, Granite flexed his giant biceps, then ran a hand through his chestnut-brown hair. *If he had been a student in the bodybuilding competition, I would have cast him as Narcissus.*

"Thank you all for coming." Dressed in a wrinkled gray suit, Manuello pulled at one of the folds of flab hanging over his thick belt. "As you know, this meeting is about the death of bodybuilding student Jonathan Toner."

"What do you know so far, Detective?" asked Brick Strong in authority mode.

Manuello rubbed his wide nose. "The cause of death was a heart attack."

Thinking of the numerous muscles on Jonathan's petite frame, I asked, "Did Jonathan Toner die from taking steroids?"

Brick Strong's crew cut nearly hit the moldy light bulb over his head. "Absolutely not! We don't permit our students to use steroids."

"Do you test them?" I asked.

I obviously had hit a nerve.

The department head said, "I say no steroids, and the students know that means *no steroids.*"

"I'll have to try that with *my* students regarding texting during class," I said with a nudge to Noah's arm.

Manuello turned to me in annoyance. "Professor Abbondanza, why are you and Professor Oliver working in this department?"

Since Noah and I helped solve a series of murders in our Theatre Department last academic year, Manuello had a soft spot for us—where he sat.

Noah waved his hands theatrically. "Nicky and I are adding dramatic elements to this year's student bodybuilding competition."

"I'm sure," Manuello answered with eyes raised to his

bushy eyebrows. "The initial toxicology report showed something in Toner's blood. The forensic team is doing further investigation, but they know it isn't steroids or testosterone."

Granite flashed his green eyes. "Is there anything else, Detective?" Glancing again at his reflection in the mirror, he added, "I'd like to fit in a workout before my morning class." His gigantic pectoral muscles contracted under his skintight green sweatshirt as Granite said to Noah, "Care to join me, Professor Oliver?"

"Noah doesn't like working out," I explained with dagger eyes aimed at Granite.

Granite responded as if helping himself to sloppy seconds, "How about you, Abbondanza?"

After removing Granite's thick hand from my arm, and lifting his chin from staring at my crotch, I answered, "I prefer to do my workouts *alone*."

"Which is how it came about that Professor Abbondanza found Jonathan Toner last evening," Manuello said getting us back on track. "Toner's parents want his body flown to them in Montana after the full coroner's report. While we wait, do any of you have any information that might be of help? We know Toner had no history of heart disease. But what about his recent state of mind? Is there anyone who might want to hurt him?"

"Detective," said Cheryl Stryker, "I don't know if this has anything to do with his death, but Jonathan has been training quite hard this semester."

"Why is that?" asked Manuello.

"I think it was because Jonathan was jealous of Jillian Flowers," Cheryl answered.

"Why was Jonathan jealous of Jillian?" I asked as Manuello raised his dark eyes to the cracks in the ceiling.

Cheryl answered, "Jonathan thought Brick had a *personal interest* in Jillian winning the competition."

"That isn't true, and you know it, Cheryl!" Brick Strong rose from his chair like a lawyer issuing a courtroom objection. "I've complimented Jillian and Mack a lot lately, because they've worked hard and made good progress. As a judge in the bodybuilding competition, I will be completely impartial." He added to Granite and Cheryl, "I hope you will be too."

Granite rested his powerful hand on Noah's knee, and whispered, "Cheryl favors Tim Sim. Tim's twin Kim is my bet to win the competition."

I removed Granite's hand from Noah's lap.

Manuello asked, "Anything else, Professor Stryker?"

Cheryl nodded. "Jonathan was a good student, and a good bodybuilder, but unfortunately he wasn't always a very good person."

Manuello took out his pad and pencil. "Can you elaborate, Professor?"

Sitting at the edge of her seat (and no doubt using her strong abdominal muscles to stay on the lightweight chair), Cheryl responded, "Jonathan was a bit...self-involved."

"I hate that in a guy," Granite said while checking himself out in the mirror.

Cheryl continued cautiously. "Jonathan wasn't always very...nice to the other students."

"I can attest to that."

"Can you be more specific, Professor Abbondanza?" asked Manuello.

I explained, "At the rehearsal last night, Jonathan outed Maria Ruiz as a transsexual. And after rehearsal, Jonathan tried to blackmail the Sim brothers."

"About what?" asked Manuello while scribbling like a doctor writing a prescription.

*How do I put this delicately?* "It was a *personal* matter between them, Detective."

Manuello asked, "Was Jonathan gay?"

"Hardly!" Brick Strong responded with a glance at Cheryl. Then he sat back down in his chair with a squeak. "Jonathan was dating our daughter."

*So Jonathan had a beard.*

"*Our* daughter?" asked Manuello.

Cheryl explained, "Brick and I are married...*were*

married. Jonathan was dating our daughter, Abigail."

"Until recently," said Brick bitterly.

"When Jonathan broke things off," added Cheryl.

"How can I reach your daughter?" Manuello asked.

Cheryl answered, "Abigail works in the Student Admissions Office at the college."

Manuello jotted down a note. "This isn't a murder investigation at this time, but I will be speaking to everyone involved with the deceased to ascertain their whereabouts last night."

Van Granite ran a comb through his wavy hair. "We were all in our offices, Detective."

"In the evening?" asked Manuello.

Strong explained, "Our department's new equipment purchase requisitions are due to the dean soon. We were each compiling our list."

I said, "I was working out, as you know, Detective."

Manuello turned to Noah. "And you, Professor?"

"I was at home, alone," Noah responded matter-of-factly.

"*Your* home or Professor Abbondanza's home?" asked Manuello with a dash of homophobia for bad measure.

Noah's wide back straightened. "As of the end of last semester, my home *is* Professor Abbondanza's home, Detective. Is there a problem with that?"

*Not in this state.*

"Actually, there *is* a problem involving you, Professor Oliver." Manuello flipped through his notepad.

That caught my attention.

Manuello scratched at the layers of fat surrounding his waist. "Before his death, Jonathan Toner filed a sexual-harassment complaint against you."

Noah's eyes bulged out of his head like waterfalls. "What!"

"Your department head has the paperwork," added Manuello.

I leapt to my feet as if my chair was on fire. "Noah, we need to talk to Martin right away!"

Noah and I hurried out of Strong's office, and headed for

our refuge from the storm.

★

"Toner was angry because Noah gave him a bad monologue performance grade in acting class—which Jonathan deserved!"

"That's what I assumed, Nicky," Martin Anderson said like a mental health worker trying to calm down a manic patient.

Noah, Martin, and I were seated on tall leather chairs next to Martin's cherry wood fireplace mantel. Melon-colored monogrammed napkins rested on our laps, and three china cups filled with steaming cocoa were perched on the cherry wood end table. As usual Shayla Johnson, Martin's sassy office assistant, was stationed at the crack in Martin's office doorway to ensure she heard every word that was said inside.

Our father-figure and Theatre Department head adjusted his melon-colored bowtie and sweater vest then rested his tiny hand on Noah's tense shoulder. "Besides, given the fact that Jonathan Toner is...deceased, his complaint will obviously go nowhere."

Noah and I breathed a joint sigh of relief, nearly causing the fire to go out in the fireplace.

"So, tell me, how are things going over in the Physical Education building?" asked Martin with a concerned look in his aging eyes.

I took a sip of cocoa. Noah wiped the mustache off my upper lip. "Noah and I have added dramatic touches to the bodybuilding competition, but the bodybuilding students seem to have enough drama of their own."

A devoted gossip, Martin slid to the edge of his chair like a priest at new altar boy training. "Do tell, Nicky!"

I explained, "Jonathan Toner was blackmailing Kim and Tim Sim to keep silent about their sexual orientation to big bucks papa Sim. Toner was also jealous of the department head's attention to students Jillian Flowers and Mack Heath."

"Not to mention Professor Granite's and Professor Stryker's support of the Sim twins," added Noah.

"And now Jonathan Toner is dead." Martin seemed lost in the amber flames. Then looking at Noah and me, he added, "It seems like Holmes and Watson will have an encore performance."

I explained, "Manuello won't know if it's murder until he gets the full toxicology report."

Martin nodded. "Well, while you two boys are here, I have a favor to ask you."

"Does it involve adding dramatic touches to the Math Matters Contest?" Noah asked with his dimples on luscious display.

Martin smiled and patted Noah's knee. "This request is a lot closer to home. The college is throwing a dinner in honor of your ancient department head's forty years of service at the college."

"Congratulations, Martin!" Noah and I said in unison.

"Oh dear, together only a few months and you are sounding alike," Martin said with a proud wink. "Anyway, the president will make a speech, meaning the president of the college, not of the US."

"We got that," we replied in unison again!

"And she has asked that, in addition to the Dean of Faculty, I ask a member of my department to say a few words. Will you do me the honor, Nicky?"

I blinked back tears. "I'd love to, Martin. Thank you for asking me."

Martin looked at me like a grandfather at a bris. "Thank *you*, Nicky." He patted his eyes with his napkin. "It means a great deal to me."

"You've mentored and supported me for years, Martin. This is the least I can do," I said, accompanied by Noah's fierce head nodding.

"Is Ruben able to come?" asked Noah, the romantic.

"He'd better!" Martin answered with a wink.

Martin's husband, Ruben Markinson, is the head of a large gay rights organization and the other father to their two grown daughters.

"Well, we should all get back to work." Martin put his

arms around us and walked us to the door. "Be careful, you two. And tell me everything!"

In the outer office, Shayla's dark skin highlighted the earth tones on her sweater. She sounded like a mother hen talking to her lost chicks. "How are my two favorite lovebirds?"

I said, "It seems like we may have another adventure on our hands, Shayla."

Noah added, "And the next chapter is set for tonight in the Physical Education building."

*We are finishing each other's sentences now too?*

"Well, solve it fast and come back home to us in the Theatre Department!"

"Yes, Shayla," Noah and I said in unison as we each kissed one of her cheeks.

Noah and I taught our classes (Noah — Acting II, me — Directing I), then graded papers and answered emails during our office hour before heading home for dinner.

Sitting in our Victorian-style dining room with its thick wainscoting, stone fireplace, comfy window seat, rose-patterned wallpaper, and long wooden table, I felt like the lead in a 1940s domestic comedy. Noah and I looked out the bay window, past our white picket fence and trellis, at the amber, crimson, and maize-colored mountains in the distance under the clear blue sky.

I squeezed Noah's hand as we ate his delicious gouda and nut-encrusted (for me) salmon, quinoa pasta with green pepper sauce, and vegetable medley. We both ate quickly, then drove to the Physical Education building for rehearsal (as I swallowed vitamins along the way).

When we got to the gym, Noah set up the columns, cloud flats, smoke machine, and lighting equipment while I rallied the six student finalists (all texting). As the cast members hustled into the locker rooms to get into their Greek god or goddess costume, I noticed Tony Piccolo sitting at his desk in the supply area with his hands covering his face. I walked over and peeked my head inside.

"Everything okay, Tony?"

The elderly man quickly wiped his hazel eyes with the loose sweatshirt covering his emaciated upper body. "Hiya, Professor. Another rehearsal tonight?"

"Yes, the first without Jonathan."

Tears dropped onto dark circles under Tony's tired eyes. "I can't believe he's gone."

I walked in and rested a hand on Tony's bony shoulder. "It was quite a shock."

He nodded sadly, and said embarrassed, "I must seem like an old fool."

Smiling, I replied, "You seem like a nice guy with a good heart, Tony."

"They may not be perfect, but I love each one of them kids, Professor. Always have. Always will."

Unable to stop myself, I looked up at the pictures of Tony's son on the bulletin board, marveling at the young bodybuilder's poses for the Treemeadow competition eighteen years ago. Staring at the tanned young man in his briefs, I couldn't help but gape at the kid's chiseled, handsome face, perfectly muscled body, and the majestic, inviting glow in his hazel eyes, so much like his father's. I'd never been so taken with someone in a picture before, and to be honest, it started to concern me.

"Does your son still do bodybuilding, Tony?"

Tony waved an arthritic hand. "Nah, he's too busy in Florida defending poor people charged with crimes they didn't commit, so the politicians look good to the top one-percenters who own them."

I couldn't stop staring at the pictures. "He was really something."

"That he was."

Noah called me, and I leapt away from the pictures like Bert and Mary Poppins. "Duty calls, Tony."

"Have a good rehearsal, Professor."

I began the rehearsal by giving a short tribute speech to Jonathan Toner (lucky for me I'm in the theatre—the world of illusion). The students didn't seem particularly choked up about Jonathan either. So I re-staged the opening sequence sans Jonathan. With the six students in their skimpy Greek costumes, I could see all of their hours in the gym were paying off. As their shaved and oiled muscles ripped, pulsated, and glowed around the set, I turned to Noah and said, "Amazing, aren't they?"

Noah squeezed my arm and whispered in my ear, "This is the only muscle for me."

Feeling guilty about gazing at young Robbie Piccolo's pictures, I kissed Noah on the cheek, and whispered back, "That's not the only muscle for you tonight."

We shared a knowing giggle, then I asked Noah to work with the students on their individual poses. After threatening to put tape over my mouth if I opened it, Noah did a good job working one-on-one with the young bodybuilders to bring out their individual personalities, characters, charisma, and stage dynamics as they executed their godlike poses.

Since Noah didn't need me, I decided to stretch my legs. Okay, I eavesdropped on the students' conversations during their breaks. After all, there was a possible murder to solve, not to mention gossip to gather for Martin.

In one corner of the gym, I pretended to tie my shoelace (though I was wearing loafers) behind a bench and heard the Sims in a heated psychic twins' exchange.

"That's like true, Kim, but why do you like care?" asked Tim Sim with his large hand resting on the gym wall behind his brother's head. After a pause, Tim continued. "Yes, I like know Poppy is, you know, your father too, and he got a bad report from the doctor, Kim." Kim dodged his brother, and Tim added rolling his dark eyes, "Oh, please! You never like paid any attention to Poppy!"

Kim paused, then glared at his brother. "Yes it um is *so* like true, Tim. Poppy never paid any attention to *me*!"

Tim grabbed his brother's powerful arm. "Yes, but um why do you, you know, think that *is*, Kim?" After a tense pause, Tim shouted, "No like way! *That* um is like a lie, Kim, and you like *know* it!"

*This is like hearing one side of a telephone conversation.*

"Hah! Are you like telling me you um never like kissed

Poppy's, you know, ass, Tim?" After a pregnant pause, Kim added in a rage, "You like liar! I like *do not*, you know, kiss every guy's ass at this college!" A beat later, Kim pushed his brother. "Are you like kidding me? Tim, I um dare you to like think that again!"

Tim laughed sarcastically. "Right like back at you, brother." Tim pushed Kim up against the wall, then said inches away from Kim's face, "Oh, like no you don't. You like can't worm your way into Poppy's heart *and* into his pockets by being like nice to him now that he's, you know, moving into hospice care."

Kim pushed his brother away.

Tim screamed, "I can't um believe you just, you know, thought that, you like heartless prick!"

After a few beats, Kim cried, "How could you like *think* that, you um selfish bitch!" Tears brimmed in Kim's enraged eyes. "The um wrong member of our family is like dying!" Following a pause, Kim added, "No, I will *never* forgive you for like thinking that, Tim!"

As the twins continued to argue like mediums in a Shakespearean tragedy, I moved on to the weight room, where Rodney Towers and Maria Ruiz were stretching out on a mat. I mimed taking an urgent call on my cell phone behind the water cooler and listened to them.

Rodney's V-shaped back was on display as he sat reaching over to touch his toes. Maria, spread-eagle, was doing the same nearby.

"Too bad about Toner, huh?" Rodney said, breaking the silence.

Maria placed her hands on the soles of her feet and pulled her chest to her knees. "Aren't you going to gloat that Jonathan is in Hell?"

Rodney sat on the leg machine and slid the pin to the heaviest weight. "God will judge Jonathan, not me."

"Just like you don't judge me, right Rodney?" Maria sat on a machine to work her pecs.

*You go, girl!*

Rodney adjusted the string T-shirt on his enormous back,

sank into his machine, and his massive legs lifted the weight like tree trunks forming roots. "So it's true then? What Jonathan said about you?" When Maria didn't answer, Rodney asked, "How the heck did Jonathan find out about it?"

Maria ended her repetition, then rested on the machine. "If it's any business of yours, Jonathan got me drunk at a party, and I spilled the whole story...and my party snacks."

"What's the whole story, Maria?"

"Why do you want to know? So you can pray for my diseased, wicked soul?"

"Maybe."

Maria started to leave. Rodney jumped off his machine and blocked her path. Rodney's giant hand grasped Maria's muscular arm, as he said, "I want to know because...I want to understand."

"Why?"

"Because you could use a friend, and so can I."

Maria said, "No judgment?"

"No judgment."

They sat together on the bench, and Maria turned back the pages of time. "We lived in Detroit. I was the youngest child of six with five older brothers." Maria didn't make eye contact with Rodney. "As Mario, I was anything but a typical boy. I had no use for sports, boys' clothes, boys' toys, or cars." After an involuntary shudder, she continued. "To survive the teasing and beatings from my brothers and the kids in the neighborhood, I took up bodybuilding at school." She added with a half-smile, "And I found out I had a real penchant for it." She cleared her throat. "When my brothers dated girls, and I refused to do the same, my parents' disappointment turned into arguments, which ultimately turned into beatings. When the hitting didn't change me, my father dragged me to our local priest for conversion-therapy sessions." She wiped a tear off her high cheekbone. "The priest showed me pictures of naked men, then squeezed and hit my genitals when I became aroused."

"I'm sorry," Rodney said.

42

"Me, too," Maria responded.

*Me, too.*

"What happened then?" asked Rodney.

"I have a gay uncle."

*Every kid should.*

"He's my mother's brother. He and his husband are lawyers. When my uncle found out about me, he threatened my parents with a lawsuit and whisked me out of Michigan to his condo in Vermont. After many late-night discussions with my uncle, and the psychiatric approvals, hormone treatments, and genital surgery, Mario Ruiz became Maria Ruiz."

Maria's and Rodney's eyes finally met.

He said, "Thank you for telling me that."

With defiance in her eyes, she asked, "Aren't you going to stone me to death, Rodney?"

"No, but you'll have to explain to God at Judgment Day why you changed what he created."

Tears filled her eyes. "I think God will understand that I didn't change anything." She walked away.

"Maria, wait!" Rodney followed her out.

I walked back to the main gym, popped some vitamins into my mouth, and swallowed them with water from the cooler. Mack Heath was right behind me.

As Mack drank, Jimmy Saline, a theatre major working as a student aide in the gym, said hello to me, then approached Mack shyly. At about a hundred pounds, Jimmy's whole body could have fit into one of Mack's muscular legs.

"Excuse me?" said Jimmy hoarsely.

Mack looked at Jimmy like a fly buzzing around his head. "Yeah?"

Jimmy swallowed hard. After clearing his throat, he wiped the perspiration off his freckled forehead, and croaked out, "You looked really up there good." Jimmy's face turned the shade of his fire-engine-red hair. "I mean you looked good up there. You should win."

Mack smiled. "Thanks."

I pretended to focus and refocus some lighting equipment near them as Jimmy handed Mack a fluffy white towel, then started to walk away.

Mack wiped the sweat off his handsome face. "What's your name?"

"Me?"

Mack nodded.

Jimmy looked like a shock victim. "James...Jim...Jimmy."

"Hi James Jim Jimmy. I'm Mack." Mack offered his thick hand.

Jimmy's face lit up like a torch as he stared at Mack's hand in wonder. Finally his sweaty hand connected with Mack's.

As they shook hands, Jimmy said, "I didn't mean to take you away from your rehearsal."

"You didn't take me away," Mack responded. "I'm on a break."

"I'm glad. I mean, it's good to have a break once in a while, because you might get tired, and then you'll need...a break." Jimmy raised his brown eyes to his mop of red hair. "I'm babbling."

As Jimmy started to leave, Mack said, "Are you a phys. ed. major?"

Laughing, Jimmy responded, "What gave me away? My skinny arms or skinnier legs?"

Mack put his strong hand on Jimmy's minuscule shoulder. "Jimmy, you shouldn't put yourself down."

"I've learned to do it before someone else beats me to it." Realizing he was still holding Mack's hand, Jimmy moved away nervously. "I'm a theatre major, working here as a student aide."

"Why do you want to work in the Phys. Ed. building if you're a theatre major?"

*I've been asking myself the same thing.*

"You don't want to know." Jimmy picked up a broom resting against the gym wall and began sweeping the floor.

Mack held the broom still. "I don't ask a question unless I want to know the answer."

Jimmy looked down at his sunken chest. "I took a weightlifting class last semester. Obviously I failed. When I was leaving class one day, I saw you coming into the weight room."

"That's why you applied to be a student aide here?" Mack asked in astonishment.

Jimmy nodded. "I hoped I could meet you."

"Why?"

Jimmy took a step backward. "Please don't get freaked out."

Mack raised Jimmy's chin from his chest. "I'm not freaked out."

"I'm not a stalker or anything. I know that someone like you would never be friends with someone like me. I just want you to know that I really admire what you've accomplished as an athlete. And I've watched the way you interact with people, how you listen to them and respect them. I think that's a really good thing. And I think you're a really good guy."

Jillian Flowers tapped Mack's perfect back, then flicked back her blonde hair. "Mack, you um want to go over our like poses together?" She pressed her strong shoulder against his. "I, you know, promise to go like easy on you."

Jimmy looked like a squirrel at a demolition site. "I'm sorry I bothered you. Good luck with the competition." He scurried off to the supply room.

"Wait!" Mack shouted, but Jimmy was gone. Alone with Jillian, Mack said, "No thanks, Jillian."

Jillian responded, "No thanks for what?"

He responded patiently, "No thanks. I don't want to go over our poses together."

"Were we um supposed to like do that?" she asked in confusion.

"Definitely not. Catch you later, Jillian." Mack walked away deep in thought.

Jillian shrugged her shoulders and practiced her poses alone.

Continuing to stretch my legs, I followed Cheryl Stryker

as she left her office, then sat down on a bench in the hallway next to a forlorn Tim Sim. Wondering if what Jonathan Toner had said about Tim and his advisor was true, I hid behind a trophy cabinet in the hallway and observed.

Cheryl looked at Tim fondly. "Tim, you know I am always here if you ever need to talk."

Tim slid to the other end of the bench. "Um thank you, Professor Stryker. I um know you are like my faculty advisor."

Sliding closer to him, Cheryl put her strong arm around Tim's muscular shoulder. "I'm not saying this just because I'm your advisor, Tim. I think you have an amazing future in bodybuilding—contests, product endorsements, educational lectures. I think you are *special*, Tim. And I'd like to help you reach your goals."

*And Mrs. Robinson's goal.*

Tim smiled shyly. "Thanks, Professor, but I'm um focused on the, you know, competition for now."

"And you should be. Especially since Professor Strong speaks so highly of Jillian Flowers and Mack Heath. And Professor Granite has been very complimentary as of late to your brother." Cheryl squeezed Tim into her mountainous chest. "Mine is only one vote, Tim, but I'd like to help you win."

His voice cracked. "Um, help me *how*, Professor?"

She grinned like a vampire entering a blood bank. "Your rehearsal is nearly over. Let me take you out for dinner and we can discuss it over some protein."

*I wonder if the Big Bad Wolf said that to Little Red Riding Hood.*

Tim Sim leaned away. "Thanks, Professor, but I um better get back to my like dorm room, to do some, you know, studying, and get some like sleep."

Stryker rested her hand on Tim's knee and coaxed her way up his sculpted thigh. "Then let's go to your dorm room to figure things out."

Tim jumped off the bench like a crocodile had bitten him. "I um better like hit the men's room then get back inside for, you know, rehearsal, Professor. Thanks. Good night."

Jillian Flowers, blonde hair bouncing behind her, collided into Tim. "I'm, you know, sorry Tim. I was like going to the bathroom."

"Um I'm like sorry too, Jillian."

"For what?" Jillian asked, oblivious.

"For bumping into you. I'm like going to the bathroom too."

Jillian asked, "How did you um know I was like going to the bathroom, Tim? I thought you could, you know, only like read *Kim's* mind."

"I'm never going to like read Kim's mind again. See you um later, Jillian." Then Tim turned to Cheryl. "Bye, um Professor."

Since it was getting late and we had accomplished what Noah and I had planned, I went back into the gym and released everyone, wishing them a good night. After a kiss or two or three with Noah, I asked my younger (twenty-eight) lover to wait up for me at home while I took advantage of the gym equipment.

Once I was changed into my sweat clothes, and reasonably convinced I was stretched out enough to avoid injury, I used the push-and-pull universal-gym torture devices in the weight room to do pec exercises. Then I moved on to the rowing machine until my chest revolted and throbbed in agony.

Next, I entered the spinning room and did fifteen minutes on the stationary bicycle. Finally, I hit the cardio room. That was where I found Tim Sim hanging lifeless over the side of an elliptical machine with open but dead eyes.

# Chapter Three

The next morning, Noah and I walked past Mary, the ancient office assistant snoozing on her desk blotter, and we took our rickety seats in Bodybuilding Department Head Strong's no-frills office. Again, sitting around Brick Strong's battered desk were Professor Cheryl Stryker, Professor Van Granite, Noah, me, then Detective Manuello.

"Tim Sim's cause of death was a stroke," said Manuello.

"The poor boy!" said Cheryl, wiping away a tear with the sleeve of her gray sweatshirt. "He was so young!"

Always compassionate, Noah asked Manuello, "Do you know what caused it?"

Manuello replied, "Not yet."

"Tim seemed troubled lately," Cheryl said with sad eyes.

"About what?" Manuello asked with his pencil pressed against his pad.

Cheryl responded between sniffles, "I asked him, but Tim wouldn't tell me, even after I offered my help."

*And to be his Sugar Mamma.*

Van Granite's handsome face sprouted a worry line. "Where is Kim?"

Manuello checked his notes. "Kim Sim is with his family in Maine."

*Where Kim now has total access to his dying father's fortune.*

Manuello explained, "Tim's body will join Kim once the coroner has completed his testing."

Granite flexed his biceps in Noah's direction, then whispered in his ear, "Kim is quite an athlete. I have given him a great deal of personal attention."

*I'm sure.*

49

Manuello flipped through his growing notes. "Do any of you know of any reason why someone would want to hurt this boy?"

I offered, "The twins were in a heated battle over their dying father's inheritance."

After making a note, Manuello said, "And once again, Professor Abbondanza, *you* found the body."

As if announced as the guest on a television talk show, I said, "That I did, Detective." Then I turned to the department head. "Brick, are you absolutely sure that Tim Sim and Jonathan Toner were not taking steroids?"

Strong rose from behind his desk like an enraged phoenix. "Let me restate this for you one more time, Nicky. None, and I mean *none*, of my young athletes are on steroids."

Noah, as usual, provided my back-up (no pun intended). "But since you don't test them, Brick, how do you know?"

"I know!" answered the department head.

Like a right-wing news reporter interviewing a liberal candidate, I said, "Brick, you said you told the students not to use steroids, but each of us in this room knows that our students don't always do what we tell them." *Just ask the lead of my play two years ago who blew kisses at the audience during the curtain call.*

Lifting his powerful hands in defeat, Strong sat back down in his creaking chair. "All right. At one time, many years ago, a few of our students took steroids."

"They *told* you?" asked Noah.

Strong looked down at his bulging thighs. "I knew because...*I* gave it to them." He pounded his mighty fist onto his scratched desktop. "But after I saw the dangerous side effects of that poison, I got in my students' faces and made sure they didn't mess with that stuff ever again. And now my athletes are *all natural*! You can tell by looking at them." Brick's eyes darted to each person around him. "Look at Mack Heath. He has a perfectly sculptured body with ultimate control. Mack doesn't look overly pumped up. There's no protruding stomach or tiny scrotum."

*How does Strong know the size of Mack Heath's scrotum?*

Brick continued. "Jillian Flowers is the perfect example of feminine muscle mass that is naturally cut with no fat and no water weight."

"I agree. Kim Sim's perfect proportions are not indicative of someone on steroids," said Granite, proudly revealing his bleached teeth.

"Tim was the same," said Cheryl, as tears careened down her cheeks.

As if finishing his closing argument to a jury, Strong said, "I pound into these kids' heads day in and day out that in *this* department at *this* college for *this* sport, natural is the *only* acceptable way to compete!"

We heard the sound of someone's throat clearing and followed it to the doorway. Tony Piccolo stood sheepishly at the department head's door holding a wrinkled folder. Given Strong's captivating performance, who knows how long Tony had been standing there uncomfortably hoping for Brick's attention?

Brick asked, "What can I do for you, Tony?"

Tony entered the office meekly. "Sorry to bother you, Brick." He handed Brick the folder. "You asked for my supply list for purchasing requests."

As if coming out a coma, Brick took the folder. "Right. Thanks, Tony."

"No problem, Brick." Tony ran a shaky hand through his gray hair, nodded to each of us as if we were royalty, then left the office unbeknownst to the still slumbering Mary.

Having seen Tony, my brain exploded with the sudden remembrance of a dream I had had the night before. In my nocturnal vision, Tony's son Robbie stood in his posing trunks and moved through his bodybuilding poses on the makeshift stage of Treemeadow's gymnasium at the bodybuilding competition eighteen years ago. I sat in the front row watching the young bodybuilder display his perfectly sculpted, tan, and hairless shoulder, pectoral, abdominal, biceps, triceps, lat, back, thigh, and calf muscles. When the competition ended, I cheered loudly as Robbie was justifiably awarded the gold cup. After Robbie posed for several pictures, people surrounded him on stage. As I was about to leave with the other audience members, Robbie looked out into the sea of faceless fans and spotted me. As our eyes made contact, he waved me toward him. Like a paperclip headed for a magnet, I rose from my seat and made my way through the crowd. When I finally reached Robbie, I woke up.

Noah shook my shoulder. "Are you okay, Nicky?"

I came back to earth. "Sure. Why?"

"Since the meeting's over, we should get to the Theatre building for our classes."

I nodded and followed Noah past the snoring Mary, who I hoped was having as nice a dream as I had just recalled.

Once out in the hallway, Noah went on ahead of me, and Manuello cornered me in front of a storage closet. "We need to talk, Nicky."

"Manuello, Noah didn't kill Jonathan Toner, and I didn't kill Tim Sim."

He rubbed his wide nose. "My wife reminded me over breakfast how you helped solve the murders in your department last year. I need you to do something for me on this case."

I replied like a starving dog at a buffet table with a wobbly leg, "What do you need, Manuello? Shall I sniff around the gym for clues? Interrogate the Bodybuilding students? Pressure the Bodybuilding faculty to tell me what they know?"

"I need you to stay out of it."

"What!"

"You heard me, Nicky. Don't get involved in this."

I placed my hands over my heart and pretended to faint backwards into the closet door (no pun intended). "After all I did in the last case, you are rejecting my offer to assist you in solving these murders?"

Manuello raised his dark eyes to the fluorescent lighting. "Cut the theatrics, Nicky. The *reality*, something you don't do well with, is that we aren't sure these are murders. You poking around and playing detective will complicate matters, cause hysteria, and impede my investigation."

I put on my Sherlock Holmes persona. "Well, my dear detective, I am utterly convinced of foul play!"

"Can we do this without the British accent, Nicky?"

"Where's your sense of high art, Detective?"

"In your department where it, and *you*, belong."

Manuello walked away, and I said to his back, "Don't you think it is too much of a coincidence that two young men in a bodybuilding competition both died of *supposed* natural causes?" Manuello turned to face me and I slipped into the guise of a television lawyer. "We know that enhancement products are popular in the sport of bodybuilding." I paced the hallway and continued with raised vocal projection and animated hand gestures. "And we *also* know those said drugs can have dangerous side effects, including heart attack and stroke. So I have come to the conclusion that both Jonathan Toner and Tim Sim were *murdered*!"

The detective picked at the rolls of fat frolicking over his belt like gelatin. "Please, Clarence Darrow, I'm getting motion sickness."

I came face to face with Manuello. "Detective, bodybuilders ingest protein every two hours. *Anyone* could have slipped a drug into something Toner and Sim ate or drank. It isn't as if there aren't any suspects. Read your notes from our meetings."

Manuello ran a wide hand through his black, wavy hair. "Nicky, I am asking you, ordering you, to stay out of this before you, Noah, or someone else gets hurt."

*Even Sherlock Holmes didn't solve a case in two days.* "All right, Manuello. Have it your way. Noah and I will stick to directing the bodybuilding competition, and let you investigate the two deaths."

Manuello nodded and his double chins collided. "I hope you mean what you say, Nicky."

Grinning from ear to ear, I replied, "Would I lie to a detective?"

Reaching for the ulcer medicine in his pocket, Manuello nodded and left the building.

I walked out to the gym, where I gravitated to Tony's alcove. Peeking my head inside, I waved at the elderly man.

Tony stopped putting away hand sanitizers. "Hiya, Professor. Sorry to barge in on your meeting. My purchase list was due to the big guy."

"No problem, Tony." Unable to stop myself, my eyes darted to the pictures of Robbie on the bulletin board. Again, I found myself taken in by the young man's warm smile, amazing physique, and charismatic presence.

Noticing my gaze, Tony smiled. "You like looking at the pictures of my Robbie, Professor?"

My face turned the color of my rose shirt. "Sorry, Tony."

He waved his blue hands in front of the craters on his face. "Everybody is taken in by my Robbie. And nobody's more proud of him than me. There has never been another student at Treemeadow like him, and there never will be."

I couldn't help but agree.

Tony began a coughing fit. He sat behind his desk and spit into a handkerchief.

"Are you all right, Tony?"

He nodded. "Just old age. It happens to the best of us."

*Tell me about it.* I took the opportunity to steal another look at Robbie's pictures. "After you retire, are you planning to move to Florida and live with Robbie and his family?"

"That's the plan," answered Tony with a doting look at his son's old photos.

I pulled myself away from the pictures, wished Tony a good day, and left his alcove. As I walked through the gym, I began to panic at my new obsession. *Is it possible for a thirty-five-year-old man to be infatuated with old photographs of a twenty-one-year-old?*

My internal investigation ended as I reached Van Granite—whispering with my Noah in a corner of the gym.

"Here you are," said Noah as if I had been lost in the jungle.

Granite smiled like the Cheshire Cat. "Hi, Nicky. I was keeping Noah company."

*I'll bet.*

54

"We should get back to the Theatre building, Nicky."

"I'm right behind you, Noah." My face painted a picture of Granite's name.

Granite clasped Noah's arm. "We'll finish our conversation later."

*Why didn't I study karate?*

"Sure, Van." Noah continued walking until I caught up with him near the door.

"What was *that* about?" I asked once we were clear of Professor Universe.

"What was *what* about?" Noah asked with a confused look on his beautiful face.

"You and Granite. What were you talking about?"

"This and that." He walked on.

I put my arm around Noah and held him still. "Noah, what were you and Granite talking about?"

"Nothing important." Noah looked at his watch. "We don't want to be late for our classes, Nicky."

"We're not late."

Taking my hand in his, Noah offered me his baby-blue eyes. "I was worried when I couldn't find you. So I wasn't fully listening to Van." He shrugged. "I think Van said something about having aspirations to be department head one day."

I replied, "Mary better wake up and order new mirrors for the department head's office walls."

"Come on, let's go back to where we belong." Noah opened the door and I followed him out of the building.

After teaching my Directing II class, attending my faculty committee meeting, grading students' papers, completing course assessment reports, planning my classes for the following week, and advising the Theatre Club meeting (planning a show the student director was certain would instantly move to Broadway), I arrived home just in time to join Noah in making dinner.

Later, as we sat in our Victorian-style dining room, digging into our lobster bisque, chicken Florentine, buckwheat fettuccine, and green salad with blue cheese, apples and walnuts (for me), I squeezed Noah's hand. "Sorry I came on so strong about Van Granite this morning."

Noah kissed me and I could taste the delectable raspberry vinaigrette. "Van's not as obnoxious as you think. He's a professor, like us."

"Well, not *exactly* like us," I replied as I returned Noah's kiss.

Noah smacked his adorable forehead. "I forgot to tell you, my parents are coming for a visit."

I choked on a walnut. "All the way from Wisconsin? When will they get here?"

"Tomorrow. You know how long it takes by stagecoach," Noah said with a twinkle in his eyes.

I swallowed some vitamins. "Do you think this is a good time for them to visit? With the murders...and the competition?"

"It's the *perfect* time." Noah squeezed my knee. "My folks want to meet you. And once they do, they'll love you as much as I do." He speared a large piece of chicken and placed it into his mouth. "I'll make up the guest room tonight."

"How long will they be staying?"

"Just a week," Noah said between chews.

"Have they ever been to Vermont?"

"I usually visit them. This is their first time coming to see me, but I'm sure it won't be their last." Noah looked at the antique clock hanging over the Victorian hutch. "Nicky, we have to go to rehearsal!"

After a quick kiss, we dropped our dishes into the kitchen sink, and rushed out the door.

When Noah and I got to the Physical Education building, Noah opened a storage closet and assembled our set and lighting pieces in the gym. After a quick visit to the men's room, I passed Brick Strong's office, noticing Mary was gone for the day (no doubt sitting wide awake at home), and heard laughter coming from inside Brick's office. Breaking my promise to Manuello, I tiptoed to the door and peeked through the seam between the door and the molding. Brick Strong stood next to the beaten up, threadbare sofa with his arms around Mack Heath.

"I love you, Mack. Never forget that," said the department head.

"I love you, too," replied his student. "And I always will."

*So our butch Brick Strong swings both ways!*

I heard Noah call me, so I hurried into the gym and assisted Noah with placement of our columns and smoke machine.

A few minutes later the cast arrived in costume, including a disheveled Mack. I gave a brief eulogy for Tim Sim, then re-staged the opening sequence with Rodney, Mack, Maria, Jillian, and Noah (standing in for Kim). For the second half of the rehearsal, Noah worked with the young bodybuilders on the emotional intensity of their characters and poses.

After rehearsal concluded, Noah and I put away our set. We locked the closet door (pun intended), then Noah kissed me on the cheek, wished me a good workout, and left the gym.

Upon hitting the locker room and smelling the familiar scent of sweat, cologne, and sperm, I put on my sweats and stretched my arms across my locker. Convinced my arms were as stretched out as a porn star's anus, I hit the weight room, where I executed my curls and triceps extensions — feeling like I should execute myself. After a number of reps, my arms begged for mercy. So I took a walk to the water cooler and downed a handful of vitamins, hoping for renewed energy.

When I returned, I noticed Mack Heath, wearing a tank top and shorts, pumping iron at the other end of the weight room. I quietly walked over and ducked behind a weight rack. Luckily, I was accustomed to staying on my knees for long periods of time (to clean my hardwood floors). After a few moments, Jimmy Saline entered the weight room and approached Mack Heath mid-pump.

Dressed in baggy brown corduroy pants and a yellow and brown flannel shirt, the stick-thin theatre major looked out from under his red mound of hair. "Excuse me, I'm not sure if you remember me—"

"I remember you, Jimmy." Mack lowered his fifty-pound hand weights.

"Wow." Jimmy's face registered disbelief. "I don't mean to take you away from your workout."

"It's okay," said Mack. "I'm due for a break."

Jimmy handed Mack a towel. "I wanted to apologize."

"For what?" Mack wiped the perspiration off his firm neck.

"Last night. I didn't mean to creep you out…about me taking the student aide job here to be near you."

Mack laughed. "It would take a lot more than that to creep me out, Jimmy." He sat on the bench and motioned for Jimmy to sit next to him.

"Cool." Looking like a peasant asked to sit next to a king on his throne, Jimmy cautiously sat beside Mack.

After taking a sip of water from a jug on the floor, Mack said, "I have a proposition for you."

Jimmy looked like he'd be the next student at Treemeadow to have a stroke. "For *me*?"

Mack nodded his princely head. "As you know, the competition is coming up soon. I've been putting all my time into my Biology and Anatomy classes, rehearsing, and working out. That doesn't leave a lot of time for…other things."

*How come this never happened to me when I was in college?*

"*Other* things?" asked Jimmy, nearly salivating on Mack's sturdy knee.

Mack nodded. "Shaving, oiling, and tanning."

"Right," answered Jimmy, pretending he knew that all along.

"After you get off work, would you be willing to help me?"

"*Help* you?"

"Shave, oil, and tan a different body part each night." He blushed. "Some of the places are…hard for me to reach. And it takes up so much time."

Jimmy looked like his lottery ticket had the winning

number. "You want *me* to do *that* for *you*?"

"I'll understand if you don't want to do it. Unfortunately, I can't pay you, but I can train you in return...after the competition is over."

"I *want* to do it!" Tears welled up in Jimmy's brown eyes. "You don't have to pay me. And no worries about training." He smiled from ear to ear. "When do we get started?"

"How about tomorrow night?"

"Tomorrow night's great!"

Mack said, "I'll meet you in the shower room at this time?"

"You got it." Jimmy shook Mack's hand.

Jimmy started to leave then returned. "I hope you don't take this the wrong way, Mack, but I can't help wondering why you are being nice to me."

"What do you mean?"

"Guys who look like *you* generally don't hang out with guys who look like *me*."

"We're not that different, Jimmy." Mack walked back to his weights.

Jimmy faced the floor-to-ceiling mirror and looked at his and Mack's reflection standing shoulder to shoulder. "Tell that to the mirror."

"Jimmy, can I tell you a story?"

"Sure." Jimmy sat on a weight rack and was all ears.

Time-traveling to the past, Mack said, "When I was growing up not far from here, I was the skinniest kid on the block, probably in the town, maybe even the state. I got teased and bullied in school...and outside of school. I cried myself to sleep every night, wishing and praying that the tormenting would end, but it never did. I had no brothers or sisters or friends to protect me. My teachers turned blind eyes and deaf ears to the mocking and beatings. It got to the point that one night in bed I asked God to take me to relieve my misery. But that didn't happen." His handsome face brightened. "When I turned thirteen my father started me on a nutrition and weightlifting program. I wasn't much interested, but I wanted my father to be proud of me, so I gave it a try. Three months later the teasing and bullying ended. Six months later I was the most popular kid in school. A year later I won the local Junior Bodybuilding competition."

"That's a great story, Mack," said Jimmy obviously moved. "But what does that have to do with being nice to *me*?"

Mack faced the mirror. "When I look in the mirror, I don't see what everyone else sees when they look at me. I see that thin, frightened kid who feared for his life. I see someone who looks pretty much…like *you*."

"You don't look anything like me."

"Maybe not on the outside, but I do on the inside."

Jimmy said, "So you want to help me like your father helped you. Kind of like giving back by donating to charity?"

Mack kneeled next to Jimmy. "That's not what I mean, Jimmy."

"I'm sorry. I don't understand."

"I'm not like most people."

Jimmy looked at Mack's body and smiled. "Obviously."

"I don't mean like that." Mack ran his strong fingers through his thick, chestnut locks. "This is harder to explain than I thought."

Jimmy said, "When I have a hard time saying something, I just blurt it out."

*I can relate.*

Mack nodded and took in a deep breath. "Unlike most guys, I've never been with anyone…sexually."

"I've never been with anyone either." Jimmy added, "I'm sure that's no great revelation."

*That I can't relate to.*

Mack looked down at the rubber floor. "I've never been interested in anyone, or even *attracted* to anybody."

"That must be tough."

Mack sat next to Jimmy on the weight rack. "I'm used to it. When other guys talk about their girlfriends or boyfriends, I keep quiet, put my energies into my training."

"The results sure paid off."

Mack messed Jimmy's hair and smiled. "I want to work

with you, Jimmy, because I want to get to know you better. And I'd like *you* to get to know *me*."

"I'd like that too...very much," answered Jimmy like Aladdin granted his first wish. "But I still don't understand why—"

Mack took Jimmy's hand in his, causing Jimmy's hand to disappear. "Last night when we met, and just now when we were talking—"

"Why do you care if I go to Heaven, Hell, Purgatory, Limbo, the North Pole, or Never Neverland?" Maria charged into the weight room like a televangelist in a wig factory.

Rodney was at her heels like a right-wing politician stalking a large corporation's funding. "Because you're my workout partner."

"Right, Rodney, not your *prayer* partner."

Maria and Rodney approached a weight rack, and Jimmy took off like a chipmunk facing a snowblower.

Mack called out, "Jimmy, wait!" and followed Jimmy out of the weight room.

Rodney jumped up on the bar to do pull-ups while Maria hit the floor to do push-ups.

Hanging from the bar with his massive shoulders bulging, Rodney looked down. "I've been thinking about what you told me."

"What I told you was a secret, Rodney," replied Maria with sweat dripping off her ripped back.

"I know." Rodney jumped off the bar. "I'm not judging you."

Maria stopped exercising and sat on the weight room floor. "Rodney, let's just stick to working out from now on. Okay?"

He sat next to her on the floor. "Maria, I prayed last night...all night." He took her hand. "And I think God spoke to me."

"You should tell that to a shrink."

"It's not like I heard a voice or anything. It was more like a...*feeling* that came over me. A message. About *you*."

"That you should stone me to death?"

"No, Maria, that's the Old Testament stuff. Jesus loved everybody, the lepers, the tax collectors, the prostitutes, the adulterers, the poor."

She removed her hand. "I'm none of those things, Rodney. And what do you care about tax collectors? Churches don't even pay taxes."

"Maria, please listen to me. The message I got was about you making things right with God. *Pray* with me. Let's ask the Lord for forgiveness. Let's tell him you will live your life as Mario, and that you will never disobey his word again."

*Ugh-oh!*

Muscles bulged in every direction as Maria lunged for Rodney's throat. He grabbed her wrists and clasped them behind her back.

"Let me go, or I'll whip your ass from here to Sunday!"

"Maria, stop!"

They looked into one another's eyes and held each other for quite a while.

"Stop closing yourself off. Let me in, Maria. Can you do that?"

She stared at him as if under hypnosis.

"Open your heart, Maria. Open your heart to…the Lord."

"Agh!" Maria wiggled free and ran out of the weight room with Rodney following, calling her name.

I rose on stiff knees and followed them into the hallway, where I heard laughter coming from Brick Strong's office. When I arrived at the door, I was surprised to find it open. So I hid behind Mary's desk (or bed), propped Mary's pillow under my aching knees, and peered into the department head's office. Strong was sitting on the sofa with his arm around Jillian Flowers.

He pressed her bulging shoulders into his solid chest. "Come on, Jillian, relax. You know I would never hurt you. I'm your number one fan around here."

*He sure gets around!*

Jillian leaned away from Brick with her hefty back pressing against the arm of the sofa. "Um thank you for your like vote of confidence, Professor, but I, you know, should like go." She started to rise.

"My vote indeed!" Brick pulled her back down and ran his powerful fingers through her blonde hair and nibbled at her neck. "And you'll need my vote since Professor Granite is supporting Kim Sim."

"I'll um need your vote to win the like competition, Professor, since Professor Granite is, you know, supporting Kim Sim," said Jillian.

"I just said that," replied Strong losing patience.

Jillian pushed against Strong's rock hard shoulders. "I um like you, Professor."

"I like you too, baby."

"But um you're like my, you know, professor."

"Don't worry about that. We're both of age." Strong kissed her substantial neck. "Though when I'm with you, I feel like a kid again." He laughed wickedly.

*A kid with raging hormones!*

"And um I kinda have my eye like on somebody else," said Jillian.

"Mack doesn't know you're alive, honey." Strong kissed Jillian on the lips.

She came up for air, and repeated obliviously, "And um I kinda have my eye on like somebody else."

"Mack still doesn't know you're alive, baby!" Brick kissed her again and his hands roved down to her rock-hard buttocks.

Jillian continued to push him away. "This um isn't like right, Professor."

"Calm down, baby. After we do it, you'll forget all about it, so there won't be any guilt." He forced his body on top of hers. "For either of us."

Cheryl Stryker came out of her office and headed in my direction. I ducked, lost my balance, and my pillowed knees slid across the floor, landing at her feet. Hearing the noise, Brick jumped up and stood at his office doorway.

Taking advantage of the break, Jillian rose and left the office. "Um bye, Professor. I'm not like sure what we, you know, talked about, but whatever it was thanks for your like time."

I scurried to my feet. "Just admiring the floor. We need to get something like that in the Theatre Department. What's it made out of?"

Strong replied through a clenched jaw, "Wood."

"Ah, wood. Thanks for the tip. See you both around."

I walked down the hall and stopped at the turn in the corridor.

Cheryl glared at Brick. "It's bad enough you fawn all over Mack, but your behavior with Jillian Flowers is abominable!"

Her ex-husband responded, "And your salivating over Tim Sim makes you Teacher of the Year? You should be ashamed of yourself, Cheryl."

"Right back at you, Brick."

Apparently leaving for the evening, they continued down the hallway as I ducked into another corridor. I heard voices coming from inside Van Granite's office. Stopping in my tracks like a cartoon character at the edge of a precipice, I walked to Granite's office, and saw Mr. In-Love-With-Himself talking to my Noah! I pressed my back against the hallway wall and listened.

Noah said, "I'm not sure about this, Van."

Granite replied, "I can tell you want this, Noah. Relax, and trust me."

"I don't want anyone to know."

"This is just between you and me."

"Do you promise, Van?"

"Cross my heart."

Before I could burst in and clobber Granite's muscle brain, I heard a loud crash down the hall. I raced into the weight room, followed by Granite and Noah, and found Brick Strong on the slant board with a barbell crushing his throat.

# Chapter Four

An hour later, in Van Granite's office, Granite sat on his desk, Manuello stood by the door, and Noah and I sat on chairs flanking Granite's bulbous thighs.

"Did anyone inform Professor Strong's ex-wife and daughter?" asked Manuello.

"I phoned Cheryl and Abigail," replied Granite. "I also sent an email announcement to our students."

"Thank you," said Manuello.

"What did the coroner say?" I asked Manuello.

"Not much," Manuello replied. "He'll need to do testing before he can tell us anything."

Granite said, "I don't need to do *testing* to tell a barbell was lodged into Brick's throat, Detective." Then he flexed his calf muscles in Noah's direction. "Noah and I heard the clang of the weights from in here."

*Where's a barbell when I need one?*

Manuello scratched at a roll of stomach fat that covered another roll of fat beneath it. "Hopefully the coroner will be able to tell us if it was an accident or foul play."

"Do you really think Strong's death could have been an accident?" I asked incredulously. "I can't imagine someone as experienced as Strong dropping a barbell on his own throat."

Manuello responded, "Strong didn't have anyone spotting him, Professor. Accidents can happen to the most experienced of athletes."

I asked, "Do you know Jonathan Toner's cause of death, Detective?"

Manuello checked his notes then said, "An overdose of

testosterone."

"I *knew* it!" *The little gray cells are never wrong.*

"Strong was right when he said his students aren't injecting steroids," said Manuello. "Instead they seem to be swallowing testosterone pills. At least one student was anyway."

"Don't you need a prescription for testosterone replacement drugs?" Noah asked with the naïveté of someone who follows the law.

Manuello laughed. "It's not hard to get these drugs on the black market, Professor. Obviously Jonathan Toner found a way."

"How about Tim Sim?" asked Granite.

Manuello responded, "No word yet, but I won't be surprised if it's the same scenario."

I said, "But Brick Strong obviously didn't die from taking testosterone."

Noah looked as if he was carrying the weight of the world on his delicate shoulders. "Three deaths in one department over three days." He shook his gorgeous blond locks. "It *can't* be a coincidence."

Manuello rubbed at the lines on his forehead. "Professor Oliver is right. For the protection of the faculty and students, I have no alternative but to close down this building until we can sort all this out."

Granite jumped up like a wealthy bidder at an auction for the crowned jewels. "Is that really necessary, Detective?"

"I'm afraid so, Professor," answered Manuello.

Granite strutted around the office like a peacock in a public television documentary. "As you know, Detective, I am incredibly saddened by the death of my esteemed colleague. But now that he's gone, I assume the Dean of Physical Education will appoint *me* as Interim Bodybuilding Department Head." Checking himself out in the mirror and obviously liking what he saw, Granite continued. "And I would like to carry on Brick Strong's policy of open access of this building for the health and welfare of our students, faculty, and staff."

"I don't think so, Professor," said Manuello with a frown.

Granite clutched at Manuello's arm like a child asking for candy. "Please reconsider, Manuello. I give you my word that nobody else will be harmed in this building. I promise to keep an eye out day *and night*." Granite glanced at Noah, and I tasted the acid in my stomach. He added, "If anything else happens, you can close us down for as long as you like, Detective."

After weighing his options, Manuello finally said, "All right, Professor Granite. You can stay open, but I am holding you personally responsible for ensuring the safety of this department."

Granite's diaphragm expanded and contracted like a helium balloon. "Thank you, Detective."

"I'll station a police officer in front of the building, and I'll ask the dean to station a security guard inside."

Not wanting to leave Noah alone with Granite, but having no choice, I said like a high school principal calling a misbehaving student out of class, "Detective Manuello, can I talk to you outside?"

As if walking to his execution, Manuello followed me out of Granite's office and around the corridor. "What is it, Nicky?"

I clasped my hands behind my back. "Detective, there appear to be a number of sharks in our midst."

"I thought you were going to stay out of this."

"It is my duty as a citizen to report what I have witnessed to the police."

Manuello readied his pad. "Please tell me without the metaphors, Nicky." He added with a sneer, "Remember I'm just a common servant of the people."

I scratched at one of my sideburns. "Van Granite wants to be department head, and Jonathan Toner was blackmailing the Sim twins who were in an inheritance battle."

"Tell me something I don't know, Nicky."

I answered like a television entertainment news reporter, "I saw Brick Strong in his office in compromising positions with two of his students, Mack Heath and Jillian Flowers.

Jimmy Saline, my theatre student, is devoted to Mack, and Rodney Towers and Maria Ruiz are reenacting the Spanish Inquisition."

"That seems to be standard behavior at Treemeadow College," replied Manuello.

A reporter from the local newspaper burst into the hallway with a reporter from the local television station at his heels.

"What's the scoop on the third death, Manuello? Did a failing, deranged student drop the barbell on Professor Strong?"

"Was Strong molesting Toner and Sim? Did Strong's ex-wife, Cheryl Stryker, lob the barbell onto Strong's throat in a fit of jealous rage?"

I turned to the news camera like Norma Desmond on her staircase. "As the theatrical director for the upcoming bodybuilding competition, I have been in very close contact with each of the deceased."

"Save it for the stage, Nicky." Manuello ushered the reporters into Strong's office and shut the door.

I walked back to Granite's office. My jaw, and every other muscle in my body, clenched at the sight of Granite and Noah talking quietly like right-wing politicians in the back room of a gay bar. As Noah turned to leave, Granite slapped Noah's shapely behind.

Nonchalantly, Noah said, "Are you ready to go home, Nicky?

Granite's pectoral muscles twitched under his tight green sweatshirt. "After finding poor Brick, I think we *all* need some rest." He winked at me. "Your metabolism changes when you hit thirty-five, Nicky. Make sure you get a good night's sleep."

I took Noah's hand. "We'll both be fine once we get to bed."

Granite unleashed his pearly whites. "Good night, gentlemen."

Granite and Noah shared a knowing smile. Noah and I walked out of Granite's office with my heart palpitating out of my blazer.

Speaking of heart palpitations, Noah drove us home, whipping around windy blue-gray mountain roads at a speed that would make a race-car driver panic. I took deep breaths in an effort to lower my blood pressure to two hundred over one hundred.

Noah put his hand on my thigh. "What a nightmare finding Strong like that. We better cancel rehearsal for tomorrow night, Nicky."

I looked at the frightened deer hovering in the shoulder of the road and felt their pain. "Noah, what were you doing in the Physical Education building tonight?"

"When you didn't come home at the usual time, given the recent murders at the gym, I got worried. So I came looking for my man." He kissed my cheek.

Moving Noah's face back in the direction of the road, I said, "Why were you in Van Granite's office?"

"I saw his office light on, so I asked him if he had seen you."

Noah sped around a steep curve. I held on to the edge of my seat like a roller-coaster rider. "Before we found Strong, I overheard you saying something to Granite about not wanting anybody to know."

"Are you spying on me, Nicky?"

"More like spying on our narcissistic Professor Granite."

Noah pressed his foot on the gas pedal like he was riding a bumper car. "Van was telling me about a technique he uses in his classes. Any student who misses class must do push-ups at the start of the next class. If a student is late for class, the student does sit-ups upon arrival. I told him I'd like to try that in my classes, and I asked him not to mention it to anyone...for the surprise element."

"Is that what you two were grinning about before we left?" I asked.

"I guess so."

"Our theatre students will be quite fit by the end of your experiment."

Noah laughed, and his blue eyes sparkled.

I took in my gorgeous, maniacally driving partner. "I don't trust Granite, Noah."

Noah shrugged. "He's a bit full of himself, but aren't we all, Nicky."

"Not like that."

Noah said, "Working on the competition I realized there isn't much difference between athletes and actors. It's all about the show."

As we thankfully turned a corner to our side street, Noah slowed down to four driving points above the speed limit.

I asked, "Why did Granite slap your behind before we left his office?"

Noah laughed. "That's what people in the sports world do. It doesn't mean anything."

We miraculously pulled up to our driveway. Noah shut off the engine and took my trembling hand in his. "Nicky, don't be jealous of Van. He may be all muscle and might on the outside, but on the inside, he's half the stud you are."

We shared a long, wet kiss, then Noah and I walked to our wraparound porch and kissed again. Once inside the hallway, we kissed and dropped our clothes as we made our way up the long flared staircase and into our four-poster bed. Lying on his back with me resting on top of him, Noah wrapped his warm arms around me and massaged my back muscles. The moment I suited up, Noah pressed my buttocks closer, taking me inside him deeper and deeper with each thrust. I kissed and caressed his smooth face, neck, and chest, then took his hooked erection inside my hand. As we climaxed, I said, "You're the only one for me, Noah."

Noah replied, "I love you, Nicky."

We cuddled in each other's arms until restful sleep ended, and the sky outside our bedroom window matched the color of Noah's eyes.

★

Noah and I taught our classes the next day, then Noah rushed home to make dinner for his parents. After listening to my students complain about their grades during my office hour, I finished my course assessment reports, and headed for home. While locking my office door, I noticed Jimmy Saline walking down the hallway.

"Jimmy, how are things going in your student aide position at the gym?"

His thin white hand scratched at his thick red hair. "Fine, Professor. Thank you for asking."

I leaned against my office door. "Why is it that you didn't apply for a student aide position in *our* department? We have a number of positions in set and prop construction, lighting, costuming, public relations."

"No offense, Professor. I like my theatre professors and classes, and it's great being involved in the shows, but Tony's a great guy to work for."

*And he has an amazing looking son.*

Jimmy said, "And I don't mind sweeping, stocking, and cleaning the gym equipment."

"*And* you have the opportunity to see Mack Heath."

Jimmy looked down at his toothpick legs swimming inside his brown corduroy pants.

Picking his chin up with thumb, I said, "Jimmy, I'd be the last person on this campus to judge you for being attracted to another man. Do you understand what I'm saying?"

His head bobbed up and down on his long, thin neck.

"Good." I walked down the hall with him.

"Mack's a terrific guy," Jimmy said. "He's working really hard on his training and his poses. He deserves to win the competition."

"Mack has an amazing physique."

"It isn't just his body, Professor. Mack's the nicest, kindest guy I know."

I smiled in recollection of first love. "Did you hear the bad news about Professor Strong?"

Jimmy nodded. "Professor Granite emailed us last night. Do they know what caused it?"

"Not yet."

"Mack was really upset. We texted about it through most

of the night. Mack's so sensitive and compassionate." He said proudly, "Mack said he really appreciated me listening." He added with concern, "Mack also told me that after Jillian got Granite's email, she texted Mack about it in near hysterics."

I stopped at the doorway of Jimmy's next class. "Mack and Jillian were close to Professor Strong?"

"Sure, Strong was their department head."

*Among other things.*

"Were Mack and Jillian upset over Jonathan's and Tim's deaths?" I asked.

"Of course. They were in competition with those two guys, but they didn't want to see them dead."

I leaned my hand against the doorway. "Are you working at the gym tonight?"

Obviously elated at the prospect, Jimmy replied, "That I am."

"Do me a favor, Jimmy?"

"Sure, Professor, name it."

I leaned in closer. "If you see or hear anything, or anyone, suspicious at the gym, will you let me know?"

"No problem, Professor." Like one of Sherlock Holmes' street urchins, he added, "Do you think Jonathan, Tim, and Professor Strong were murdered?"

"Something is going on over there. I have the distinct feeling that it isn't very good. Watch out for yourself at the gym, will you?"

"Don't worry, Professor, I'll be careful." Jimmy smiled like a prom queen. "And I'll look out for Mack too."

I arrived home. Noah introduced me to his parents, a dairy farmer and his bookkeeper wife from Wisconsin.

Noah had set the dining room table like the cover of a beautiful homes magazine for virgins. Fresh cut white flowers hung delicately from the crystal chandelier. The window seat was adorned with soft, white rose pedals. The long wooden table was covered with a white lace tablecloth adorned with vanilla-scented candles in stunning silver candleholders, delicate china plates sporting pictures of white lilies of the valley, polished silver cutlery, and white satin napkins bound in silver leaf-patterned napkin holders.

My boyfriend and I, wearing white shirts, blue pants, and blue blazers, sat at the heads of the table like the lords of the manor. Noah's parents sat at the center of the table wearing sweatshirts, Bermuda shorts, and sneakers, looking like the hired help dining with the Queen of England (or in our case — queens). The first of seven courses that Noah had prepared was sitting on a small china plate in front of each of us.

Scott Oliver peered over his barrel of a stomach, afraid to touch anything on the table. Bonnie Oliver ran a nervous hand through her short, gray-blonde hair, looking at her crystal water glass and crystal wine glass, not sure which to use.

"What is this dish again, Noah?" asked his father like Columbus speaking to a Native American.

"It's a blue cheese and pear tart with a fig and olive tapenade," replied Noah.

"How…nice, honey." Noah's mother glanced at the three forks next to her plate, trying to decide which one to select.

Noah announced, "After the appetizer, I have avgolemono soup, pumpkin-parsnip ravioli, roasted asparagus in a beet-avocado reduction, chicken scarpariello, seven-mushroom risotto, and flambéed vanilla-poached pear crêpes with powdered sugar and cinnamon."

"I hope there aren't nuts in any of that, Noah," said his mother with lines deepening on her smooth face. "You don't want to set off your allergy."

"No nuts, Mom," replied Noah.

"Noah, you shouldn't have gone to all this trouble just for us," said Scott.

"It's my pleasure, Dad," replied Noah, beaming with pride.

Bonnie raised one of her spoons, put it down and raised another. After tasting a few bites of her appetizer, she smiled like a baby with gas. "Mm, it's delicious."

Mirroring his wife, Scott used the same spoon and took a taste. Looking as if he had eaten glue, Scott said with a plastered smile on his face, "You're a great cook, Noah. You take after your mother."

Having had enough of this charade, I picked up our appetizer plates. "Everyone, come with me."

Noah and his parents followed me through the double doors into the kitchen. I put the plates in the sink then set the breakfast nook with four cotton orange place mats, paper napkins, and department store plates, silverware, and glasses. After I emptied our refrigerator, Scott stood at the counter happily cutting green peppers, onions, mushrooms, sweet potatoes, and cheddar cheese, while Bonnie joyously whipped eggs with milk in a bowl. At the oven, I tossed a pad of butter onto the skillet and asked Noah to pour four glasses of milk.

When we were all seated at the breakfast nook eating our omelets, we looked out the kitchen window and complimented the sun setting magenta, indigo, and marigold garlands around the house.

Bonnie kissed my cheek. "Thank you, Nicky. This is the best omelet I've ever tasted!"

"Hear, hear!" Scott said, shooting me a high-five. Then affectionately messing his son's hair, Scott said, "We appreciate all the time and energy it must have taken to make that avioli soup and chicken scarparini, Noah, but that's just not our kind of food."

Bonnie added, "Maybe you can donate it to a homeless shelter, honey."

Disappointed but understanding, Noah answered, "It's fine Mom, Dad. Nicky and I will eat it tomorrow night, and we'll get take-out for you."

I winked at Bonnie and Scott. "Make that three for take-out tomorrow night."

Noah nudged my side and I blew him a kiss.

After a sip of her milk, Bonnie said, "Thank you both for letting us come visit."

"We're thrilled to have you, Mom," Noah replied.

"You two boys have a beautiful home," she said.

"Thanks, Mom," said Noah.

"How long have you two guys been living here?" asked

Scott with his mouth full.

"Nine months," I replied.

"Did you buy the baby bassinet yet?" asked Scott with a wink
at his son.

We all laughed, though I noticed Noah's laugh was forced.

"Oh, that reminds me!" Bonnie pulled her iPad out of her purse. "I want to take a picture of all of us to show Judy back in Wisconsin." After we all posed together, Bonnie aimed and pressed the iPad, then emailed the picture to her friend. "Noah, you know Judy and Jack at the next farm from us."

"Sure," Noah replied.

Bonnie looked at her iPad screen and laughed. "Judy said she was worried that since Noah is a big college professor, dinner might be something French, but she says it looks delicious." Bonnie continued reading. "Judy likes the kitchen curtains too." After more staring at the screen, she added, "And Judy says that Nicky and Noah make a nice couple."

I kissed Noah's cheek, and he squirmed like a kid out on a date with his parents driving.

Bonnie said, "Judy also said you need to go on a diet, Dad."

Scott laughed and helped himself to another omelet. "Take a picture of this for her," said Scott, and Bonnie obliged.

Trying to follow the Oliver family logic, I asked, "What does a baby bassinet have to do with Judy and Jack in Wisconsin? Did they just have a baby?"

"Ah!" said Bonnie nearly choking on a green pepper. "At their age! Noah, do you remember their son, Timmy?"

"Sure. We played together as kids," Noah said.

After a nod and a swallow, Bonnie said, "Timmy went away to college, then to graduate school, then to another graduate school."

"And now he's home without a job," added Scott helping himself to yet another omelet.

Bonnie continued. "Timmy is back, like Dad said, and he

brought Tommy with him!"

"Hopefully Tommy has a job," I interjected to thunderous laughter from Scott.

"You two!" Bonnie said with a scolding look at Scott and me. "Before Dad and I flew here, Judy told me that Timmy and Tommy are getting married next month. They rented that big catering hall on the highway. You know the one, Noah."

Noah nodded.

"I hope Jack sells a lot more milk," said Scott with a wink at me.

Stifling a laugh, I said, "That's terrific. Are you two going to the wedding?"

"Of course," replied Bonnie. "Noah, if you were home, you could have come too."

Noah's face reddened. "I haven't seen Timmy in many years, Mom."

I asked, "Noah, when you and Timmy...played together, were you —?"

"Isn't that the sweetest thing?" Bonnie said to her son. "Nicky's jealous!"

"Answer the question, Noah," Scott said as if my attorney.

"They were just children for heaven's sake," said Bonnie coming to Noah's defense.

"We fooled around together," Noah said. Hearing himself, he added, "We played games together."

After a nudge from Scott, I said, "What kind of *games*?"

Noah raised his eyes to the orange curtains. "Timmy and I never did *anything*. I didn't even know he was gay."

Bonnie took another omelet. "Noah, you didn't *know*?"

"No. Did *you*, Mom?" asked Noah in astonishment.

"Of course, honey," said Bonnie.

"How?" asked Noah.

"Mothers always know. It's our momdar," said Bonnie proudly.

Scott explained, "Timmy told Judy when he was ten. And of course Judy told your mother." Scott smiled at his son. "I always say God makes us how he makes us, and God doesn't make mistakes."

"Amen!" said Bonnie as if she was at a revival tent meeting. She swallowed a piece of omelet, savoring the delicious taste, then said, "Judy told me that Timmy and Tommy have already made plans to adopt a baby...from Vietnam! Timmy and Tommy have to go all the way over there to get her! I told Judy that since Timmy and Tommy are making such a long trip, they should get a second one while they are there. I mean the cost of airfare and hotels nowadays is outrageous, even in Vietnam. And who would want to go to Vietnam anyway, except for a war, or to get a child? How many people plan their vacations saying, 'Let's go to Vietnam this year?' Besides, a child should grow up with a sibling."

"I'm an only child, Mom," interjected Noah.

"We tried for more, but the first one broke the mold," said Bonnie with a kiss to her son's cheek.

Scott winked at me. "We tried and tried and tried."

"It took us a while to have *this* one," Bonnie said, pointing at Noah. "He was a breech baby. We were all so worried. I was in *agony*...for *hours*!" She kissed Noah's forehead. "The *pain* you caused me! It still hurts on a rainy day."

"My little breech baby," I said kissing Noah's scarlet cheek.

"Do you have a brother or sister, Nicky?" asked Bonnie.

"One brother, "I answered.

"How nice," said Bonnie.

Noah said, "Nicky told me his brother got the good looks in the family, so I'm *very* anxious to meet him."

I squeezed Noah's knee. "Down, boy. My brother and his wife work in my parents' bakery in Kansas."

"Do they sell flambéed vanilla-poached pear crêpes?" asked Scott, pinching his son's nose.

"They'll probably have that at Timmy and Tommy's wedding," said Bonnie. "Unless the whole menu is Vietnamese in honor of the baby." She took her son's hand. "When Judy was going on and on, as only Judy can do, about Timmy's wedding, and now seeing you and Nicky living here so compatibly, I know it isn't any of my business, but I can't help but wonder…and I'm certainly not trying to push anything…and I will totally understand and my feelings won't be hurt one iota if you say to me, 'Mom just butt out,' but I was just—"

"Are you going to make an honest man out of my son, Nicky," said Scott, cutting to the chase.

"Oh, Dad, that's not what I meant," Bonnie said pushing her husband's shoulder.

Noah said, "Thanks for your support, Mom and Dad." Sounding like an independent politician running for office, he added, "It means a great deal to both of us. The truth is Nicky and I haven't talked about marriage and children. But when we do, you two will be the first to know."

"Ditto." I raised a glass of milk to my potential future in-laws…and my evasive future husband.

After dinner Noah and I put away the leftover food from Noah's planned dinner while Bonnie and Scott loaded the dishwasher (a future and thankful addition to our Victorian kitchen).

"Noah walked us through your beautiful campus, Nicky," said Bonnie as she stacked plates in the dishwasher. "I took pictures of all those white stone buildings, wooden arches, cobblestone bridges, and that gorgeous mountain view! Judy in Wisconsin said she wishes Timmy could get a job in such a nice place."

"Are you doing a production now, guys?" asked Scott dropping forks into the dishwasher's silverware casket.

"Not in our department, but we *are* doing a show," Noah said.

Scott leaned on the counter and posed dramatically. "You need a young leading man?"

His wife poked his ample stomach and they shared a laugh.

"Actually, it's a bodybuilding competition in the gym," explained Noah.

Ripping plastic wrap and handing it to Noah, I said, "Our department head loaned us out this semester to add dramatic touches to the Bodybuilding Department's annual competition."

"That sounds exciting," said Bonnie. "Are you boys enjoying it?"

"We were until the three deaths," answered Noah while covering bowls of food with plastic wrap.

Bonnie clutched her husband's arm. "Three deaths!"

Noah nodded. "Two students and the department head."

"What caused them?" asked Scott closing the dishwasher door.

My inner Sherlock Holmes was happy to make an appearance. "I found each of the victims in the Physical Education building. The first student had an overdose of testosterone. The word isn't in yet on the second student. The department head had a barbell lodged on his throat."

"Oh my heavens!" said Bonnie as she plopped down on the kitchen stool. "With the murders in your department last year, and now people being barbelled to death in the next department, it's a wonder any parent sends their child to that college. I hope you two boys are careful!"

"We look out for one another." I hugged Noah's back.

Scott seemed thrilled by the chase. He sat up on the counter (thankfully the Victorians made sturdy countertops). "Who are the suspects, guys?"

After swallowing a stack of vitamins at the sink, I replied, "The other five students in the competition." I added, "*And one of them was in an inheritance war with his deceased brother.*"

Taking it all in, Scott asked, "How about the faculty? No offense, you two."

I responded, "Van Granite is full of himself and desperate to be department head."

Noah added, "There's also Cheryl Stryker. She's the ex-wife of the deceased department head."

"Cheryl Stryker?" said Scott as if he had seen the entrance to a time tunnel.

Having put away all the food, Noah shut the refrigerator door and leaned his back against it. "Does that name mean something to you, Dad?"

Scott seemed lost in the past. "I knew a Cheryl Stryker back in college…in Wisconsin. I think she moved up north after graduation."

"How did you know her, Dad?" asked Noah with a glance in my direction.

"I was an Agriculture major. She was in Physical Education. We met in a required class for both our majors, Public Speaking." He smiled in recollection. "For our first speech we had to interview, then introduce someone else in the class. Cheryl and I happened to be sitting next to one another, so we interviewed each other. She stood up and said I was a freshman Agriculture major who liked fly-fishing. I got up and said Cheryl was a gorgeous blonde who was wasting her time in Physical Education and should be a model. Everyone laughed, except Cheryl. After class she called me a sexist pig, and I called her a women's lib lackey. After the next class I asked her out for coffee to apologize. To my surprise she said yes." He laughed nostalgically. "She was something. Tough as nails on the outside, but soft and sweet as butter on the inside."

"How long did you two date?" Noah asked before adding, "Sorry, Mom."

From her stool, Bonnie said, "Don't worry about me. Your father told me all about his peccadilloes, and I've told him about mine."

Scott said, "Cheryl and I dated through college. Things ended when she moved up north. Lucky for me I met your mother at the local drive-in." He kissed the top of Bonnie's head.

"Do you think it's the same person, Nicky?" asked Noah at my side.

"It sure sounds like it," I replied shifting my gaze between Noah and his father.

"Would you like to come with us to the gym sometime and find out, Dad?" asked Noah.

Scott jumped off the countertop. "Sure."

Bonnie rose from the stool and cleared her throat.

"She probably won't even remember me, Bonnie," said

Scott.

"And if she does?" asked Bonnie.

"We'll have a chat about the old days. Then she'll go back to her life and I'll go back to mine," replied Scott.

Bonnie pressed her chest against her husband's. "Just remember that she's divorced and you're *not*." She kissed his cheek. "At least not yet."

Noah's parents retired to the guest room (thankfully Noah didn't make it up with white flowers), and Noah and I straightened up the dining room.

Carefully stacking the china plates, Noah said, "Sorry I went overboard with dinner."

"It's the thought that counts." I slowly placed the crystal glasses onto their shelf in our Victorian hutch.

Noah put the plates back inside the hutch. "What do you think of my mom and dad?"

"I adore them as much as I adore you." I kissed his delicious neck.

Noah collected the silverware and placed it inside a drawer in the hutch. "Wasn't it funny how Dad got so engrossed in the deaths at the gym?"

"And they say boys don't marry their fathers."

We kissed.

I came up for air. "Speaking of marriage, wasn't it wild how your folks practically asked us to set the date?"

"Yeah." He smiled.

"What do you think about that?"

"What do I think about what?"

"Marriage." I held my breath.

Noah collected the flowers, looking ready to walk down the aisle. "I think it's great. When the time is right."

I helped him gather the rest of the flowers. "Is the time right, Noah?" I smiled. "You don't want your parents to be one-upped by Judy and Jack in Wisconsin."

He put the flowers in a large bowl then took my face in his hands. "Nicky, I love you more each day. But let's wait to have this discussion."

"How many more days?

"When we both feel ready. Okay?" He kissed my nose.

Miffed but understanding, I said, "Okay."

Noah placed the napkins and napkin rings inside a hutch drawer. "Can you believe that Dad knew Cheryl Stryker?"

I folded the tablecloth. "A college town is a small world."

Noah took the tablecloth, finished folding it, and put it inside the hutch. "I hope Cheryl and Dad will connect while Dad is visiting." Always the compassionate soul, he added, "With Brick's death, it might be good for Cheryl to have an old friend around."

Since the dining room was back to its old self, I asked, "Speaking of the gym, since there's no rehearsal tonight, do you mind if I zip over there for a quick workout?"

"Sure, just be careful, Nicky."

"Always."

We shared a long, deep kiss, then I slapped his behind.

"What's that for?" Noah asked.

"That's what we do in the gym world."

He slapped my butt, and I was out the door.

When I got to the gym locker room, I changed into my sweats, then stretched out my leg muscles on a nearby bench. Upon reaching the weight room, I sat in a leg machine, like a woman at the gynecologist, and yanked, pulled, and pushed my legs in and out again and again. Moving on to the next machine, I crouched my body into a ball, then lifted my legs like someone trying to escape a shrinking room. When my legs threatened to go out on strike, I limped over to the cardio room and struggled out twenty minutes on the running machine—or in my case, hobbling machine.

Feeling like George Jetson on speed, I jumped off the machine and leaned against it to catch my breath. When I heard voices, I ducked behind the machine to listen.

"Tony asked me to wipe down the machines in here before I log out," said Jimmy Saline.

"I'll help you," replied Mack Heath.

"You don't have to do that."

"I want to help you, Jimmy."

I crawled out of the cardio room on shaky legs, unnoticed

by the two students as they began wiping the machines.

After I changed back into my shirt, slacks, and blazer, I heard Mack and Jimmy headed for the locker room. Feeling like a magician's assistant, I squeezed into my locker, keeping the door open just enough for me to see outside.

Wearing his sweat clothes and carrying a gym bag, Mack sat on the bench in the shower room and asked Jimmy to join him. In his usual brown and baggy flannel and corduroy clothes, Jimmy happily took a seat next to the handsome bodybuilder.

"Thank you for texting with me last night, Jimmy. I was a total mess," said Mack.

"No problem, Mack. I was glad to do it." Jimmy looked at Mack compassionately. "Are you feeling better tonight?"

Mack shrugged his strapping shoulders. "First Jonathan, then Tim and now Professor Strong." He put his handsome head in his thick hands. "I can't believe it!"

Jonathan raised his bony hand to put it on Mack's back, thought better of it, and rested his hand at his own side. "I'm sure you really miss them."

Fighting back tears, Mack replied, "Professor Strong was my...mentor."

*Among other things.*

"He really cared about me, and I cared about him. I'm going to miss him so much."

"I'm really sorry, Mack."

Mack took his hands away from his face and looked at Jimmy. "I know you are, Jimmy. And I appreciate it."

"Is there anything I can do to help?" Jimmy asked.

"You already helped by meeting me here tonight."

Jimmy smiled. "That's great."

Mack wiped a tear from his high cheekbone. "Professor Strong would want me to keep training hard to win the competition, and in his honor, that's what I'm going to do."

"That's the spirit!"

Mack mussed Jimmy's red hair. "You want to help me?"

"You know it!"

Mack rose and took off his sweat clothes, wearing only

small green posing trunks. He opened his gym bag and placed a razor, can of shaving cream, bottle of olive oil, and tanning spray on the bench. "I worked legs tonight, so let's do those."

*Don't remind me.*

Mack explained, "The shaving cream goes on first. After you shave and oil, the tanning spray is last. Can you do that, Jimmy?"

"Sure!" Jimmy answered like a contestant on a game show.

"Thanks again for helping me."

"My pleasure!" Jimmy got down on his knees in front of Mack, shook the shaving cream, and sprayed the foamy lather up and down Mack's legs. Next, he took the razor and carefully shaved both of Mack's legs from top to bottom, periodically washing the razor in the nearby sink.

Mack asked, "Do you like being a Theatre major?"

"Yeah. Professor Abbondanza and Professor Oliver are really cool."

*Smart student!*

"I've always been a ham, telling jokes, making goofy faces, doing impersonations. It started out as a way to entertain the big kids, so they wouldn't beat me up. Then I kept doing it, because I like to make people laugh. It feels good inside when other people are happy." His face turned as red as his hair. "And I like the applause."

"I know what you mean. I'll admit I like the applause I get in bodybuilding too." Mack added, "Hey, you've seen me posing. Now it's my turn to see *you* perform."

Jimmy impersonated a few celebrities and Mack cracked up.

"You better stop, or I'll accidentally get cut."

"I'll watch out for you, Mack."

Mack started to put his hand on Jimmy's head but stopped himself. "Have you been in any of the plays on campus?"

Jimmy nodded, and his hair flew all over his face. "Most of the comedies. Professor Abbondanza is a great director."

*I always liked that kid.*

Mack responded, "He's done a great job working with us for the competition too."

*I always liked Mack too.*

After shaving Mack's legs, Jimmy wiped them with a towel from Mack's bag. Next Jimmy poured some oil onto his hands then slowly applied it to Mack's legs. Jimmy spent extra time massaging Mack's muscular calves and thighs until the oil was fully absorbed. I noticed a lump growing in the front of Mack's posing trunks.

Mack looked down then turned his back to Jimmy. "Thanks, I can spray the tan on myself."

"You sure? I don't mind doing it."

"I'm sure," said Mack, obviously nervous.

Jimmy sat on the bench and put the supplies back inside the gym bag. "I'm sorry if I made you uncomfortable."

"What?" Mack sat on the bench with the towel draped over his lap.

"It's obvious that I'm attracted to you." He waved his skeletal arms. "But I totally get that nothing can ever happen between us. And I'm completely fine with just helping you win the competition." He smiled. "And being your friend." His eyes bore into Mack's. "I want you to know that I'll never cross the line."

Mack started laughing.

"What did I say?"

After a deep breath that further expanded his mountainous pectoral muscles, Mack said, "Jimmy, remember I told you that I've never been attracted to anyone?"

"Yeah?"

"That's not totally true."

"Okay."

*Tell him about Brick Strong.*

Mack moved the bag to sit closer to Jimmy. "It was true for most of my life, but it's not true anymore."

"How come?"

"Everything changed a few days ago."

"Why?"

"Things changed when I...met *you*."

Jimmy put his hands over his mouth. "Did I say...or do something wrong?"

Mack laughed again. "Actually, you said and did something *right*." Moving Jimmy's hands away from his mouth, Mack leaned over and placed his lips over Jimmy's.

Jimmy looked like a shock victim. "Did you just kiss me?"

"Yes."

"Is this a practical joke or something?" Jimmy got up and looked around the shower room. "Is there a hidden camera or a bunch of kids watching somewhere?"

Mack stood next to him, wrapped his muscular arms around Jimmy's skinny body, and Jimmy's body sank into Mack's. They shared a long, passionate kiss.

While they were otherwise engaged, I slipped out of the locker room and drove home.

When I walked into our bedroom, I found Noah sitting in the wingback chair next to the fireplace. I bent down to give him a kiss and his spine stiffened.

"What's wrong?" I put my wallet on the dresser and starting to get undressed.

Noah blushed like a virgin bride, and whispered, "It feels weird with my parents right down the hall."

I laughed. "Noah, we're not teenagers, and your parents aren't homophobes."

"I know it's ridiculous, but it's how I feel, Nicky."

Tossing my clothes into the closet hamper, I said, "Maybe we should make it legal. Then you'll feel better." I kissed the top of his strawberry-scented head.

Noah rose. "I think I just need a little fresh air."

"Now?" I stood naked in front of Noah.

"I feel kind of antsy with everything going on at the gym...and with my *resounding success* of a dinner. I'll be back up soon."

"Okay, be careful."

"I will." Noah blew me a quiet kiss and was gone.

Exhausted from my workout and my stint as a locker spy,

I quickly showered, slipped on my nighttime gym shorts and T-shirt, then crawled into our four-poster bed. My body sank into the high-thread-count sheets, and I drifted off to sleep the minute my head hit the hypoallergenic pillow.

My dreams were distorted images of Rodney Towers wrestling with Maria Ruiz, Kim Sim waving his father's millions over the coffin of his deceased brother, the ghost of Brick Strong chasing Jillian Flowers, and Mack Heath seducing Brick for his vote while Jimmy Saline ghost-busted Brick. They continued with Noah's father kissing Cheryl Stryker, Van Granite arm-wrestling Cheryl to become department head, and Granite slapping Noah's naked backside like a cowboy at a rodeo. My final dream, however, was the most vivid.

As in my previous vision, I sat in the front row of the Treemeadow Bodybuilding Competition eighteen years ago. Tony Piccolo's son at twenty-one won the gold cup. Camera flashes went off, then fans cheered and congratulated the handsome young bodybuilder on stage. As the audience began to disperse from the gymnasium, Robbie motioned for me to join him on stage. I made my way through the throngs and landed at Robbie's side. I found myself inches away from his perfectly sculpted body as Robbie stood next to me in his posing trunks. Being so close to Robbie's perfect musculature made me quite aroused. I was also drawn in by Robbie's shiny black hair, piercing hazel eyes, and strong nose and chin. Robbie Piccolo put his strong hand on my shoulder, leaned in to me, and placed his soft mouth against my ear. I felt Robbie's warm breath on my neck as I took in his scent of clean pine. Robbie whispered in my ear, "Please help me."

I woke in bed with my erection nearly ripping a hole in my gym shorts.

JOE COSENTINO

88

# Chapter Five

By the time I got up the next morning, Noah and his parents had eaten breakfast and left to go sightseeing around our quaint college town. As I sat in the breakfast nook eating my cereal and a stack of vitamins chased down by cranberry juice, I thought about the night before. *Can people communicate to one another through their dreams? If so, what was Robbie trying to tell me? Was he in trouble back then? Is he in some kind of trouble now? What can I do to help him? And why I am obsessed with the younger image of a straight married man with kids!*

Not a fan of psychiatry, I opted for the next best thing, a chat in the hallowed office of my department head. Perched on high-backed leather chairs flanking the cherry wood fireplace, Martin Anderson and I sipped hot cocoa from china cups, enjoying the warmth of our drinks and the fire.

Martin rested his cup on a nearby cherry wood end table. After dabbing at the corner of his full lips with a monogrammed violet cloth napkin, and adjusting his violet bowtie and sweater vest, he said, "It sounds to me like your subconscious mind is telling you something, Nicky."

I rested my cup next to Martin's. "What do you think it means?"

Rubbing his large bald head with his tiny fingers, Martin answered like a wise alien, "Perhaps Robbie embodies, no pun intended, the current crop of young bodybuilders in Treemeadow's competition, asking *you* to protect them." He leaned in my direction like a televangelist spotting a good-looking cameraman. "Tell me *all* about the student bodybuilders."

"Rodney Towers and Maria Ruiz are involved in a

love/hate relationship. Kim Sim is due back from Maine today, no doubt to Van Granite's delight. Jillian Flowers has eyes for Mack Heath, but Mack seems otherwise engaged with Jimmy Saline."

"*Our* Jimmy Saline from *this* department?"

"The one and only."

Martin chuckled. "Will wonders never cease?" Then he said seriously, "You've got to watch over those students, Nicky."

I nodded. "I also have to watch over Noah."

"Is Noah in danger?"

My spine stiffened. "It seems Professor Granite has taken a liking to my boyfriend."

Martin patted my knee like a nanny scolding a toddler. "Don't be silly. Noah has eyes for only you." His dark eyes twinkled. "Though I can't see why."

I sat at the edge of my seat. "Martin, I want more than anything to marry Noah and have a million years with him, like you and Ruben."

"A million? Please, Nicky, I'm not *that* ancient."

I smiled. "I'm probably making too much of this, but I get the feeling that Noah isn't interested in tying the knot."

"Everything in its time, Nicky. You boys will know when the time is right. And when that time comes, I better be invited."

"Me, too!" Shayla shouted from her seat at the crack in the office doorway.

I asked, "Speaking of big events, how are things going with your fortieth-anniversary gala at the college?"

"Things are moving along slowly but surely, just like me. Have you written your speech yet?"

"I've been tossing around a few ideas." *I completely forgot about it.*

"Thank you again for doing it, Nicky. The guest list appears to be growing each day. Even Detective Manuello is attending." Banging the palm of his hand against his forehead, Martin said, "I almost forgot! Detective Manuello was here to see me shortly before you arrived."

"What did my favorite detective have to say?"

He took another sip of cocoa then wiped his mouth. "After discussing the anniversary gala, Manuello told me the second bodybuilding student, Tim Sim, died of an overdose of *Tribulus terrestris* and creatine, whatever they are."

"They're herbs touted as muscle enhancers and penis enlargers."

"From what I've heard, you won't be needing *those* herbs, Nicky," said Shayla from her outer office.

My face reddened.

"Good one, Shayla," said Martin, followed by, "And Brick Strong died from a contusion."

I leapt to my feet like the grand prize winner on a television game show. "I knew it! Strong was murdered!"

Martin nodded sadly. "It appears so."

"And I think Toner was *given* his overdose of testosterone, as was Sim his large dose of *Tribulus terrestris* and creatine."

"By whom?"

I stared into the amber and burgundy flames beckoning me to solve the case. "That is the question."

After thanking Martin for his time, I walked past Shayla's desk in the outer office. "What do you make of all this, Shayla?"

She moved a strand of black hair back into the bun at the back of her head. "I don't trust the professors over there in Physical Education."

I sat on her desk and she shooed me off like a fly at a picnic. "You think this is about a feud between Van Granite and Cheryl Stryker?"

"Maybe it sits closer to home."

"Meaning Van Granite and Noah?"

Shayla lifted her eyes from her computer monitor. "Everybody wants to do what's right, Nicky, especially Noah. But each of us is the star of his own play. As the other characters come and go, they can change us, sometimes for the better, sometimes...not." She looked out her office window at the trees, meadows, and mountains surrounded by the lake. "Look at the radiant yellows, oranges, greens, reds, and purples out there. You know why those colors are so vibrant?"

I shrugged my shoulders. "Because it's fall?"

Shayla shook her head. "Because the sun, air, rain, and soil have joined forces to create those magnificent leaves. *But* in about a month from now, the leaves will all be *gone*."

After leaving Shayla and pondering her comments, I taught my class and did my office hour, meaning I listened to my students' fabricated reasons for missing classes.

At dinner that evening in the kitchen nook (turkey meatloaf, mashed potatoes, and peas and carrots), Bonnie said while passing the potatoes, "Nicky, you have such a charming village!" (as if I had single-handedly built all of Treemeadow). "We *loved* your historic town hall with the white columns, the wood-paneled library with the turreted reading nook, that quaint community theatre, and the cozy village green." She patted the iPad at her side. "I took lots of pictures. Judy said she doubts that Timmy and Tommy will live in such a nice place."

"Timmy and Tommy will live in Judy and Jack's garage." Patting me on the back, Scott added between bites, "That little white church with the tall steeple is a great place to get married, guys."

Noah gulped down his last bite. "Nicky, we need to get changed. The funeral starts in half an hour."

"Can we come, too?" Scott said like a kid asking to go clubbing with his parents.

Noah responded, "Dad, you can't go to a funeral wearing a sweatshirt and shorts."

"We brought nice clothes too, for heaven's sake," said Bonnie to her son. Then she said to her husband, "Why do you want to go to a funeral?"

Unlike his son, Scott didn't have finely tuned improvisational skills. "Well, ah, as they say, when in Rome."

"What does *that* mean?" asked Bonnie with a hand to her ample hip.

Scott scratched his bald head. "It means that one of our

son's colleagues passed away and we should support our son."

Not buying it, Bonnie came face to face with Scott. "Especially since our son's colleague was once married to your old flame who will no doubt be at the funeral."

"Then there's that," said Scott sheepishly.

Happy to have such entertaining (hopefully) future in-laws, I swallowed my last vitamin, and said, "Everyone put your plate in the dishwasher, then follow me upstairs to get changed."

Fifteen minutes later we all walked down the flared wooden staircase looking like the cast of an old black and white movie. Bonnie Oliver was decked out in a black chiffon dress, and Scott Oliver was bursting out of the seams of an old black suit. Gazing at Noah in his dark suit, I wanted to ravish my mystery man on the banister. I leaned in to kiss Noah on the lips and he kissed the cleft in my chin instead, glancing over at his parents awkwardly.

Bonnie took a selfie of us, and Judy responded that she hoped Timmy and Tommy would look as good in their wedding suits as Noah and I looked in our funeral attire.

Then the four of us piled into my car with Scott (who insisted) at the wheel, and away we flew. And boy did we fly! I thought Noah drove like maniac, but his father had Noah beat by a mile — driven in about ten seconds! Forget dairy farming, Scott Oliver should have been an ambulance driver, or a European. He screeched and skidded around every curve and corner and got us to the funeral home in five minutes flat.

Noah, Scott, Bonnie and I entered the funeral home's main sitting room with its clustered sofas and wingback chairs arranged for grieved conversation. I led the way to the center of the room. In that area chairs were stationed in rows for easy viewing of the mini stage up front, where Brick Strong's ashes were displayed in a gold urn on a black table under a blue pin spot.

We offered our condolences to Cheryl, standing in the front row. The deceased's ex-wife, dressed in a black pantsuit, dabbed a dry handkerchief to her tear-free face and thanked us for coming. She did a double-take when Scott Oliver placed his large hand in hers. "Cheryl, do you remember me?"

Tears finally brimmed in Cheryl Stryker's eyes. "Scott! I can't believe it!"

The two old paramours embraced as Bonnie Oliver's face turned ashen.

"What are you doing here, Scott?" asked Cheryl, losing twenty years.

With a pink glow in his flabby cheeks, Scott answered, "My son, Noah, teaches in the Theatre Department at Treemeadow."

"I didn't know Noah was your son!" said Cheryl eyeing Scott like a loin of pork in a butcher's window.

"Dad's here for a little visit," said Noah like a kid whose father had crashed his party.

I put my arm around Bonnie. "And this is Noah's mother, and Scott's *wife*, Bonnie Oliver, here with her *husband*, all the way from Wisconsin, where they will be *returning* after their visit." *Subtlety has never been my strong point.*

Cheryl shook Bonnie's petite hand and bones cracked. "It's so nice to meet you, Bonnie."

"Likewise," said Bonnie with an unsuccessfully stifled sneer. *Try saying that three times fast.*

Cheryl said to Bonnie, "Scott and I went to college together." She waved her masculine hand. "A million years ago."

"But it seems like only yesterday." Scott rested a hand on Cheryl's strong shoulder. "Please accept our condolences."

"Thank you, Scott." Cheryl added with a twinkle in her eyes, "Please come to see me at the college. I'd love to catch up on old times—" She looked around the room. "—under better circumstances."

"It's a date," said Scott conspiratorially.

Before Bonnie could scratch Cheryl's eyes out, Van Granite joined our group, standing in front of the mirror on the wall. Granite flexed his biceps in Noah's direction as he took Cheryl's hand. "Cheryl, as you know, I will miss Brick a great deal."

"We all will," said Cheryl with her eyes locked on Scott's.

"Mom, Dad, this is my colleague and friend, Van Granite," said Noah as Granite shook Scott's and Bonnie's hands.

*Friend?*

Granite aimed his pectoral muscles at Noah. "Noah is doing a great job working with our bodybuilding students on their posing routines for our upcoming competition."

*And what am I, chopped barbells?*

"I'm sure it will be a fine competition," said Scott with a smile at Cheryl.

"The students look like strong, *young* gods and goddesses." Granite offered me a look filled with pity. "Don't they, Nicky?"

I put my arm around Noah. "Noah and I have enjoyed working with them."

After checking himself out in the mirror and moving a strand of gelled hair back into place, Granite said to Cheryl, "I'll take Brick's class for the remainder of the term."

Cheryl's back stiffened. "No need, Van. I've already hired an adjunct instructor."

Granite's green eyes doubled in size. "*You* hired an adjunct?"

Cheryl smiled victoriously. "Yes, the Dean of Phys. Ed. appointed me Interim Department Head of Bodybuilding."

Granite developed TMJ on the spot. "Is that so?"

"That's so," replied Cheryl like a general after a winning battle.

"Excuse me." Granite hurried away as if to escape an explosion—his own.

Noah said, "Nicky, Mom, Dad, I'll catch up with you later." To my chagrin, Noah followed Granite out of the room.

Bonnie excused Scott and herself, then led her husband away from Cheryl Stryker to a sofa in the back of the room.

As the next group of mourners gave Cheryl their condolences, I moved to the young woman standing beside her. She had stringy hair and a huge nose. Wearing a navy-blue dress that drooped off her thin body, she blew her runny nose and wiped her wet eyes.

"I'm very sorry for your loss," I said not sure of the woman's identity.

"Thank you," she answered with a sniff.

I offered my hand. "I'm Nicky Abbondanza. I teach at Treemeadow in the Theatre Department."

Laying her wet hand in mine like a dead fish on a sushi plate, she said, "I work in the Admissions Office at the college. I'm Abigail Strong."

*Brick and Cheryl's daughter and Jonathan Toner's beard/girlfriend.* I said consolingly, "What a week it has been for you. First Jonathan and now your dad."

She nodded. "Even though Jonathan and I were...estranged at the time of his death—"

*Meaning he dumped you.*

"—I miss him very much." Abigail moved a clump of straw-like hair behind her cauliflower ear. "Jonathan really left his mark on me."

*As he did with the Sim twins in the shower room.*

"Jonathan and I had a relationship very much like my parents did. They were divorced but still very much in love." She cried into her wet handkerchief.

*Is that why I caught Brick with Mack Heath, then with Jillian Flowers in his office?*

"I'm not well myself," Abigail said with a sympathy seeking gaze. "Things have been crazy busy at work with all the new administrative hires in my department. Losing Jonathan and now my father is the last straw. How could they do this to me?" She wailed on my shoulder like a baby with colic.

Seeing Noah and Van Granite re-enter the room, I patted Abigail's bony back, offered my condolences again, and excused myself.

As I met them at a brick fireplace toward the middle of the room, I heard Noah say to Granite, "It's different, but I like it."

I put my arm around Noah. "What's different?"

Noah responded, "Working with the bodybuilding students as opposed to our theatre students."

Granite said, "Our students are more buff." He patted my stomach. "As are our faculty."

Before I could clobber Granite with the fireplace poker, Bonnie and Scott approached and Noah slithered out of my grasp.

As if a guest at a coming-out party (no pun intended), Bonnie said, "Noah, introduce us to the rest of your little friends and co-workers."

"We want to tell them how proud we are of our son," added Scott with a pinch to Noah's cheek.

Bonnie took the iPad out of her purse. "And I want to get pictures of me posing with some college professors. Wait until Judy sees that!"

As if a tour guide, Noah said, "The tour starts here. Follow me, folks. And we're walking…"

Alone with Granite, I said, "Noah and I are enjoying his parents' visit."

"That's not what Noah said," replied Granite with a smirk.

"It's an awkward time for him."

"When *isn't* it awkward to have your parents around?"

"Where are *your* parents, Granite?"

Granite shrugged his broad shoulders. "Who knows? I was brought up in foster homes. Raised in poverty, as they say, by people who were more interested in their monthly check than in me. Bodybuilding was my ticket to college, and ultimately to a job here."

"How fortunate for all of us." I unleashed my best fabricated smile.

A young man dressed in a very expensive turquoise suit and vermilion tie joined us. As he dropped his black leather coat on a nearby chair, I noticed he wore more gold rings on his fingers than a televangelist during a fundraising drive.

Our jaws dropped when the young man said, "Hello, um Professors. I'm, you know, back from Maine. Kinda leaving one like funeral for another."

Granite threw his sculpted arms around Kim Sim. "Welcome back, Kim! It's terrific to see you. We have to get you back into the gym to work out for the competition!"

"Um thank you, Professor," said Kim, out of breath from Granite's bear hug.

"My condolences again about your brother," I said. "I hope everything is all right at home."

Kim nodded. "Like right after the, you know, funeral for Tim, my father like passed away. As his um heir, I settled Poppy's like affairs, then came back to like school."

*With bulging pockets in your fancy new pants.*

With his arms still around Kim, Granite said, "Tell me all about it, Kim."

"Yeah, like tell our professor, you know, all about it, Kim," said Jillian Flowers with the stench of beer on her breath.

Granite released Kim. "Have you been drinking, Jillian? You know that's against the rules of the competition."

Jillian laughed bitterly, and some spittle landed on her black dress. "What's the like point of, you know, following the rules, Professor? I can't um win the like competition now." She pointed at Kim Sim as if he was Exhibit A in a courtroom. "You'll um obviously be like voting for your, you know, boy Kim. And with Tim like gone to, you know, twin heaven, Professor Stryker will no doubt like vote for Kim too." Jillian flicked back her blonde hair and locked eyes with Kim. "Looks like you, you know, won a fortune, a um bodybuilding contest, and a like sugar daddy, Kim."

Kim Sim's eyes became sticks of dynamite. "Take that like back, Jillian."

"Take what like back?" asked Jillian, not recalling what she had said.

Granite stood between the two students. "Let's take this outside, shall we?"

As Granite and the students left the room, I noticed Martin, Ruben, and Shayla sitting on a sofa at another section of the room. I walked over and greeted my department head, his spouse, and our department office assistant.

"Nicky, I understand you are the keynote speaker at my husband's fortieth anniversary tribute," said Ruben with a proud look at Martin. "Have you finished your speech?"

*I have to get started on that!* "Finished and perfected, Ruben," I said with a smile at the well-dressed elderly man.

Martin said, "Noah introduced us to his parents in the hallway. They are quite charming, just like their son and his partner."

Shayla asked with a raised eyebrow, "How come you and Noah aren't together, Nicky?"

"Noah is busy introducing Bonnie and Scott to everyone from the college," I replied. "I already know the cast of characters, including you, Shayla."

I heard a giggle and followed the sound to a pretty middle-aged woman sitting in a chair nearby. Her face seemed familiar, but I couldn't place her.

"I offered her my hand. "Nicky Abbondanza."

"Sue Heath," said the woman with a bat of her long eyelashes.

*Heath?* "Are you Mack Heath's mom?" I asked.

"Guilty as charged." Sue rose from her chair with a warm smile.

"I'm working with Mack on the bodybuilding competition," I explained.

"I know. It's all Mack talks about. I've never seen Mack so excited, and so singularly focused on something." A line formed on Sue Heath's alabaster forehead. "I sure hope he wins."

Shayla cleared her throat. I introduced Sue to Martin, Ruben, and Shayla.

"How do I know you, Sue?" asked Shayla, motioning for Sue to sit back down.

"I work in the cafeteria at the college," explained Sue as she obliged. Then she added with a smile, "I've noticed French fries are your favorite food group, Shayla."

Shayla pulled her brown skirt over her ample hips. "Which I give to poor orphaned children."

Sue smiled.

"There's my son's boss!" Noah's parents joined us, as Scott continued to Martin, "Are my boy and his future husband pulling their weight, Martin?" Scott winked at me and Bonnie kissed my cheek.

"They are more than pulling their weight," answered Martin. "If I get any older, they'll be pulling *mine* too."

Everyone laughed.

Bonnie said, "Judy from Wisconsin said you don't look a day over seventy, Martin."

Ruben nudged Martin's side. Martin forced a smile.

My theatre student Jimmy Saline motioned for me to meet him across the room. I excused myself and made my way through the crowd, but not before Martin grabbed my arm and whispered in my ear, "Come and tell me everything tomorrow!"

Joining him in a corner of the room next to a bulletin board covered with pictures of Brick Strong, I asked, "What's up, Jimmy?" *No pun intended.*

"Professor, I sniffed around as you asked, and I have some news to report," he said à la Jimmy Olsen.

Taking on the character of Clark Kent, I replied, "Shoot, Jimmy."

After making sure nobody was eavesdropping, Jimmy said, "Before the funeral...Maria Ruiz gave Jillian Flowers beer in Maria's dorm room, which thanks to Jillian's brain problem caused Jillian to act aggressively."

"Check." *So that's why Jillian behaved so badly with Van Granite and Kim Sim.*

"Before you got here, Professor Stryker, Abigail Strong, and Jillian Flowers had an argument over who will take home Professor Strong's ashes after the service tonight."

"Got it," I replied as I searched for a phone booth to turn into Superman. "Anything else?"

Jimmy looked at me sheepishly. "I'm sorry to say this, Professor, but I overheard Professor Oliver talking to Professor Granite in the hallway."

My fists clenched. "And?"

"I didn't hear everything, but Professor Oliver said that

he 'enjoyed it,' and that Professor Granite was 'the best.'"
Trying to soften the blow, Jimmy added, "With all the noise
out there, I might have heard wrong."

*Let's hope Jimmy is addicted to rock music and losing his
hearing.*

"Oh, and Professor Oliver asked me to tell you he'd 'had
enough of this' and Professor Granite was driving him home.
He also said you should stay and not worry about his parents,
because he asked Professor Anderson to drive them back to
your house after the service."

"Thanks, Jimmy." *I think.* "You did good work. I'll take
care of everything." *Especially Professor Granite.*

Mack Heath made his way over to us.

"Hi, Jimmy," said Mack like a teenager on his first date.

"Hi, Mack," replied Jimmy with everyone else fading
from the room except Mack.

Jillian made her way back into the room and stared
longingly at the old pictures of Brick Strong on the bulletin
board. Noticing Mack was there, Jillian divided her lustful
gazes between Brick's pictures and Mack in the flesh.

Examining the pictures, it was no surprise to me that
Brick Strong was once a handsome, muscular, athletic looking
youth. However, Brick as a youth couldn't hold a candle to
Tony Piccolo's son, Robbie. As I thought back to those
amazing old photographs of Robbie in Tony's office, as if by
conjuring, Tony Piccolo appeared at my side in an old dark
suit and dark sneakers.

"Hiya, Professor. It's good of you to come."

"Hello, Tony. How are you holding up?"

Tony Piccolo shook his emaciated head from side to side.
"I can't believe it, Professor. I feel like Job in the Bible.
Jonathan and Tim were like sons to me. Brick was a terrific
boss." He wiped the tears from his prune-like face with the
cuff of his jacket.

I patted his bony back. "I'm sure it's been rough, Tony."

Tony looked at the pictures of Brick Strong from
youngster to middle age. "Brick was a great athlete. Look at
that form." He smiled at me. "Not as good as my Robbie

though, right, Professor?"

*No argument from me.*

Jillian said with her arm around Mack's waist, "Who like cares about Robbie Piccolo's ancient, you know, pictures, and Professor Strong's um pictures from his glory days? You're like hotter than, you know, both of them, Mack."

Mack wiggled free. "That's not nice to say, Jillian."

"What's like not nice to say?" Jillian asked.

Spotting Detective Manuello standing at the back of the room, I excused myself to join him.

"Detective, are you here to pay your condolences to the *grieving* widow and daughter?"

Manuello rubbed his nose and looked around the room. "Nice turnout."

"Brick Strong was admired by many, especially those who wanted his job." I moved in closer like a private detective in a crime noir film. "Van Granite was miffed when Cheryl Stryker announced her appointment as Interim Department Head of Bodybuilding."

"As I recall, you were going to stay out of this, Nicky."

I responded in true high drama, "It is my civic duty to come forward with what I know, Detective!"

"We wouldn't want you to shirk your civic duty." Manuello took out his notepad. "Go ahead."

"Kim Sim is back, minus a father and a brother and *plus* a fortune and a new wardrobe. Van Granite's green eyes are all over Kim, which has Jillian Flowers' nose out of joint, especially since Maria Ruiz plied Jillian with alcohol before the funeral."

Manuello stroked the numerous layers of fat under his suit jacket. "I'm sure you've heard the cause of the three deaths?"

"Testosterone, *Tribulus terrestris* and creatine, and contusion," I answered like a crime lab physician. "Any leads on who killed Strong?"

"DNA testing wasn't helpful since so many people use the gym and the equipment. I'm closing down the Bodybuilding Department's classes and competition until further notice."

"Will the gym remain open?"

"For now." Manuello cased the room. "I'm going to take a walk around.

"What should I do?"

"Enjoy the funeral."

I added over my shoulder, "I wouldn't leave early, Manuello. I hear there will be fireworks at the end of the service."

I zigzagged my way out of the crowded room and meandered around the hallway. Noticing Maria Ruiz and Rodney Towers perched on a leather couch, I ducked behind a large potted plant and observed.

"I know some people use the Bible as a weapon, Maria, but that's not what I'm doing," said Rodney with his gigantic arm stretched around the top of the couch.

"Then what *are* you doing, Rodney?" Maria asked with her dark eyes piercing into his.

"I want to *share* with you how I came to know the Lord. Will you let me do that without any backtalk?"

Maria rested her broad back on the couch cushion. "I'm not stopping you."

Rodney's face became childlike. "When I was a kid, I bullied the other kids in school."

"Why doesn't that surprise me?" said Maria.

"You agreed no talk back."

She motioned for him to continue.

"I bullied them because I felt inferior to them. It was like I was afraid to let them see the real me 'cause if they did, they'd know I was...not as good as them." He planted his powerful elbows on his giant knees. "Deep inside I wanted to be friends with the kids I tormented, but I didn't know how. So I kept calling them names and beating them up."

"What does this have to do with the Bible?"

Rodney nodded. "Since my mother worked at a diner and my father...wasn't always around, my aunt picked me up after school each day. One afternoon she saw me whopping the crap out of another kid. When we got home, she gave me her fancy Bible, which was given to her by her grandmother. My aunt told me to read the section where Jesus calls the little children to him." Rodney's thick lips spread into a huge smile. "She told me that even if nobody else wanted to be my friend, Jesus would always be there for me. All I had to do was ask him. So that night before I went to sleep, I asked Jesus to be my friend. And you know what, Maria? Jesus has been there for me ever since. In happy times and desperate times, including when my mama passed. When I'm at my lowest, I can talk to Jesus, and he always listens...like a good friend."

Maria softened. "That's nice, Rodney, but what does this have to do with me?"

Rodney took her hand. "Jesus can be your friend too. I searched my Bible and found this." He took a piece of paper out of his dark pants pocket. "'There are eunuchs who were born that way, and there are eunuchs who have been made eunuchs by others. There are also those who choose to live like eunuchs for the sake of the kingdom of heaven.'"

The muscles on Maria's back knotted, pressing through her dark blouse. "Are you calling me a eunuch, Rodney?"

He rested his hands on her bulging shoulders. "As I said, Jesus loved everyone. The poor, widowed, orphaned, the eunuchs, the concubines—"

"Um I think Maria's more like a concubine," said Jillian approaching them.

Maria rose and backed Jillian up against the wall. "You won that role, Jillian, given your *standing* with Professor Strong."

"Calm down, ladies," said Rodney, surprised to hear himself refer to Maria as a woman.

"Um calm down about what?" asked Jillian in confusion.

"You're both pathetic," Maria said, then stomped off with Rodney following her.

Leaving the holy wars, I walked to the other side of the hallway, where Mack sat hunched over on a loveseat with Jimmy sitting next to him. I stood behind a column and observed.

"I'm sorry you lost your mentor, Mack," said Jimmy.

Mack shook his head and his chestnut hair swept across his forehead. "He was more to me than a mentor, Jimmy."

"I don't understand," said Jimmy with questioning eyes.

Mack took Jimmy's hand. "Strong meant everything to me."

*Confession time?*

"And he wanted more than anything else for me to win the bodybuilding competition. So no matter what I have to do, I intend to honor his wishes. Do you understand?"

Jimmy nodded. "What can I do to help you?"

"You are helping me right now."

Mack cupped his thick hand on Jimmy's emaciated cheek, and Jimmy wiped the tears from Mack's face with the sleeve of his flannel shirt. Mack smiled and mussed Jimmy's hair, and they sat holding hands, gazing into each other's eyes.

Still testing the waters, Jimmy said, "Jillian seems to have her eye on you."

"Not interested," replied Mack.

"You sure?"

"I'm sure," answered Mack with a smile. "There's somebody else I'm interested in."

"Who might *that* be, sir?" Jimmy asked like a Tennessee Williams' heroine.

Mack laughed. "Oh, I don't know, let me see."

They shared a sweet, tentative kiss, then a longer, deeper kiss.

"I'm really glad I found you, Jimmy."

"This is like a dream come true for me. Don't wake me up, Mack."

They kissed again even more passionately. Then again.

"Mack?" Sue Heath stood in front of her son.

Mack jumped to his feet, nearly giving Jimmy whiplash.

"Mom, this is my…new friend, Jimmy Saline."

Jimmy rose awkwardly, then offered his skeletal hand to Sue. Sounding like a marine talking to his commander, he said, "Hello, Mrs. Heath. It is my honor to meet you."

Sue shook Jimmy's hand. "Well, Jimmy Saline, it seems that you and I should get acquainted." She turned to her son. "Would you like that, Mack?"

After Mack nodded cautiously, Sue sat on the loveseat, motioning for Mack to sit on one side of her and Jimmy to sit on the other. She put her arms around the two boys. "Good, because I can't think of anything I would like better."

Mack and Jimmy looked at each other and glowed.

*I like Sue Heath.* I went back into the sitting room. Realizing the minister was nearly ready to start the service, I sat next to Bonnie and Scott up front, with Noah and Van Granite noticeably absent.

The minister was so old he looked as if he might follow Brick Strong into the next world. He began the ceremony by mumbling a brief prayer, followed by the eulogy. He characterized Brick Strong as a loving husband, devoted father, and dedicated professor — with no mention of Brick's divorce and lecherous behavior with his students. Given Jillian Flowers' state, I was thankful the minister didn't ask if any of us would like to say a few words about Brick. *Speaking of Jillian, where is she?*

Bonnie whispered in my ear, "I have to use the little girl's room."

I nodded and tucked my size-ten feet underneath my chair.

After she left, Scott whispered to me, "Get used to it, Nicky. You and Noah will have to seat her next to the bathroom at your wedding."

*Hopefully Noah won't be off somewhere with Van Granite when we say our vows.*

After giving the "ashes to ashes" speech, the minister said, "Dear friends and family of Brick Strong, I conclude this service with the bestowing of the urn. It was Brick's expressed wish to me that someone very special to him be awarded this urn."

I noticed Cheryl and Abigail sit forward in their seats.

The minister struggled to lift the urn in his shaking, feeble hands. "And that individual is…Mack Heath."

Mack slowly made his way from the back of the room. When he reached the minister, he said, "I am truly honored," and reached for the urn.

Cheryl Stryker rose from her seat like an erupting volcano. "There must be some mistake."

Abigail blew her giant nose. "Calm down, Mom. I don't need any more dramatics."

"That urn belongs to us, Abby," said Cheryl like a tribal warrior. Then she strode next to the minister and reached for the urn. "This belongs to my daughter."

Abigail rose and grasped at her mother's arm, pulling it away from the urn. "I don't need this aggravation, Mom."

With Mack, Cheryl, and Abigail each pulling in different directions, the delicate minister lost his balance. The urn flew out of the minister's hands with the contents landing all over the room—and all over everyone in it like fairy (no pun intended) dust.

Bonnie screamed and rushed back into the room. "A girl is lying on the bathroom floor. She's not moving!"

It looked like Ash Wednesday gone wild as we all raced into the women's bathroom with ash marks on our faces. There we found Jillian Flowers lying on the green tile floor with a bar of soap lodged inside her mouth. Manuello felt the pulse in Jillian's neck and pronounced her dead (but clean).

# Chapter Six

The next morning over breakfast in the kitchen nook, the four of us dug into our buckwheat banana pancakes (with walnuts for three of us) and chewed over (no pun intended) the funeral from hell.

Bonnie dribbled maple syrup on her pancakes. "What a shame. What a horrible tragedy! A young woman drops dead right in front of me and I forget to take a picture to show Judy back in Wisconsin!"

"Did you take a picture of the pancakes for Judy," I asked Bonnie facetiously.

Nodding as she chewed, Bonnie replied, "Judy said Timmy and Tommy make good pancakes too."

"Not as good as these," said Scott admiring his huge stack.

In Watson mode, Noah sat staring at his plate. "I wonder why Brick Strong left his ashes to Mack Heath?"

"Maybe Mack was the professor's favorite student," offered Scott as he plopped a dollop of whipped cream onto his plate.

Taking on my Sherlock Holmes persona, I leaned back in my chair. "Or perhaps there was more to Brick's and Mack's relationship than mentor and student." I turned to my lover. "Speaking of relationships, why did you leave so early last night, Noah?"

Bonnie licked a line of syrup off her wrist. "Noah, you missed *everything*! Even the ashes flying all over the room like confetti at New Year's Eve!"

Not looking me in the eye, Noah said, "I'm not big on

funerals. Van told me he was angry about Cheryl being named Interim Department Head and he was leaving. So I asked him to drop me home on the way."

"I was worried about you." I ran my hand through Noah's blond curls.

Noah squeezed my hand affectionately, then looked at his parents and his neck muscles stiffened. "I'm fine, Nicky."

In full armchair-detective mode, Scott Oliver said, "That...what's the dead girl's name?"

"Jillian Flowers," said Bonnie.

"Right, Jillian Flowers," said Scott. "She sure isn't fine." He stuffed a forkful of pancake into his mouth. "I suspect...what's the guy's name who likes mirrors?"

"Van Granite," answered Bonnie.

"Right, Van Granite," said Scott. "There's something...laminated about that guy."

*Yeah, his teeth, and his personality.*

"From what I could hear," said Scott waving his fork at us, "Granite wants that rich kid..."

"Kim Sim," Bonnie said.

"...to win the competition," said Scott. "Maybe knocking off Jillian Flowers was Van's way of making sure that happened." His round face wrinkled. "But Van couldn't have done it, since he left early with Noah."

I replied, "Elementary, my dear Scott. After dropping off Noah, Granite could have come back to the funeral home in time to murder Jillian."

"No, he couldn't because Van was..." With six eyes staring at Noah, he thought fast, and said, "Van said he was going straight home to bed."

*Hopefully alone.*

Bonnie helped herself to more pancakes. "I suspect Cheryl Stryker. What kind of a woman doesn't take her husband's last name?"

Noah replied, "Plenty of women, especially divorced ones."

Quickly changing the subject, Scott said between bites, "On the drive home, Martin's husband...what's his name?"

"Ruben," said Bonnie.

"Right, Ruben," said Scott. "Ruben mentioned that after..."

"Mack Heath," Bonnie replied.

"...got the ashes, and Cheryl and..."

"Abigail," said Bonnie.

"...made the fuss with the urn and the minister, Mack's mother..."

"Sue," said Bonnie.

"...looked defiantly at Cheryl," said Scott.

Coming to Sue's defense, I said, "Sue seems like a very nice woman. She was probably just looking out for her son. I doubt she meant Cheryl any harm. Besides, Jillian was killed last night, not Cheryl." I swallowed a handful of vitamins with a chaser of orange juice. "Jillian was missing throughout the service, so the murderer must have done it when everyone was meandering around the main room and the hallway prior to the service. Meaning *anyone* could have killed Jillian Flowers."

I left for the college with lots of questions and no answers. When I arrived at the lab theatre classroom for my Directing I class, the students weren't texting on their cell phones as usual. They were engaged in animated discussions about the four murders on campus. Utilizing their energies, I separated the students into groups and asked each group to stage an improvisation on how the murders might have been committed and by whom. I asked them to pay particular attention to their characters' motives, relationships, and methods of achieving their goals.

As I watched from the back of the lab theatre, the first group presented a Leopold/Loeb scenario, where a young man committed the murders to please his charismatic male lover. Ironically, Jimmy Saline played the Loeb character.

The next group presented a *Macbeth* plot, where a woman cajoles the man who loves her to kill for power and wealth. Maria Ruiz and Rodney Towers immediately came to my mind.

A Cain and Abel story line was next as a young man

killed his brother due to jealousy and greed. Kim Sim fit that bill.

In reminiscence of *The Front Runner* with an added murder twist, the next group highlighted a professor training an athletic student for competition, falling in love with him, then sabotaging the other competitors. *Van Granite and Kim Sim? Brick Strong and Mack Heath?*

The last group's scene featured a domineering mother determined to secure power for herself and her child à la *Manchurian Candidate*. I cast Cheryl Stryker in the leading role with Sue Heath as her understudy.

Still having no answers, after my faculty committee meeting I went home. Since Manuello nixed our rehearsals for the competition, after dinner with Noah and his parents, I headed over to the gym for a workout.

Recalling Van Granite's aside at the funeral home about my abs, after changing into my sweats, I rested my back on the slant board in the weight room, placed a ten-pound weight on my stomach, and did sit-ups. During my third set Maria Ruiz came into the weight room followed by Rodney Towers. To the relief of my aching stomach muscles, I slid off the slant board and hid behind a fitness ball to observe.

Maria did arm curls with fifty-pound hand weights. Rodney stood behind her and pulled back her muscular shoulders.

"Stop adjusting my shoulders." Maria rested the weights back in their sockets on the rack. "You can't change my form, and you can't change me."

"*You* did that already," said Rodney with his massive hands lifting sixty-pound hand weights.

"What I do is none of your business," Maria said with a snap around Rodney's large face.

Rodney executed his hand curls. "It's my business when you give alcohol to someone with a brain injury."

"And why is that, Rodney?" she asked with her black eyes ablaze.

"Because Jillian is our classmate."

"*And* our competition in the contest."

Rodney put his weights back on the rack. "Is that why you did it?"

Maria pounded her fist into her hand. "I did it because Jillian got me mad, just like you!"

Sitting Maria down next to him on the bench, Rodney asked, "How did Jillian get you mad?"

"Jillian came into my dorm room going on and on about how Professor Strong favors *her* and Mack for the competition. Then she said, since Professor Granite and Professor Stryker will probably vote for Kim Sim, you and I have no chance to win and should drop out of the competition. Of course she quickly forgot what she had said, but *I* didn't." Maria held Rodney's mountainous shoulders. "Rodney, we've been workout partners for over three years. All the weight training, dieting, shaving, tanning, oiling, working on our routines, all the hours, all the sacrifice, for what? You're the biggest and strongest in the competition. I have the best proportion and technique. Yet the dark folks don't have a chance in hell to win!"

Rodney's eyes doubled in size. "Maria, did you...were *you* the one who killed Jillian...and Professor Strong?"

Maria began to cry.

He put his powerful arm around her giant shoulders. "You can tell me, Maria. We'll pray about it...together. The Lord will tell us what to do."

*Yes, spill it for the Lord, Maria!*

She rested her head in her hands. "I know what you think of me, Rodney."

He pulled her into his strapping chest. "I want to help you."

"You want to help me say I'm a murderer...and a eunuch...and a deviate sinner who God is waiting to punish."

*Saying "I'm a murderer" will suffice!*

"Please, Maria, whatever you've done or haven't done, let your anger, fear, and resentment melt away like dirty ice on a highway when the sun finally shines. Don't hide from grace. It's not cool to shield yourself from love!"

Maria pressed her hands against Rodney's chest. "Why

do you care about how I feel?"

"I care about your salvation, and I want you to make yourself right with God."

"No, Rodney, tell me, why do *you* care so much about what I did or didn't do to Jillian, how I identify in terms of gender, and if I'm sad, happy, open, or zipped up like a sandwich bag?"

Looking like a stumped game-show contestant, Rodney said, "You're my workout buddy."

She rose from the bench like a psychic seeing a powerful vision. "No, that's not it." She banged her fist against her forehead. "How could I not have seen this long ago?" As if picking Rodney out of a police lineup, Maria pointed at him. "You! You have *feelings* for me!"

"Of course I do. You're my classmate and my friend."

She shook her head wildly and her dreadlocks nearly blinded him. "No, that's not it. You're in *love* with me!"

"I want you to receive the Lord's love and blessing, Maria. I want to help you move from darkness into the light."

"Ugh, ugh, Rodney. This is about *you* wanting *me*. Me, who is repulsed by your superior attitude and nauseating self-righteousness. Me, who would rather die alone than ever be coupled with a fanatical, judgmental, bigoted, Neanderthal like *you*! Someone who devotes his every thought and emotion to changing me, molding me like a potter with his clay, and robbing me of my very essence and core!"

Rodney's eyes locked into Maria's. "You're wrong, Maria. I could never be in love with someone like you who didn't commit herself, body, soul, and spirit, to the Lord. I would never fall for a woman who...wasn't born a woman. And I'd never partner with a stubborn, arrogant, self-centered, angry person who doesn't appreciate my integrity, my compassion, and my fortitude."

The two bodybuilders threw their arms around one another, and their lips joined like trucks crashing from opposite directions on a highway. As their tongues explored one another's mouths, their hands stroked and kneaded each other's backs and buttocks.

As the temperature in the room rose to the level of extremely hot, I crawled on all fours until I reached the doorway, then made my way to the locker room.

After changing back into my street clothes, I heard Mack Heath and Jimmy Saline coming into the locker room. I dodged behind a locker and watched as they walked through the locker room and into the shower room, where Jimmy placed Mack's gym bag on the bench near the sink. À la Mary Poppins, Jimmy took out each item and placed it next to the bag: Mack's razor, shaving cream, towel, oil, and tanning spray. Then Jimmy spread shaving cream all over Mack's chest and abdomen and carefully shaved, then discarded the black hair into the sink.

"I like your mother," said Jimmy with a warm smile on his emaciated face.

"She likes you too," answered Mack, grimacing briefly when Jimmy accidentally nicked his chest.

"I'm going to visit her in the cafeteria."

*They say men marry their mothers.*

Tears welled up in Jimmy's big brown eyes.

Mack rested his thick hands on Jimmy's bony shoulders. "What is it?"

"I'm sorry," said Jimmy, wiping Mack's chest with the towel.

Mack held the towel still. "Tell me, please."

Jimmy sat on the bench. "The last few days have been...perfect. I've felt like a fairy tale character with a prince."

"I'm no prince," said Mack, sitting next to Jimmy with his muscular arm wrapped around Jimmy's narrow shoulders.

"You are to me."

Mack kissed Jimmy's cheek. "Then why are you upset?"

After a shaky breath, Jimmy said, "I'm a junior, and you're a senior."

"So?"

"So after this school year, you'll be moving on to professional bodybuilding competitions, while I stay here and finish college."

Mack took Jimmy's hand. "Jimmy, I'll be spending next year right here."

"You will?" Jimmy replied like a big lottery winner.

"I will."

"To be near your mother?" Jimmy asked.

"And to be near *you*."

"Mack!"

They kissed, then Jimmy rested his red head on Mack's muscular shoulder.

Mack explained, "I can use next year to continue training and competing in amateur contests in our area."

"And after that?" Jimmy asked, clearly praying for the right answer.

"After that, we can talk about our future."

"*Our* future. I like the sound of that."

Mack mussed Jimmy's hair. "Me too."

They kissed more passionately.

Jimmy said, "I know you'll make it big one day, Mack."

"I'll be the next Rob Kearney, and you'll be the next Neil Patrick Harris."

They shared a laugh.

"But while we're still commoners, we better get ready for the competition." Mack handed Jimmy the oil bottle, like the Tin Man needing a fix.

Jimmy squeezed some oil onto his fingers, then slowly applied it to Mack's wide pectoral muscles, taking extra time at Mack's protruding nipples. "I'm sorry about Professor Strong."

"Me too."

"He must have really liked you to leave you his ashes."

Mack turned away so Jimmy couldn't see the emotion in his handsome face. "He taught me so much...about so many things."

*Obviously!*

Once the oil disappeared from Mack's chest, Jimmy rubbed oil on Mack's six pack, working his fingers in and out of each layer of muscle. "Professor Stryker and her daughter didn't seem too happy about it."

"I can understand their feelings," said Mack.

"Poor Jillian wouldn't have liked it either."

"I guess not."

Finished with the oil, Jimmy raised the tanning spray, aimed it at Mack's torso, and hit the nozzle. "It's too bad the competition has been postponed."

"It'll come around soon enough. And when it does, I need to be ready. I have to win it for you and for my mom." Mack looked over Jimmy's shoulder like a warrior headed for his most important battle. "And for Brick Strong!"

As they packed up to leave, Mack said, "Jimmy, I have to tell you something about Professor Strong."

*Poor Jimmy!*

Mack looked down at the tile floor. "I've been keeping something from you. Strong was more to me than just my professor."

Jimmy zipped up the bag and followed Mack out of the shower room. "I don't understand."

As they walked through the locker room, Mack said, "This will come as a big surprise, and I hope you understand, but he and I..." And they were gone.

*So Brick Strong did swing both ways. I wonder if it had something to do with Strong getting killed? A lover's spat with Mack perhaps? Cheryl Stryker or Jillian Flowers in a jealous rage?*

When I got to the hallway, Mack and Jimmy were gone, but I heard voices coming from Cheryl Stryker's office. So, I stood to the side of her open door and peeked in.

Noah's dad sat next to Cheryl on her brown leather loveseat. Her large hands squeezed his.

"As they say, those were the good old days," said Cheryl, unveiling her molars.

They shared a giggle.

She continued. "We were so full of ourselves, and we didn't have a care in the world back then."

"Except to pass our classes and get out of there," said Scott.

Cheryl pinched Scott's knobby knee. "We had a great

time and you know it." She sat at the edge of the loveseat. "Remember when I did weightlifting for my Demonstration Speech, and that kid in the class asked me if I was strong enough to beat him up?"

"And you did!"

They laughed.

Scott said, "And remember when I did my Persuasive Speech on the health benefits of milk, and that girl asked me how you make chocolate milk?"

"And you said by milking brown cows?"

They guffawed.

Cheryl said with a double meaning, "And remember all of our late nights studying Biology and Chemistry?"

"We were some pair, Cheryl."

"That we were." Cheryl cuddled up closer to him. "What happened, Scott?"

"What do you mean?"

"With us?" She pressed her firm torso against his flabby chest.

"We grew up," Scott said. "You came east to achieve your goals, and I stayed put in Wisconsin to achieve mine." He looked around the office. "Seems like we both did just fine." As Cheryl leaned in closer, Scott broke the mood. "Cheryl, I'm so sorry about…"

"Brick." Cheryl's face gained twenty years of age. "Thank you. He was a good man and a good father."

"Tell me if I'm being too nosey, but what went wrong with you and…"

"Brick." She rested her strapping back on the loveseat. "What went *right*? It's hard being married to someone when you both desperately crave the same thing."

"And what's that?"

"Control."

Scott smiled. "I can't believe that any man could control you, Cheryl."

"Brick could…until I had enough."

"What happened?"

"I found out some things about Brick…that I didn't like.

After that, our marriage became a tug of war."

"Since he was department head, I guess he won, at least at work."

Cheryl looked at the department head sign on her office door and grinned like a champion. "But not for long."

Crossing his chubby leg, Scott said, "I'm so sorry about what happened with the ashes at the funeral. Your daughter seemed very upset."

Cheryl cringed. "Mack Heath won the battle, but not the war."

"Go easy on him, he's just a kid."

"He's the same age we were when we first..." She whispered something in Scott's ear, and Scott turned beet red.

"Well, I better get going, Cheryl. It was great seeing you, but my wife will be worried."

"Stay a bit longer. Bonnie's probably sound asleep in front of her favorite television program."

*Or taking a picture of a voodoo doll of Cheryl to show Judy back in Wisconsin.*

Looking like a priest meeting his new altar boy, Cheryl licked her full lips and smiled. "Don't you want to comfort a lonely old woman, Scott?"

He replied, "I'd like to stay and continue reminiscing about old times, but my son drove me here, and he'll want to get home soon."

*Your son? My Noah?*

"Noah's a terrific guy." She pressed her mountainous shoulder against his droopy one. "Very much like his father."

"Thanks, Cheryl." Scott rose.

Cheryl pulled him back down beside her. "Let's pretend we're young again, Scott...confident, free, without a care in the world." She threw her massive arms around him.

"I really need to get—"

As Cheryl leaned in for a kiss, Scott backed away and landed on the floor. "Aghhhhhh!"

"What is it, Scott?"

"My back! I hurt my back!"

While Cheryl helped Scott to his feet, I tiptoed past the

office, and heard voices coming from Van Granite's office nearby. Standing in Granite's doorway, my heart did a somersault when I saw Van Granite with his hands on Noah's waist.

*Like father, like son!*

# Chapter Seven

"Noah, what are you doing here?"

My boyfriend quickly stepped away from Granite's bulging biceps. "Nicky, are you still working out this *late*?"

Granite sat on his desk and flexed his powerful thigh muscles. "Shouldn't you be in bed by now, Nicky?"

Coming to my side, Noah said, "Dad needed a lift to visit with Cheryl. While I was waiting for him, I noticed Van's light on."

*And his motor running.*

Noah led me into the office. "When I heard a noise in the hallway, I jumped back and Van caught me."

*How convenient.*

"Aghhh!"

Our heads whipped around faster than an anti-gay politician's on thong day at Key West. Scott Oliver stood at Granite's doorway with his chubby hands pressed against his flabby back.

Noah rushed to his father. "What's wrong, Dad?"

"Cheryl and I were…talking and I fell off her couch."

Noah put his arm around his father. "Where's Cheryl now?"

"She went to get an ice pack. I need to get home and into bed," replied Scott.

"We better get going, Van," said Noah.

"Of course," replied Granite with a glance at his wall mirror.

"Help me, Nicky," said Noah with a concerned look on his handsome face.

Noah and I took Scott's arms as if we were club bouncers

with a poor patron. As we walked Scott out of Granite's office, Scott bent over and moaned like the leader of an ex-gay ministry on the beach in Provincetown.

"Get home safe, guys," said Granite with a wink at Noah.

After gently placing Scott into Noah's car, I followed Noah and Scott home.

Amidst Bonnie scolding Scott for visiting "that woman," Noah and I helped Scott up the stairs and into bed.

When Noah and I finally crawled into our four-poster, Noah rested his blond locks on my chest, said he loved me, and was out like a light.

I lay awake looking up at the moon's lavender and gray reflection on the ceiling. Images of Noah and Granite, Mack and Brick, and Cheryl and Scott raced through my mind. Eventually I relaxed into my hypoallergenic pillow with visions of a young Robbie Piccolo, and I fell asleep.

The next morning, Noah and I served Scott breakfast (whole-wheat waffles and bananas) in bed while Bonnie took pictures for Judy in Wisconsin.

After finishing our breakfast in the nook, I swallowed my vitamins, kissed Noah goodbye (after his mother left the room), and headed to my own oracle of contemplation.

Martin Anderson looked like a shark at a nude beach. "How fascinating, Nicky!"

I had filled in my department head on the recent scandals in the Bodybuilding Department. As we sat next to the glowing fireplace covered by the cherry wood mantel, Martin adjusted his lime bowtie and sweater vest, then placed a monogrammed lime cloth napkin on his tiny lap. "Compared to the shenanigans going on in the Bodybuilding Department, we seem like *monks* in the Theatre Department."

Shayla interjected from the outer office, "Bad analogy, Martin."

"Good one, Shayla," Martin responded.

I took a sip of hot cocoa, then rested the rose-patterned

china cup on the cherry wood end table. "The Bodybuilding faculty have conveniently forgotten the college's policy prohibiting faculty-student romances."

"It appears so." Martin tented his slight fingers. "Cheryl Stryker hawked the late Tim Sim. Poor Brick Strong was after Jillian Flowers and Mack Heath. Now Van Granite is taken with Kim Sim!"

*And I'm obsessed with the eighteen-year-old image of Robbie Piccolo!* "Martin, do you think that people can communicate with one another telepathically?"

"Sure. I know everything Ruben is going to say and do long before he says or does it."

"I mean someone we don't know, sending us a message?"

The wrinkles deepened on his thin face. "What's this about, Nicky?"

I shared my *encounter* with Robbie Piccolo.

Martin stared at the dancing flames. "'Please help me.' What could it mean?"

"If Robbie had a problem eighteen years ago, there's not a lot I can do about it now. Maybe he's in some kind of trouble now in Florida."

"Surely Tony would have mentioned it." Martin said like an old sage, "I believe the subconscious mind speaks to us in our dreams and visions. Can other people infiltrate them? That is for bigger minds than mine." He patted my knee affectionately. "Speaking of your obsessions, how are things with you and Noah?"

My back stiffened against the tall leather chair. "Fine — when Van Granite or Noah's parents aren't around."

He laughed nostalgically. "I remember a thousand years ago when Ruben and I were newlyweds. He refused to kiss me or even touch me when his parents visited us from Ohio."

"What did you do?"

With a twinkle in his brown eyes, Martin replied, "One night at dinner, I used my theatre chops and pretended to choke on a broccoli floret. Ruben forgot all about his parents, gave me the Heimlich maneuver, cradled me in his arms, and hugged and kissed me back to health."

"Maybe I should try that with a bagel at breakfast, or better yet with a protein shake in Van Granite's office."

"Do tell!" Martin rubbed his tiny hands together like a scout at a campfire.

"I found Granite and Noah in Granite's office in a...compromising position."

"And you didn't take a picture?" asked Shayla.

Martin shook his bald head. "There's more to this than what you are seeing, Nicky. Have faith in Noah. I do. This will reveal itself when the time is right." He stared into the scarlet flames. "In the meantime, our narcissistic colleague has been striking out on other fronts."

"What do you mean?"

Martin leaned forward in his chair. "You know we never spread stories in this department—"

*And the Middle East never has wars.*

"—but I heard, through the department head grapevine, that Van Granite and Cheryl Stryker had quite the falling out over Cheryl being appointed Interim Department Head."

I raised my eyes to the wood-beamed ceiling. "I'm not surprised. The both of them are like barracudas in a goldfish bowl. Just ask Noah's father."

"Which one of them came on to *him*?"

"Cheryl Stryker, Scott's old college flame. Scott's home now with a pulled back."

"Ah." Martin took a sip of cocoa, then wiped the corner of his mouth with his napkin. "Scott better be careful not to hurt more than his back. Given Detective Manuello's penchant for crime solving—"

Martin and Shayla said in unison, "—or the lack thereof—"

"—there no doubt will be more murders soon," said Martin.

"Have you spoken to Manuello recently?" I asked.

He nodded. "Detective Manuello told me that Jillian Flowers was killed by suffocation. After the full autopsy, her body will be returned to her parents in Arkansas."

I rubbed my forehead as if I had hives. "Jonathan Toner dead from testosterone. Tim Sim overdosed on *Tribulus terrestris* and creatine. Brick Strong with a barbell on his throat, and Jillian Strong with soap in her mouth. Who is doing this...and why?"

Martin placed his china cup on the end table. "You can figure it out, Nicky."

I threw my hands up in the air. "I'm not a detective, Martin."

"You did pretty well last semester."

"Noah and I got lucky."

He took my hand. "No, Nicky. You and Noah used your theatrical backgrounds to catch the killer, and you can do it again." Martin sounded like Mama Rose prepping Louise before her first striptease. "Trust your instincts, Nicky. And trust Noah. Think of your investigation like directing a play, and the killer's motives as objectives in a scene. Use the theatre skills of concentration, listening, observing others, and role-play to nab the killer!"

Running my hands through my hair, I said, "But where do I start?"

After thinking a moment, Martin answered, "Start with Jimmy Saline. I've been watching that boy in my Theatre Management class. Our Jimmy knows more than he lets on. Talk to him. Follow him." Martin stood and walked me to the door. "And keep an eye on Van Granite." His small elbow poked my side. "And on Noah."

After thanking Martin and promising to do my best, I stopped at Shayla's large desk.

"How's your speech coming for Martin's tribute dinner?" Shayla asked as she tucked a black strand of hair back inside the bun at her neck.

"It's coming along great!" I said, again reminding myself to get started on it.

Shayla nodded. "Just like my new play." She pointed to a blank piece of paper.

"Looks like we both better get to work, Shayla."

"Mm, hm," she replied, looking back at her computer

monitor.

I looked out the office window at majestic shades of sapphire, crimson, coral, and goldenrod. "I love this time of year. Everything is so beautiful outside. And inside too."

"Thank you, Nicky." Shayla puffed her earth-toned sweater.

"Even the flames in Martin's fireplace look radiant."

Shayla said, "That's from the ashes I placed in there this morning."

"Ashes?"

"They fell on my coat at Brick Strong's funeral. Don't they burn nicely?" She winked at me.

I kissed Shayla's cheek and headed to my office.

When my Theatre History class ended and the students piled out of the lecture hall as if it was on fire, Jimmy Saline entered the room like a fish swimming upstream. He finally reached the front of the room, and said softly, "Professor, can I talk to you?"

"Sure, Jimmy. What news does the Thin Man have for me today?" I sat on the computer console.

Jimmy scratched at the brown corduroy pants dangling from his skeletal hips. "Professor, if you know a secret about somebody you love, should you always keep the secret?"

Feeling like the father in an old sitcom, I replied, "That depends, Jimmy, on whether or not telling the secret would harm the someone you love."

He swept a clump of red hair off his forehead. "I'm not sure."

"But it could help our investigation?"

Jimmy nodded, and the hair fell over one eye.

"Is it a secret about Mack?"

He nodded again, and hair covered the other eye.

"Is it about Mack and Professor Strong?"

Breathing a sigh of relief, Jimmy said, "You know about it, Professor?"

I nodded. "I saw them together in Professor Strong's office before Strong...left us." Noticing Jimmy's twitching knee, I asked, "Are you okay with it, Jimmy?"

He looked around to make sure we were still alone. "I was really surprised when Mack told me."

"Does it make you think any less of Mack or of Professor Strong?"

"At first I was disappointed that Mack hadn't told me sooner. But after thinking about it, I can understand why Mack and Professor Strong wanted to keep it a secret." Jimmy shuffled from foot to foot like a kid needing a bathroom. "But now that I know, I'm worried about Mack."

"Why?"

"Professor Strong, when he was alive, would have voted for Mack to win the competition given their...relationship. So what if one of the other kids in the competition found out about Professor Strong and Mack, and got jealous?" Alligator tears slid from Jimmy's cheeks onto the flannel shirt hanging from his frail chest. "He or she could have killed Professor Strong. And Mack may be the next target!"

I put my arm around Jimmy's narrow shoulders and walked him to the door. "Keep snooping, Jimmy, and continue sharing with me what you know. And don't worry. We'll find the murderer and protect the people we love."

Since Noah's dad was still recuperating, that evening Noah and I ate dinner together at the kitchen nook (filet of flounder in olive oil and lemon, cauliflower au gratin, and three bean salad with goat cheese and walnuts—for me) while his parents ate in the guest room (takeout southern fried chicken, mashed potatoes, gravy, and biscuits). Noah looked fetching in a gold cashmere sweater and black slacks. He was as affectionate as usual, and we held hands and caressed all through dinner. When it came time for me to swallow a handful of vitamins, then leave for the gym, Noah walked me to the door and looked at me with loving eyes.

"I'll miss you, Nicky." Noah handed me my jacket from the antique coatrack in the hallway.

"I'll only be gone an hour or two."

"Every minute I'm not with you is lonely for me, Nicky."

I scooped up Noah's firm, round bottom, and he clasped his arms around my back. Then we shared a long, sensuous kiss.

"You're all I'll ever need, Noah. I can't imagine myself with anyone else. After your parents leave, let's talk about—"

Bonnie called for her son, and Noah slid out of my grasp. After wishing me a good workout, Noah flew up the stairs, and I went out the front door.

When I arrived at the gym, I saw Jimmy Saline with his boss in Tony Piccolo's alcove. Unseen by them, I rested my back against the outside alcove wall. Unfortunately, from my vantage point I couldn't see the pictures of Tony's son on the bulletin board, but I could hear what Jimmy and Tony were saying.

Jimmy said, "I laundered the towels and put out fresh ones, mopped the floors, and cleaned the lockers. Is there anything else you need me to do, Tony?"

Tony replied, "You're a terrific kid, Jimmy. Just like all my boys, though you're a lot skinnier." Tony laughed. "Go have fun with Mack, and I'll see you same time tomorrow."

"Thanks, Tony."

"And, Jimmy, take care of my boy, Mack."

"I will."

"That a boy."

I ducked back as Jimmy headed for the weight room to, no doubt, shave, oil, and tan Mack's arms—and watch over him.

Entering the alcove, I tried unsuccessfully not to stare at Robbie's pictures. "Hello, Tony."

Tony closed a box of resin. "Professor, sorry to hear the competition's on hold."

"Me too."

He rested his bony buttocks on his desk. "Here to work out?"

"That's the plan. Care to join me?"

The elderly man laughed and pointed to a small stack of prescription slips on his desk. "I wish I could."

Trying to shift my gaze from Robbie to his father, I asked, "Are you okay, Tony?"

His liver-spotted hands waved me away. "Just old age. It

ain't fun getting old, Professor."

I thought about Van Granite's remarks. "Tell me about it."

The craters on Tony's face softened. "You ain't old, Professor. You're about the same age as my Robbie."

At last I was free to openly stare at Robbie's pictures. "How is he doing?"

Tony answered proudly, "Terrific! He's trying a big case for the state of Florida."

*If he still looks like this and the jury is made up of gay men and straight women, he'll win hands down.*

"Thanks for asking about him, Professor." Tony put a hoodie on over his sweat clothes. "I better get going. Have a good workout. If you need anything, just ask Jimmy." He winked at me. "Though I get the feeling Jimmy may be preoccupied."

We shared a laugh and Tony was gone. Alone in the office, I gazed into Robbie's gorgeous hazel eyes, and I was transported back to my latest dream. Sitting in the front of the audience, I cheered as Robbie Piccolo won the gold cup. After being summoned to the stage by Robbie, I worked my way through the crowd. Standing next to the incredibly muscular youth, I took in his smooth skin, perfect proportions, and warm smile. When he leaned in to whisper in my ear, I breathed in deeply and savored his woodsy scent, as he said, "It's up to you!"

"He was really something."

I came to like a coma victim after a miraculous healing and discovered Cheryl Stryker standing next to me.

"Cheryl, hi." I cleared my dry throat. "Yes, the pictures are amazing."

She nodded. "Robbie deserved every award he won. Brick was really proud of him." Cheryl poked my side and nearly broke a rib. "And Tony never lets us forget."

We shared a laugh.

"How's Noah's father?" Cheryl asked with sentimental eyes.

"Resting in bed."

"Give him my best will you, Nicky?"

"Of course." *Not on your life.*

Her large shoulders squared. "I better get back to my office. The administrative work of a department head is never done."

"That's what Martin says."

"Martin's right. Have a good workout, Nicky."

"Thanks."

As I changed into my sweat clothes in the locker room, I noticed that Jimmy was spray-tanning Mack's arms in the shower room. So I nonchalantly sat on a bench within hearing range. As I tied my sneaker — for the third time — I overheard Mack tell Jimmy to meet him in Brick Strong's office in five minutes, and to make sure nobody followed him.

Relieved that I didn't tie my two laces together, I hurried out of the locker room and hightailed it to Brick Strong's office. After searching for a safe hiding place, I inched the bookcase away from the wall, took in a deep breath, and slid behind it. Luckily, I found a good lookout space between an almanac of bodybuilding competitions and a book on shaving without chafing.

Moments later Mack entered the office and stood in the doorway, looking both ways. When Jimmy arrived, Mack led him into the office and shut the door behind them.

"Is it safe, Mack?" asked Jimmy.

"I used to come in here all the time," replied Mack.

*A kiss-and-tell man.*

"It's a lot safer than the dorm," said Mack. He led Jimmy to the couch, where they sat massive shoulder to puny shoulder. Then Mack wrapped his hands around Jimmy's. "Are you sure you're ready for this, Jimmy?"

Jimmy nodded, and his red hair fell over his forehead. "Are you sure *you're* ready, Mack?"

"I'm sure." Mack put his muscular arm around Jimmy's slight shoulders like a boa constrictor wrapped around a twig. "I've never loved anyone before, Jimmy, but I know I love you. And I want to be with you, now and always."

Jimmy's pale face lit up like a Christmas tree. "Mack, I've

always felt so alone." He looked down at his sunken chest. "So totally unlovable." Gazing into Mack's dark eyes, he said, "But a miracle happened when a guy I worshipped from afar talked to me, was kind to me, shared his life with me, and let me share my life with him. I love you so much, Mack, and I always will."

The two young men smiled at one another. Their lips touched, and they shared a tentative kiss. They kissed again, much more passionately. Mack unbuttoned Jimmy's yellow and brown flannel shirt and rested it on the arm of the sofa. Next Mack took off his blue sweatshirt and placed it on top of Jimmy's shirt. Then Mack kissed Jimmy's thin neck and slight chest. Jimmy let out a moan when Mack licked his nipples and navel.

*I feel like a voyeur, but I can't leave now. I guess I could look away. But I won't.*

Jimmy stroked Mack's massive shoulders and bulging, high-peaked biceps. Then he squeezed Mack's mountainous pectoral muscles and kissed all six of Mack's abdominal muscles.

Rising from the sofa, Mack kicked off his sneakers then pulled off his sweatpants. Still sitting on the couch, Jimmy did the same with his sneakers and brown corduroy pants. Mack stood in front of him and Jimmy buried his face into Mack's groin as his hands rubbed and caressed Mack's rock-hard buttocks, thigh, and calf muscles. Mack ran his thick fingers through Jimmy's hair and groaned in pleasure when Jimmy took Mack inside his mouth. As Jimmy's head bobbed up and down, Mack's cries became louder and more fervent. When Mack looked ready to explode, Jimmy released Mack's thick organ and the young men switched positions.

Mack caressed Jimmy's lanky torso, buttocks, and legs as he serviced Jimmy's thin member. When Jimmy begged for release, Mack slipped on lubed protection and pressed his muscular body on top of Jimmy's emaciated form on the sofa. Jimmy cried out first in pain, then in pleasure as Mack gently entered him then thrust his manhood inside of his lover again and again. Holding on to Jimmy's slight organ, Mack continued his rhythm until they both shouted in ecstasy, reaching simultaneous orgasm.

Looking into Jimmy's eyes and smiling, Mack kissed him. "I love you so much, Jimmy. You mean everything to me."

"I'd do anything for you, Mack. I love you forever," said Jimmy, hugging Mack's strapping, V-shaped back.

Someone pounded on the office door. Looking as frightened as rabbits facing a lawn mower, Mack and Jimmy quickly got dressed, and Mack opened the door.

"I thought I heard voices." Cheryl Stryker entered. "What do you think you are doing in here, Mack?"

"Jimmy and I were just..."

She pounded her thick finger into Mack's strapping chest. "I *know* what you and Jimmy were just *doing*." Cheryl looked at Mack in disgust. "This is a college, not a bordello! Brick's office is off limits to you now, Mack. You lost your *special privileges* when we lost Brick. Do you understand me?"

Mack nodded begrudgingly.

A sadistic look overtook her manly face. "And don't think I won't take your irresponsible behavior into consideration when I vote at the competition."

From the couch, Jimmy said, "Professor Stryker, this was all *my* fault."

"There's no use, Jimmy," said Mack.

Cheryl confronted Jimmy like the Wicked Witch to the Scarecrow. "That's right, Jimmy, there's no use. What you two have done is unconscionable and abhorrent." She glared at them. "Now both of you get of this office, and if I see you back in here again, I'll call Security *and* Detective Manuello. Do you understand me?"

"Professor Stryker, please don't take this out on Mack. I—"

"Jimmy, let's go," Mack said with an icy glance at Cheryl.

As they walked by Cheryl, Jimmy gave her a pleading look, and Mack hurried him out of the office.

Cheryl went back into her office, and I slowly released myself from the confines of the bookcase then bumped into Noah in the hallway—leaving Van Granite's office.

"Noah, what are you doing here?"

His face flushed. "Mom asked me to give her a lift to the gym."

"Why?"

"Dad told Mom about his visit with Cheryl. How Cheryl came on to him in her office, and how Dad fell off Cheryl's sofa." Noah ran his smooth fingers through his golden locks. "I tried to talk her out of it, but Mom insisted on visiting Cheryl to ask her to leave Dad alone."

I looked back in the direction of Cheryl's office. "Bonnie's not in there."

Throwing his arms up in the air, Noah said, "She's probably taking pictures all over the building to show Judy back in Wisconsin."

Not letting him off the hook so easily, I asked, "What were you doing in Granite's office?"

Noah's eyes moved in his head like a malfunctioning slot machine. "When I passed by his office, Van was feeling sorry for himself about not being appointed department head. So I tried to lift his spirits."

*Hopefully that was all of his you lifted.*

"I better go look for Mom. Have a good workout. I'll see you back at home."

Before I could object, Noah was gone. As I headed for the weight room, Kim Sim walked down the hallway, knocked on Granite's office door and entered. Noticing that Kim left the door open a crack, I gratefully postponed my workout and peered inside.

Granite was seated on his desk with his chiseled face in his beefy hands. Kim Sim placed a strong, consoling hand on Granite's herculean shoulder.

"It's so unfair," Granite said. "All the butts I kissed around this place, including the Dean's, and he appoints Cheryl as Department Head and not *me!*"

"You're like a much better professor, you know, than um Professor Stryker. I like wish there was, you know, something I could like do to help," said Kim.

Granite stopped feeling sorry for himself, and took in

Kim Sim, standing loyally at his side. "Thank you, Kim. You've been a good student, and a good friend."

"That's like the least I can um do, Professor, after how you like mentored me and, you know, gave me such like good advice about so many things. I don't like know how I would have um gotten through everything, you know, like with my brother and my father if it like wasn't for you."

Granite rested his hands on Kim's muscular shoulders. "It was my pleasure, Kim." Then Granite looked in the mirror and combed a lose strand of gelled hair back into place. "I'm glad everything is settled for you back at home. Now we have to make sure you win the competition here."

Kim answered, "Um that doesn't like matter as much anymore, Professor. I like still want to, you know, win the competition, but now that I'm, you know, rich, I don't like need the scholarship money."

"*Of course* it matters, Kim!" Granite stood and looked into Kim's dark eyes. "Kim Sim, you are a champion. You are the best student athlete in the competition. Kim Sim deserves to win the gold cup, and as your mentor, I'm going to make sure that happens." Granite walked over to his favorite thing in the room beside himself—the mirror—and checked his profile. "If only I was department head, I'd have more clout."

Kim stood behind him. "Um maybe you like will be department head, you know, someday, Professor. You're a lot younger than Professor Stryker."

"That I am." Granite smiled in the mirror and checked out his laminates. "Thank you for being in my corner, Kim."

"Um always, Professor."

"It means a great deal to me."

"Um you like mean a great, you know, deal to *me*, Professor."

"Do I, Kim?"

Kim nodded like a puppy faced with a treat.

"Good, because you mean a great deal to me too." Granite moved closer to Kim. "Do you know the reason I picked you out of all the other bodybuilding students, Kim?"

Kim Sim shook his head and his crew cut bristled.

Granite's eyes bore into Kim's. "I picked you because I sensed that you would be loyal to me, like a private to a sergeant in battle. Are you loyal to me, Kim?"

"Um yes, Professor," answered Kim like a cultist in a cabin in the woods.

"Good. Because when someone is loyal, he'll do anything his leader needs him to do. Isn't that so, Kim?"

"That's, you know, true, Professor."

Not losing eye contact, Granite asked, "Will you do *anything* that I need you to do, Kim?"

"Um yes, Professor."

"You sure, Kim?"

"Any like time. Any like where."

Granite smiled then said matter-of-factly, "Okay, Kim. What I need you to do now is take off your clothes."

"Um take off my like clothes, Professor?"

"That's right, Kim. Are you loyal enough to do that for me?"

"Like here?" asked Kim as he looked around the office.

"You said anytime, anywhere, Kim. This is what the sergeant needs from the private, right here and right now." After a pause, Granite added, "Is there a problem doing what I need, Kim?"

Kim Sim shook his head and self-consciously took off his designer clothes, standing naked in front of Granite. Moving in closer to the mirror, Granite slowly pulled off his sweat clothes. Not taking his eyes off his own reflection, he lowered Kim down to his knees. "You know what I need, Kim."

*I have to stop watching. But I won't.*

As Kim tentatively, then greedily licked and sucked Granite's large tool, Granite gasped and grunted, never losing contact with the mirror. Kim's hands gratefully massaged Granite's washboard abs and rock-hard buttocks, as Granite flexed, then stroked and squeezed his own shoulders, biceps, and pectoral muscles.

Next Granite lifted Kim off his knees, turned him around, and bent him over. Granite slipped on a condom and slid his erect penis inside the young man. As Kim pressed back against Granite in ecstasy, Granite thrust again and again, each time with more force and fervor, as he smiled into the mirror. Finally, Granite let out a shout of release as he leaned past Kim Sim and kissed his own reflection.

After they were dressed, I ducked behind a rubber plant as Granite led Kim out of the office and down the hall. Then I spotted Noah hurrying down the hallway.

"I can't find Mom, Nicky!"

"She has to be here somewhere."

"I know, but where?"

"Have you checked the weight room and the cardio rooms?"

"Yes."

"How about the women's locker room?"

"I opened the door and called her name, but nobody answered."

"What about the spinning room and the aerobics room?"

"Check. Check. No Mom."

"And the main gym where we rehearse?" I asked.

"The first place I looked, Nicky."

We heard a woman scream. Realizing it was Bonnie, we looked at one another in fear then raced down the hallway. When we came to the gymnastics room, we sped past the parallel bars and pummel horse and found Bonnie staring upwards in a state of shock. Following Bonnie's gaze, we saw Cheryl Stryker's limp body hanging from the rings.

I put my arm around Bonnie to console her, and she said, "It's okay, Nicky. I got a picture this time." She looked down at her iPad. "Judy said Cheryl Stryker can't hold a candle to me!"

# Chapter Eight

An hour later, Bonnie, Noah, and I sat on a bench in the hallway outside of the gymnastics room in the Physical Education building. Detective Manuello stood in front of us, writing his last entry on his notepad.

"It's still early, but at this point the coroner believes the cause of death was air obstruction," said Manuello with a rub of his red nose.

Thinking of Cheryl Stryker hanging by her neck from the rings, I said, "I wonder how long it took him to figure *that* out?"

"Speaking of figuring things out, how was it again that you came upon the body, Nicky?"

"That was me, Detective," said Bonnie, raising her hand like a brown-nosing student. "I was giving myself a picture tour of the building."

"Had you spoken to Professor Stryker prior to finding her?" asked Manuello.

"No, though I had intended to give her a piece of my mind," said Bonnie, oblivious to the fact that she was talking to a detective about a probable murder victim.

"What was it you wanted to speak with Professor Stryker about, Mrs. Oliver?" asked Manuello with a tug at one of the rolls of fat dangling over his belt buckle.

Bonnie replied, "I wanted to tell her to keep away from my husband." She rose and handed her iPad to her son. "Detective, would you mind posing for a picture with me to show my friend back in Wisconsin?" She put her arm around Manuello. "Say cheese, Detective. Okay, Noah, hit it."

Bonnie smiled grandly and Manuello looked like he'd seen a ghost. Noah took the picture, and gave his mother back her iPad. "Detective, Cheryl Stryker and my father were old friends from college. Dad had visited Cheryl here yesterday and hurt his back. My mother was concerned about him."

"Detective Manuello—" said Bonnie looking at her iPad, "—Judy says you don't look like the detectives on television."

"I'll keep that in mind," said Manuello with dagger eyes in my direction.

Bonnie continued. "But speaking of your father, Noah, I better give him a call to make sure he's all right." She added joyously, "And to tell him *I* found the body!"

Once Bonnie was down the hall and out of earshot, I said to Manuello, "Bonnie had nothing to do with Cheryl's death."

"Of course not. But somebody killed Cheryl." Noah stood and rested his foot on the bench.

From my vantage point sitting on the bench, I wanted to ravage Noah. However, since duty called, I slipped into my Holmes character and stood next to Manuello. "I've been sniffing around. And I've uncovered a number of possible suspects."

"Let me stop you right there, Nicky," Manuello replied. "I've led a thorough investigation. People told me that Jonathan Toner and Tim Sim had been talking about trying muscle enhancement products, and Cheryl Stryker was not happy about Brick Strong's infatuation with Jillian Flowers." Like the dimwitted detectives in British cozy mysteries, Manuello announced, "And I have come to the conclusion that Jonathan Toner overdosed on testosterone and Tim Sim overdosed on *Tribulus terrestris* and creatine. In both cases the boys accidentally killed themselves in an overzealous attempt to try to win the department's bodybuilding competition, perhaps even encouraged by their department head."

"What about Jillian Flowers, Brick Strong, and Cheryl Stryker?" asked Noah in true Watson form.

Manuello patted his distended stomach in satisfaction. "I believe Cheryl Stryker killed Jillian Flowers and Brick Strong in a jealous rage, then killed herself out of guilt and remorse."

I replied, "I spoke with Cheryl earlier this evening, Detective, and she didn't seem the least bit guilty or remorseful. As a matter of fact, she read the riot act to Mack Heath and Jimmy Saline when she caught them in Brick's office with the door shut."

"How do you know that?" Manuello thought better of it. "Never mind."

Noah said, "Van will be happy now."

"Why?" asked Manuello and I in unison.

Noah explained, "He's the only full-time faculty member left in the Bodybuilding Department. The Dean of Physical Education will have to make Van department head now."

*And you care about this because...?*

"That doesn't matter now. The students, parents, and the members of the college's Board of Trustees are in a panic." Manuello announced like Caesar talking to the Roman army, "I am closing down the Physical Education building. No classes, no office hours, no competition, and no working out until further notice from me."

I pressed my hand against the wall and crossed one leg over the other. I was going for a cocky gumshoe effect, but instead I nearly fell on Manuello. After regaining my balance (and ego), I said, "Detective, in addition to Van Granite, the students in the competition also have motives for committing these murders. The winner of the bodybuilding competition gets a one-year scholarship and a big, fat gold cup toward fame and fortune. Aren't you going to continue to question them?"

He looked at me with tired eyes. "The mayor, the governor, and everyone else, including my wife, are all pressuring me to solve this. I believe I have done that. And unless you have more solid proof for me than *theatrical intuition*, I'm sticking with my theory. Once things blow over, I'll let them reopen the building."

I thought I was meeting my maker as a strong white light permeated the hallway. Seconds later members of the local press were stationed around us with cameras and microphones pointing at us from several directions.

"Is it true that Brick Strong, Cheryl Stryker, and Jillian Flowers were lovers in a demonic cult that worshipped barbells, soap, and rings?" asked one young reporter who looked like a model.

A more seasoned reporter, who appeared about twenty-three, asked, "Is the mystery woman who found Cheryl Stryker's body a terrorist whose real goal was to blow up the Physical Education building?"

"That's me! I'm the mystery woman!" Bonnie cried as she ran toward us. "Wait until I tell Judy I will be on the news!"

Seeing a camera in our midst, I immediately offered my best side. "I was also with the mystery woman when she found Professor Stryker."

"As was I!" said Noah with a radiant smile to the camera and a shoulder covering mine.

Waving his arms like a flight attendant facing a coach passenger stepping into first class, Manuello shooed Bonnie, Noah, and me away to speak with the press alone.

Like actors rejected after a cattle call, Bonnie, Noah, and I headed back to our cars and drove home.

Given our action-packed night, my dreams were the usual conglomeration of disturbing images: Granite whipping Kim Sim into submission and making out with Noah at the mirror, the bodybuilding students throwing heavy hand weights at one another, a jealous Brick Strong coming back to haunt Mack and Jimmy à la the play *Private Lives*—with Bonnie taking pictures of it all for Judy in Wisconsin.

My final dream led me back to young Robbie Piccolo's bodybuilding competition. Again I stood on the stage next to the gorgeous young athlete. I gazed at his rippling muscles, thick dark hair, and handsome face as I breathed in his heavenly scent. Robbie rested a strong hand on my grateful shoulder, flashed his piercing hazel eyes at me, and said, "Stop it, Nicky. Please, stop it!"

I woke with a gasp. Noah was in the shower. Bonnie and Scott had left a note on our bedroom door saying they had taken Noah's car for a photo tour of the new supermarket in town. Noah had placed my breakfast (granola cereal, apple juice, and a stack of vitamins) on a tray atop my night table.

*"Stop it?" "Help me?" Why can't I figure out what Robbie is trying to tell me?*

I devoured my breakfast in two minutes flat then headed for our bathroom, where I joined Noah in the shower (an added feature post-Victoriana).

"Are my parents here?" asked Noah like a teenager caught in his basement smoking a joint.

"Noah, relax. Your parents went sightseeing."

His shoulders dropped.

"Noah, your folks are loving people who approve of their son's sexuality." I kissed his cheek (not his face).

Massaging strawberry-scented lather into his golden curls, Noah said, "I know it's irrational. It just feels so weird having my parents here with us."

I poured some strawberry body wash on my hands and rubbed it into Noah's smooth back as he rinsed his hair. "Do you think it's internalized homophobia?"

"I think I'd feel the same way if you were a woman, Nicky." He looked down at my family jewels. "And you definitely are not."

Moving down to wash Noah's legs, I said, "You have to get over this, honey."

"I know. I will. I just need a little more time to get used to the whole thing." He rubbed the shampoo into my hair and long sideburns. "I knew my parents would like you, Nicky."

"How could they resist?" I said with one eye open.

"They have good taste."

"Like their son's lover."

"And their son."

As I rinsed my hair, Noah slowly rubbed body wash on my hands, arms, back, chest, stomach, buttocks, legs, and feet. Saving the best part for last, Noah got down on his knees and applied the soapy liquid to my genitals.

I washed the soap off and started to leave the shower.

"Ugh, ugh," said Noah with a naughty look in his gorgeous blue eyes. He pulled me back, and we kissed. With the water spraying on top of us, Noah wrapped his arms around my back and curled his legs around my waist. I slipped out a condom from my secret hiding place, and rested Noah's back against the shower wall. As we kissed and caressed, I grasped Noah's firm buttocks, then entered him to welcoming shivers. Pressing deeper and deeper inside of him, I whispered in his ear how much I loved him. Squeezing my back and buttocks tighter, Noah nibbled at my ear and returned the amorous whispers. Noah rubbed himself against my stomach, then shouted in ecstasy as I cried out in released pleasure.

After we washed and toweled off, since it was Saturday, we dressed in our sweat clothes. Then Noah and I sat on our four-poster and went over the events of the prior evening.

"We can't let Manuello give up the investigation, Nicky. I don't buy his theory, and I know you don't either. I think there's a murderer loose on our campus again, and nobody is safe...including us!"

I pressed my back against the oak headboard and rested my legs on Noah's lap. "Martin thinks we should investigate like last time...using our theatre savvy."

Noah looked like an alcoholic in a brewery. "Let's do it, Nicky!"

Pressing my feet against his warm thigh, I said, "But where do we start?"

Noah tented his long fingers. "Let's see, we know what the victims had in common. They were all bodybuilding students or faculty."

"But they were each killed with a different weapon: testosterone, *Tribulus terrestris* and creatine, a barbell, soap, and rings. It's relatively easy to obtain each of those items, but you need a prescription for testosterone and access to a health-food store for the herbs."

Noah rubbed my feet. "Can't you get those things online nowadays?"

"Why wait for delivery when you can pick them up locally?"

"Do you think we should call the pharmacies in the area

and ask who brought in prescriptions for testosterone?"

I shook my head. "They won't give us that information. Besides, all we'd get are names of aging men with erectile dysfunction."

Noah patted my package. "Thankfully not a problem for you."

"Or you." I patted back.

I lifted the phone and began pressing numbers.

"Who are you calling?" asked Noah with his ear pressed against mine.

"Our local health-food store." I said into the phone, "Hello, do you sell *Tribulus terrestris* and creatine?"

After the noise of shuffling papers, the young woman on the other end of the phone replied, "Yeah."

I tried to sound matter-of-fact. "Are they popular items?"

"Not so much lately...after the bad press about side effects and junk."

"Can you tell me if anyone has purchased them over the last week or so?"

After discussion I assume with her manager, she replied, "It's not cool for me to say junk like that on the phone."

Noah whispered into my ear, and I said into the phone, "How about if I come to the store?"

The young woman and her manager had a longer discussion then she said, "You a cop?"

"Why?"

"My manager said it's only cool for me to tell a cop."

Noah motioned for me to hang up the phone.

I said, "Thank you for your time."

After I disconnected, Noah stood up and pulled me off the bed. "Nicky, you have to go down there."

"I can't, Noah. I shop there all the time. They know I'm not a cop."

With a maniacal look in his baby-blue eyes, Noah said, "They know *you* aren't a cop. But they have never met Officer Dick Danghammer!"

"Noah, no."

"Nicky, yes!" Noah stood and performed to the third

balcony. "Martin is right. Manuello be damned. It's time for you and me to throw up the curtain, beam the spotlight, slap on the greasepaint, and catch a killer!"

Amidst my comments on the illegalities of impersonating a police officer, Noah pushed me into my car, drove us to the campus in a flash, and led me into the Theatre Department costume shop. After rummaging through the racks of clothing, Noah selected the tightest navy-blue shirt and pants he could find. "Take off your shirt, pants, and underpants, and put these on."

While I finished changing my clothes, Noah hurried me into the prop closet, where he fastened a holster with a billy club in it around my waist, and another holster laden with a fake gun around my chest. Then he slipped a walkie-talkie on a belt around my waist, a silver badge and notepad inside my shirt pocket, and a pair of dark sunglasses over my eyes. After practically dragging me to the makeup room next door, Noah gelled my hair back, then rubbed a tan base into my face and hands. Finally, he led me to a floor-length mirror in the corner of the room. "Viola! What do you think, Nicky, or should I say Police Officer Dick Danghammer?"

I looked into the mirror and couldn't believe what I saw. "Noah, am I supposed to be a police officer or a male stripper?"

"Whatever works, Nicky. Let's go!"

Given Noah's driving habits, we arrived at the health-food store before my makeup was dry. Noah whispered in my ear, "Butch it up!" then led me inside the store, where he pretended to peruse natural remedies for menopause.

I quickly created my character as I walked toward a young woman standing behind a desk labeled "Customer Service." The woman appeared to be in her early twenties, with dyed purple hair and numerous nose rings. Focused on her cell phone like it was manna from heaven, she texted busily, unaware of my presence.

Dropping the pitch of my voice down an octave, I said, "Excuse me."

Continuing her fascinating texting exchange, she said

without looking up, "Yeah?"

"I need you to answer a few questions, young lady," I said feigning authority.

"Yeah?" she replied mid text.

I placed the badge over her cell phone then removed it before she could read the insignia, "Little Boy Sheriff."

She looked up. "Cool."

"As an officer of the law, I need to know the following information."

"Yeah?"

"What is your name?"

"Carob."

"Like the food coating?"

She raised her brown eyes to the carob bars stacked on the rack above her. "My parents are health freaks."

"How long have you worked here, Carob?"

"Forever."

"We need to be more precise in the police business. How long is forever?"

"Three months."

I took the notepad out of my shirt pocket and realized I didn't have a pen. Carob caught on and handed me hers. After I wrote "I am going to kill Noah" on the pad, I asked her, "During the time you have been working in this store, how many people have purchased large quantities of the herbs *Tribulus terrestris* and creatine?"

"One." She opened a pack of fruit-juice-sweetened gum. After sticking a piece in her mouth, she offered me one.

"No, thank you," I replied. "Not on the job."

"Whatever," she said then chewed like a free-range cow in an organic meadow.

"Who purchased the herbs, Carob?" I asked officiously.

Receiving a text, Carob went back to her phone. "Don't know his name."

"Can you look it up somewhere?"

Carob replied as she texted, "Don't keep junk like that."

I placed my hand over her cell phone, praying my makeup wouldn't rub off on it, then stepped to the side of the desk. Carob looked up from her phone. Taking me in from head to toe, Carob noticed my policeman's package and nearly popped a nose ring.

Pressing an elbow against the desk, I said, "Tell me everything you know about this customer, Carob."

Carob swallowed her gum. "He said he came from the college."

I spread my legs apart. "What else, Carob?"

She licked her lips. "He said he worked in the Bodybuilding Department."

I pressed my hips forward. "What else?"

Carob wiped a sweat bead from her forehead with a tattooed finger. "He said he was the department head."

Noah, having worked his way over to perusing multivitamins for senior citizens over eighty, flailed his arms in my direction. "Help! Police! Citizen's arrest! That man out there stole my…leather chaps!" Then he grabbed my arm and pulled me out of the store.

Once back in my car, I said, "Leather chaps?"

"It's what came into my head."

"What's *that* about?"

"Can we save the psychoanalysis for later, Nicky? We got the information we wanted. Now I have to get you away from here before Carob catches on to us…or coats your nuts!"

Noah sped out of the parking lot, nearly running over a three-hundred-pound woman carrying a huge bag stuffed with organic chips, cakes, and pies.

When we got home, after showering off the makeup and hair gel, I put back on my sweat clothes and came down our flared oak staircase. Noah and I cooked dinner together then served it in the kitchen nook. With Scott's back on the mend, Bonnie and Scott salivated over our latest gourmet creation: tuna, macaroni, and peas casserole.

As we sat enjoying our family dinnertime, Bonnie told us about their excursion to the new supermarket in town.

"It was amazing," said Bonnie scooping a large helping of casserole onto her plate. "I've never seen so many aisles in one store. They had an Asian aisle, a health-food aisle (*don't remind me*), a gourmet aisle, an Italian aisle, a Jewish aisle. I emailed Judy a picture and she asked me to bring her back some canned salmon. We don't have that at our supermarket."

"I'm glad you had a good time," I said, pouring us each a glass of milk.

"I sure did." She looked at her husband. "That is until we were leaving the parking lot."

"What happened there?" asked Noah apprehensively.

Bonnie said like a librarian reading a favorite children's story, "Dad and I were walking back to Noah's car, and I noticed the car parking next to us had a sticker reading, 'Marriage = 1 Man & 1 Woman.' I emailed a picture of it to Judy, and Judy said I should slash their tires."

"Mom, did you?" asked Noah with terror in his eyes.

"Of course not, sweetie," answered Bonnie. "I would never damage anyone's property."

Noah breathed a sigh of relief.

"But I couldn't just ignore something so hurtful. What if a child with gay parents saw that? So as the elderly couple were getting out of the car, I said, 'Excuse me, but I couldn't help noticing the sign on your car. My husband and I certainly agree that a man and a woman in love should be able to marry, but since we have a gay son, we also believe that any two people in love should have the same right to happiness.'"

"Ugh-oh," said Noah with a frightened look in my direction.

Bonnie continued. "The woman told me that she respects my concern for my son, but only God makes the rules. So I asked her when it was that God talked to her. The husband replied that God talks to them every day in the Bible. So I asked if they had children. The woman replied that they have a daughter. Then I asked, 'Have you sold your daughter to slavery as it says in the Bible?'"

"Oh my God." Noah pressed his fork into his peas.

"Exactly," said Bonnie proudly. "And I asked if the woman lies out in the fields during menstruation, and how many wives the husband has." She added with a giggle, "As you can imagine, that didn't go over too well."

"What did they do?" asked Noah, clearly afraid to hear the answer.

"The woman told me she would pray for me, and I told her I would pray for her too." After an officious nod, Bonnie said, "But here's the interesting part."

"There's more?" asked Noah.

Bonnie nodded. "The man stopped cold in his tracks, turned to his wife, and said, 'The lady has a point.' Can you imagine! He said, 'The lady has a point.' All because of what *I* said!"

"You're a gay ally, Bonnie!" I said with a wide grin.

"You know, I think you're right, Nicky. That's what I am." Bonnie laughed. "I am a gay ally!" She poked her husband. "I should join that group, Dad, 'Parents and People of Latins and Gays!'"

"That's 'Parents and Friends of Lesbians and Gays,' Mom," said Noah drowning in his milk.

Bonnie replied, "I should join *that* group too." She poked her husband again. "I should head a chapter!"

I kissed her cheek. "You're head of our chapter in *this* house, Bonnie."

"Thank you, Nicky," Bonnie said as she enjoyed a large forkful of casserole.

Noticing that Scott was sitting and eating quietly, I asked, "Is everything all right, Scott?"

Noah picked up my cue. "Is your back still hurting, Dad?"

Bonnie waved her hands at her husband. "His back is fine. He's just brooding about his old girlfriend."

After swallowing a huge mouthful of casserole, Scott said morosely, "Cheryl didn't deserve to die that way. Nobody does."

"I'm sorry, Scott," I replied.

"Thank you, Nicky," said Scott, holding back a tear.

"We're trying to figure out who killed Cheryl, Dad," said Noah.

"Can I help?" Scott asked.

"Nicky and I are on it," Noah said.

"What about that detective?" asked Bonnie.

"Manuello thinks Cheryl killed Brick Strong and Jillian Flowers in a jealous range," explained Noah.

Scott slammed down his fork. "You can tell…"

"Manuello," said Noah.

"that Cheryl didn't kill…"

"Brick Strong," said Bonnie.

"and…"

"Jillian Flowers," I said.

Scott wiped a tear from his puffy cheek. "Cheryl had her problems, but she would never kill anyone."

Noah said, "Manuello may have given up on the case, but Nicky and I haven't."

Helping myself to more casserole, I said, "I hate to admit it, but it seems that Manuello was right about Brick Strong giving a large amount of *Tribulus terrestris* and creatine to Tim Kim."

Noah said, "Cheryl favored Tim to win the bodybuilding contest. Maybe Brick was jealous."

"Or perhaps Strong wanted to clear the way for Jillian or Mack to win the competition," I said. "Brick may have given testosterone to Jonathan Toner as well."

"Then why didn't Strong kill Rodney, Maria, and Kim too?" asked Noah.

"Maybe Brick was planning to do just that, but somebody killed Brick first…and killed Cheryl." I swallowed a stack of vitamins then looked at Noah. "Maybe somebody who wanted to be department head."

Bonnie gulped down her milk. "This is so fascinating. I feel like Jessica Fletcher!"

Noah did the same. "Well, as *fascinating* as this is, I have to go to campus."

"Why?" I asked while collecting the empty drink glasses.

"I need to grade some Acting I papers I left in my office. I shouldn't be gone too long."

"Be careful, honey." Bonnie loaded the dishes into the

dishwasher.

I walked Noah to the door and handed him his jacket from the coatrack. "Drive safely."

"Don't I always?" Glancing over at his parents, Noah gave me a peck on the cheek and left.

With Bonnie and Scott cleaning up the kitchen, I excused myself and went upstairs into the study. Sitting at the rolltop desk, I turned on my computer to answer emails and noticed a stack of students' papers in the corner of the desk. I picked up the top paper and read, "Jenny O'Halloran, Acting I, Professor Noah Oliver."

Racing down the stairs three at a time, I grabbed my jacket, and called out, "I'm going for a ride. See you later."

I leapt into my car and sped down the side streets. I drove faster than lightning and reached Noah's car only two cars ahead of me. As we sped through the winding roads overlooking steep cliffs and Rocky Mountains in the distance, I wondered why Noah had lied to me, and where he was going.

Keeping a safe but viewable distance of Noah's car, I followed him onto a street like ours full of homes owned by the college for use by the faculty. As Noah pulled into a driveway, I parked on the street under a large maple tree.

Once Noah went inside the house, I noticed a light go on toward the side of the house. I made my way to the side window and peered inside. The window was open, and I could hear voices, but I wasn't able to see anyone. So I rested my knee on the windowpane and hoisted myself against the window frame. Spotting two men at the corner of the room, I leaned in further, but lost my footing, and fell inside the room. As I looked up from the floor, I saw Van Granite with his hands resting on Noah's shoulders.

# Chapter Nine

"Nicky, what are you doing here?" Noah looked down at me—sprawled on Van Granite's rec room floor.

Making my way to my feet, I said, "More importantly, what are *you* doing here, Noah?"

In his skintight sweat clothes, Van Granite took his thick hands off Noah's shoulders. "Looks like we've been busted, Noah. Time to fess up."

"Yes, time to fess up, Noah," I said with a voice as shrill as a television entertainment news anchor's.

Noah looked down at his sneakers. "I'm sorry I lied to you."

Staring into his (I thought) true blue eyes, I said, "That's all you have to say to me?"

"Please don't be upset," said Noah with a hand on my shoulder.

I pushed away his hand. "Wouldn't *anyone* be upset in my position?"

"We came over here because Manuello closed down the Phys. Ed. building," explained Granite with a flex of his pecs in my direction.

My heart nearly stopped. "So *this* is what you two have been doing together at the Phys. Ed. building all this time?"

"Noah's a fast learner," said Granite with a wink at my lover.

"It sure seems like it." I dropped onto Van's sofa.

Noah sat at my side. "I didn't tell you, because I thought you would make fun of me."

"Make fun of you. I'd have done a lot more than that." I

blinked back tears.

Granite sat on the arm of the sofa and flexed his thigh muscles. "There's nothing wrong with what we were doing. Noah will be a better man for it."

"And I'll be six feet under." I took in deep breaths to avoid passing out.

Noah took my clammy hand. "I'm doing this for *you*."

"For me! I'd prefer a nice necktie, thank you." I swallowed my bile. "How could you do this and with *him*?"

Noah squeezed my hand. "Van has been helping me grow in a whole new direction."

I blinked back the tears forming at the corners of my eyes. "What about *me*? What about *us*?"

"I know we could have done this together, but it's less stressful with someone who isn't your partner."

"Noah's stronger and more limber than I thought," added Granite with an affectionate poke at Noah. "You want to join us? Based on what Noah's been telling me, I can teach you a few new tricks too."

I put my throbbing head in my shaking hands. "Pardon me if I am terribly old fashioned and don't want to share my lover."

"It's only every other night," said Noah with a hopeful look on his face.

Granite added, "We can meet here, no problem. And once the Phys. Ed. building opens up again, we can go there."

I began hyperventilating. "I need to go home."

Helping me up, Granite said, "At your age a full night's sleep is important. Noah will be home after we finish."

"Is that okay, Nicky?" asked Noah.

I stopped before falling over a mini trampoline. "No, it is not okay. None of this is anything near okay."

Noah turned to Granite. "I better drive him home. Can I leave my car here overnight and pick it up tomorrow?"

"Sure." Granite placed a hand on Noah's shoulder. "Missing one night won't set us back too far."

*How generous of you.*

Van flexed. "We'll do some extra biceps tomorrow

night."

*I'll drop dead if I have to hear about Noah's muscle worship of Van Granite!*

"My body has been sore lately." Noah rubbed his buttocks muscles. "To be honest, I can use the night off."

*I'll bet!*

"You look pale," said Noah with an alarming look on his Jezebel face. "I'm getting you home right away, Nicky."

Noah led me to the doorway and said over his shoulder, "I'll pay you tomorrow night."

I froze. "Noah, you are actually *paying* him for this?"

Granite winked at me. "Don't you think I'm worth it?"

Noah said, "He's a professional. I can't expect him to do this with me for free."

*College professor by day. Hustler by night!*

"Besides, I'm getting free use of Van's equipment in his house."

*Spare me the tour of the dungeon room with the sling!*

I tripped over a gym ball and landed in Noah's arms. For the first time I looked around the room and noticed the hand weights, barbell, and gym mat. *I'm a muscle head.* "Van has been training you...as a personal trainer."

"Of course," Noah replied.

"You two haven't been...fooling around?"

Noah's eyes tripled in size. "What! Of course not."

Granite admired his own reflection in the wall mirror. "I'm not into blonds."

Pressing my face against Noah's chest, I wailed like a baby.

"I better get him home right away," said Noah.

"Probably male menopause," Granite said with a sympathetic pat to my heaving back. "See you guys tomorrow."

After Noah got me home and into bed, we sat together under the white quilt turned gray by the moonlight from our window. Noah put his arm around my still quivering shoulder. "You always teased me for not working out, and I was too embarrassed to ask you to help me. I thought I would hire Van, then surprise you with the results."

"Noah, I think it's fine that Granite is training you, but please promise me that you will never lie to me again, no matter how trivial or how noble the reason."

"I promise." He kissed my cheek. "Will you promise never to jump to conclusions about me again, and instead just ask me?"

"Sure." I kissed his forehead.

He kissed the cleft in my chin.

I smiled. "And by the way, I love your body just the way it is."

Noah returned my smile. "Ditto for your body."

We shared a tight, passionate embrace. Then, disappearing under the comforter, we kissed and made love well into the starry night.

★

The next morning after returning home from church (Noah's parents had led us to an open and affirming one), the four of us sat in the breakfast nook eating French toast covered in cinnamon.

"I emailed a picture of the church to Judy," said Bonnie, stacking her plate with French toast. "Judy said it's *almost* as nice as the church where Timmy and Tommy are getting married." She patted her closed purse. "I won't be emailing Judy any more pictures today."

"Mom, during the spreading of the peace, did you have to tell everyone you have a partnered gay son?" asked Noah.

"Why not? Everyone I know talks about their straight children and their straight children's spouses and their straight children's straight children until I'm ready to climb the walls," answered Bonnie.

Back to his old self (and back to his old appetite), Scott said, "Speaking of spouses, I heard your bed thumping like a wild buck at a rodeo last night, guys." He winked at Noah and me.

Noah's face turned beet red.

"Your son and I had make-up sex last night," I explained.

Noah's face turned beet red—if the beets had been injected with blood.

"That's the best kind," said Scott poking his giggling wife. "Have you two guys given any more thought to tying the knot?"

"That church would make a beautiful place to get married." Bonnie added with a sneer, "Regardless of what Judy says." She smiled. "And that lesbian minister sure has a captivating way about her."

"How do you know the minister is a lesbian?" I asked.

"A mother knows," replied Bonnie, looking like Methuselah.

Stuffing a huge piece of French toast into his mouth, Scott added, "And a woman at the church introduced herself to us as the minister's wife."

Bonnie waved a forkful of French toast at Noah. "Judy said that Timmy and Tommy are going to Kauai on their honeymoon."

"That'll cost Jack a pretty penny." Scott helped himself to more French toast.

Bonnie continued. "Hawaii is a lovely place for a honeymoon." She glared at Scott. "Or so I've heard. We went on a brewery tour of Wisconsin for *ours*."

"It was a good trip," said Scott.

Noah replied, "Nicky and I aren't going anywhere until we find out the real reason for the five murders on campus."

"Thank goodness they closed down that Physical Education building," said Bonnie, sprinkling more cinnamon on her French toast.

After swallowing my vitamins with a chaser of grape juice, I raised my glass. "Here's to us solving the case so the bodybuilding competition can resume, and young men and women everywhere can admire perfect gym-trained bodies."

I winked at Noah, and his face changed from red to green.

The rest of our day was spent going bowling with Noah's parents (their favorite pastime). Bonnie was thrilled when she scored the highest, but miffed when her announcement to the

155

other patrons that she has a gay, partnered son didn't go over as well as it did at the liberal church.

That evening at dinner (lamb chops, baked potato, and spinach) in the kitchen nook, Scott asked, "What's the latest on the investigation, guys?"

"Nothing new to report, Dad," said Noah.

"Maybe you guys need a new angle," replied Scott.

"What do you mean?" I asked, removing a piece of spinach from between my teeth.

"On television—"

"He watches a lot of television," interjected Bonnie, placing a huge slab of butter on her potato.

"—it seems that *greed* is often the motive for murder," said Scott. "If I was running this investigation—"

"Which thankfully he isn't, since he can't remember any of the victims' names, except his old girlfriend's," added Bonnie.

Ignoring his wife again, Scott reached for his fourth lamb chop. "I'd be asking who has the most to gain *financially* from the deaths."

Feeling the stirrings of Sherlock Holmes in my (tired) groin, I said, "With Tim Sim and the blackmailing Jonathan Toner out of the way, Kim Sim inherited his father's money."

Noah added à la Watson, "And Abigail Strong no doubt inherits her parents' money."

Scott asked, "How about..."

"Jillian Flowers?" said Bonnie.

"Nicky, could Brick Strong have left something in his will to Jillian, as he left Mack his ashes?" asked Noah.

I sat back in my chair. "It seems like we need to talk to the elusive Abigail Strong and find out."

The next day, after breakfast with the family and teaching my class, I sat for my office hour at the college. After the last student finished complaining about his grades while texting his girlfriend, Jimmy Saline appeared at my office door.

"Professor, can I talk to you?" Jimmy asked with his red hair covering his forehead.

"Take a seat."

Sitting in the chair next to my desk, Jimmy said, "I don't have any more news for you, Professor."

"That's okay. Is everything all right?"

Jimmy rubbed his thin fingers against his brown corduroy pants. "Professor, if somebody you love asks you to do something, should you always do it?"

Feeling like the father in a Victorian family movie, I asked, "Is this something you *want* to do?"

"I'm not sure."

"If you don't do this, could you jeopardize your relationship with Mack?"

"I think so, Professor."

"Is this something that will hurt someone else?"

He nodded sadly.

I pulled up his narrow chin. "Jimmy, love is an amazing thing. We all crave it. We all need it. And we all make fools of ourselves to get it, and to keep it." *Like me last night at Granite's.* But don't ever compromise yourself for love. Because in the end, though we love others, all we really have is ourselves and our conscience." I smiled. "Do you understand what I'm saying, Jimmy?"

Jimmy replied, "I think I do, Professor. Thank you for your time."

Thinking back to the frailties of young love, I shut my office door and sat back down at my desk. After punching a few numbers on the phone, I was connected to the college's Admissions Office. I asked to speak with Abigail Strong, and the woman on the other end informed me that Ms. Strong was out due to the recent deaths in her family. When I requested Abigail's home phone number, I was politely told that the college did not give out personal information on its employees, including to other employees, and Ms. Strong's home phone number was unlisted. Hanging up the phone and staring at the brick fireplace across from my desk, I realized it was time to pay a visit to Mickey Minor.

Mickey works in the Human Resources department on campus. He has blond hair, blue eyes, bulging muscles, and a sweet disposition. Mickey and I dated early on in my career at Treemeadow, and I found him quite charming. The problem was that when we went out to dinner, the waiter asked if Mickey wanted a children's meal. You see, though Mickey is about my age, Mickey is under five feet tall.

Like most other four-year colleges and universities nowadays, Treemeadow is on a hiring rampage — of administrators. While the number of full-time faculty members dwindles, the barrage of new administrators on campus grows like weeds popping out of an old stone patio. Nobody on campus seems to know what any of these administrators do at the college, but there are certainly a large number of them doing it. So, after I made my way through countless cubicles of Human Resource workers busily processing new administrative employee accounts for payment and benefits, I finally reached the end cubicle of Mickey Minor.

"What brings you down to the bowels of the college?"

I searched around the seemingly empty cubicle. "Mickey?"

Blond hair popped up behind a stack of pension applications on the desk. "Sit your gorgeous body down and talk to me."

Sitting on the chair next to his desk, I said, "It's good to see you...sort of."

After he moved the stack of forms to a side table, I found my old friend. He sat back in his chair with his legs dangling in the air. Mickey looked as handsome, muscular, and tiny as ever. "What do you want?"

I smiled my most genuine theatrical smile. "Now, do I always want something when I come to visit you?"

"Yes." Mickey narrowed his blue eyes.

Leaning forward in my chair, I said, "All right. There's an employee at the college — "

"I knew it." He threw his little hands up in the air. "You know I adore you madly, Nicky, but how many times do I have to tell you that I cannot give out personal information about college employees." He winked at me. "Unless the employee is *me*."

I spread my legs farther apart. "Please, for your old pal?"

Mickey crossed his muscular little arms over his strong tiny chest. "I'm not falling for that one again."

I rested my hand on his petite knee. "I'll be honest with you."

"That would be a nice change."

"I'm sure you've heard about the five murders in the Physical Education building."

"Of course. That's why they closed down the building."

"Exactly." I lowered my volume. "I need to find out who is behind those murders. And the only way I can do that is to contact a college employee who works in our Admissions Office."

Mickey scratched his diminutive chin. "I don't know. I could get into big trouble for this."

I offered Mickey my most stoic look — and my most open-kneed pose. "You could be saving a life…maybe even mine."

"Always the drama teacher." Mickey typed Abigail's name into his computer, wrote down her address and phone number, and leisurely placed it in the palm of my hand. "You better not tell anyone I gave that to you, Nicky, or your main asset will be no more."

"You have my word as a gentleman."

He smiled naughtily. "Well, let's not go too far."

I laughed. "See you around, Mickey."

"Give me a call sometime. Anytime!"

After Noah's class, he met me in my office, and we looked out my office window at the bronze statues of Tree and Meadow, surrounded by fallen leaves of coral, persimmon, and amaranth. Thinking of the gay lovers who founded the college, Noah and I shared our days, and we shared a kiss.

Noah whispered in my ear, "So when are you going to

call Abigail?"

I shut my office door. "How about right now?"

As Noah sat on the chair next to my desk, I punched in Abigail's phone number and sat at my desk. Noah pressed his ear against mine just in time to hear Abigail's voice.

"Hello?" Abigail said, obviously bothered by the ring of the phone.

"Abigail, this is Nicky Abbondanza."

"Who?" she replied as friendly as a conservative politician at a women's rights rally.

I said, "We met at your father's funeral. I'm a theatre professor at Treemeadow. Your dad hired me to direct the bodybuilding competition."

"What do you want?"

*To talk to someone with manners.* "I am terribly sorry about the loss of your mother."

"Thank you, now I have to—"

"May I pay you a visit...to speak to you about your parents?"

She sighed into the phone. "I don't need this right now."

Noah whispered in my ear. I said into the mouthpiece, "I have a little gift for you."

"Look, I'm sure you're a nice guy, but I'm not well enough right now to receive visitors."

Noah whispered again, and I said, "Then can I ask you a couple of questions over the phone?"

"I really can't do this right now."

"But—"

"Goodbye, Professor."

She hung up the phone. Noah and I stared at one another like shock victims.

"I've never seen anyone so rude," said Noah sitting in his chair.

"Her parents did die recently...as did her closet gay ex-boyfriend." I hung up the phone and sat in my chair. "I guess that's that."

Noah had that 1950s sitcom "I have an idea" look in his eyes. "Maybe not, Nicky."

"She won't talk to me."

"Abigail met *you* at the funeral, but she didn't meet *me*."

I patted Noah's shoulder. "If she won't talk to me, she won't talk to you."

"That's true." Noah rose from his seat like a cyclone ready to unfurl.

"Where are you going?" I asked, afraid to hear the answer.

"*We* are going to the costume shop, prop closet, and makeup room." He opened my office door and posed like an opera diva welcoming entrance applause. "Abigail won't talk to Nicky Abbondanza or Noah Oliver, but she *will* talk to *Marvin Meekbottom!*"

An hour later Noah was dressed in a dark suit and tie. His pants ended at the top of his white socks, and his suit jacket finished at his waist. His hair was blackened, greased, and slicked back. A pencil-thin mustache was nestled just above his upper lip. His face and lips were pale, and dark circles underscored his eyes. Dark shading on the side of his face caused it to look thin, and yellow highlighting on his cheekbones made them appear sallow.

I stood outside Abigail Strong's first-floor apartment, looking inside her open window as if a front-row seat for Noah's command performance.

After ringing the bell and being led inside, Noah sat on a white loveseat in Abigail's stark, modern living room. Abigail sat opposite him draped on a small black chair flanking a thin silver end table.

Wearing a brown terry-cloth robe and slippers, Abigail wiped her enormous nose with her soggy tissue. "I have an appointment with Mr. Darkmeister in an hour at the funeral home."

"Of course you do, Ms. Strong," Noah said in a nasal, whiny, weasel voice. "However, Mr. Darkmeister had a sudden emergency...a death to occupy him, so he asked me to visit with you here instead."

Not totally convinced of Noah's charade, Abigail said between nose wipes, "Isn't death a common occurrence for people in your profession?"

Noah slouched in his seat and his head dropped to one side. "In this case, Mr. Darkmeister's entire family of... fourteen were killed in a...helicopter accident."

Scratching her stringy hair, Abigail said skeptically, "How did fourteen people fit inside a helicopter?"

"Oh, they didn't." No doubt using his years of improvisational acting training, Noah added, "The helicopter crashed down *on top* of them. During a picnic in the park. A family reunion with all the relatives. Grandparents, parents, aunts, uncles, cousins." His chin hit his chest, and his voice deepened. "It was a tragedy of the highest order."

Though Abigail didn't seem to buy Noah's act, ultimately laziness won out. "It's easier for me to do this here anyway. The last thing I need now is to go to the funeral home again."

Noah waved his white hands and painted black fingernails. "And *that*, Ms. Strong, is precisely why I am here. As we say in the funeral business, 'A new day, a new death.'"

"I hope you don't want anything to drink," said Abigail wiping her eyes. "I haven't had the energy to go shopping."

"Please do not put yourself out."

*Moving off the chair would put out Abigail Strong.*

Noah, rather Marvin Meekbottom, continued. "At Darkmeister's Funeral Home, your bereavement is our business." He grew more frenzied with each slogan. "We want to be the salve to your sorrow. When you grieve, mourn, and wallow in fear, anger, and loneliness, let us be your asylum!"

Abigail adjusted her robe over her tree trunk legs. "Mr. Meekbottom, last week I lost my ex-boyfriend, my father, and now my mother. I don't have the strength or the patience to prolong this. So please arrange for my mother's funeral to be exactly like my father's."

*Minus the ashes over the guests' heads, and the murder in the bathroom I assume.*

Noah clicked his yellowed teeth. "Your father's demise. Such a tragedy. I believe I still have a few ashes." He reached inside his pants' pocket.

"That won't be necessary." Abigail blew her nose, which sounded like a train whistle.

Noah pressed his knees together and covered them with his hands. "Your father, how sad to lose him. He met his maker due to ingesting herbs from a health-food store, as I recall."

"That was his student, Tim Sim. My father never bought any herbs."

*It seems Abby doesn't know Daddy dear as well as she thought.*

"My parents both died in the gym. Dad with a barbell, and Mom on the rings." Abigail wiped a tear off her pimply cheek.

"Such a shame." Noah dislodged a worn leather notepad from his jacket pocket and a bitten-down pencil from inside his white sock. He opened the notepad and scribbled something. "And now Van Granite is Department Head of Bodybuilding, I understand."

Abigail blew air through her chapped lips. "Pity the Bodybuilding Department. Granite can't hold a candle to either one of my parents."

"And why is that?"

"Let's just say Granite is more interested in his own physique than in his students'."

"And how do you know this?"

"I know." She squirmed in her chair. "Can we finish up here? I'm not feeling well."

"Of course." Noah looked down at his notes and giggled.

"What's wrong?" Lines sprouted on her forehead.

"The client before you. A plumber. He wanted a faucet on top of his casket." He giggled louder.

*A little undertaker humor, Noah?*

Not enjoying the joke, Abigail said, "Are we finished, Mr. Meekbottom? I'm really not strong enough for this."

"And yet your last name is *Strong*." Noah giggled more robustly. "I'm sorry to hear you aren't well, Ms. Strong. Perhaps we should discuss *your* final resting place. It's never too early." As if starring in a television commercial, Noah added, "You may think today is a new beginning, but it could very well be the end."

She plunged the tissue inside the pocket of her robe. "Please just arrange cremation for my mother."

Noah waved the palms of his hands like a medium with a crystal ball. "Wait just a moment." He looked at his notepad. "Before I can arrange for cremation, a gold urn, a minister, no limousine, and an evening service as your father had, I will need to see your mother's will."

"What for?"

"To make sure we are following the exact wishes of the dearly departed of course. What if the lost loved one requested a white casket with a picture of a horse on it, and instead we arranged for a picture of a chicken? We would be stuck with egg on our faces?" He giggled again.

Abigail looked like a steam engine ready to explode. "My parents told me their exact wishes, and I am following them. Mr. Darkmeister was satisfied with that. You should be as well."

"I am." Noah slid to the side of his chair like a claustrophobic snake in a newly opened basket. "I simply want to make sure that your mother did not desire an alternative method of traveling to the great beyond." He flipped through his notepad. "For example, we can offer a closed casket ranging from one to fifteen thousand dollars. Or we can embalm the dead darling by injecting chemicals into her veins, putting makeup on her face, then propping her up in an open casket. Then her friends and family members can admire how wonderful she looks for days to come, just as one might admire a moose over a fireplace. And it's only twenty thousand dollars."

*Get to the investigation, Noah!*

"My mother wanted to be cremated," said Abigail.

"Did your mother mention this in her will or health care proxy?" asked Noah.

Grabbing a tissue from the dispenser on the end table, Abigail said behind crooked, gritted teeth, "No."

Noah readied his pencil and notepad. "Did your mother's will leave *any* instructions for after her demise?"

Abigail picked her nose with the tissue. "Mom named *me* as executor."

"But not your father?"

"My parents were divorced, Mr. Meekbottom."

"How sad. That happens so frequently in heterosexual marriages these days, doesn't it? Pity." Noah shook his head fussily and made an entry in his notepad.

*Rein it in, Noah!*

Abigail rolled her bloodshot eyes. "My mother's will allocate who should get her belongings."

"And who is that?" Noah asked.

*I held my breath.*

"Why do you need *that* information?" Abigail asked.

Noah smiled. "It is all part of the picture, Ms. Strong. The mindset and the makeup of the loved lifeless one."

Abigail rose and approached Noah. "I really don't need this, Mr. Meekbottom. Everybody I know and love died last week."

"Oh, you poor dear," said Noah. "Here I have been going on and on about the adored atrophied ones, and I haven't thought a moment about the one person left behind to pick up the fallen, finished pieces." Tears came to his mascara-enhanced eyes. "How thoughtless of me!"

She sat next to Noah on the loveseat and blew her nose. "And I'm alone with nobody to help me."

"What a nightmare! To be the one survivor of the storm, meandering lost and frightened through a forest laden with the dead bodies of every human being you have ever loved!"

She nodded and sniffed. "And I don't have the stamina for it, or the patience. I really don't."

"Of course not, Ms. Strong. Very few would."

Tears filled Abigail's bulging eyes. "And I miss my old boyfriend. I don't care if he dumped me, or if he was gay, straight, bi, trans, or an alien."

"Either way he would need a funeral."

She opened the floodgates. "And I miss my parents."

"It's no wonder you miss the two people who birthed you, raised you, and coddled you. The mother and father who were the embodiment of stability, protection, home, and safety for you."

Abigail wept loudly.

Noah rested Abigail's head on his shoulder and patted her on the back. "And the only saving grace in this tragedy is that your parents left everything to you in their wills."

She nodded between sobs. "My mother did. My father left his money to me and to my half-brother."

*Your half-brother?*

Noah asked, "Your father left half his fortune to your brother, yet your brother wasn't at the funeral to lament his father's loss?"

Abigail sobbed into Noah's neck. "Yes, he was. My father had arranged for the minister to give Dad's ashes to him."

"Your brother is Mack Strong?"

Abigail nodded and bawled against Noah's chest as he looked out the window and smiled.

# Chapter Ten

That evening at dinner in the kitchen nook, Bonnie filled her plate with turkey, brown rice, and string beans. "Their little blue breasts were so beautiful!"

*Try saying that three times fast.*

Bonnie continued. "And the red ones and orange ones were gorgeous."

Scott smothered his plate with brown gravy. "They're birds. Just like in Wisconsin."

"These were prettier," Bonnie said.

"I'm glad you enjoyed the bird-watch walk, Mom," said Noah, sipping his soy milk.

Scott said, "My legs ached. My ankles hurt. My knees buckled. And my back went out again."

"I don't know why. You just had to walk around and watch them," Bonnie said to Scott. "The birds had to fly around, pose, and put on a show!"

"I don't understand why we had to go on a bird tour anyway," said Scott.

Doggedly cutting her turkey, Bonnie replied, "Because Judy loves birds."

Before a family feud erupted, I said, "Noah and I did a bit of sleuthing today."

Scott ripped into a turkey leg. "What's going on, guys?"

Noah explained, "I, or rather my alter ego, talked to Abigail Strong."

"That's the daughter of the dead department head and his dead ex-wife," Bonnie explained to Scott as she speared a string bean.

"I know who she is," replied Scott, helping himself to another turkey leg.

"Okay, then tell us the names of Abigail's parents," said Bonnie.

"Will you let your son tell the story?" said Scott.

Noah continued. "It seems that Cheryl Stryker left her money to her daughter Abigail, but Brick Strong willed his to Abigail *and* to Brick's son."

"Who is—?" Scott asked.

"Brick's," Bonnie said.

"—son?" asked Scott.

Noah explained, "Brick had Abigail with Cheryl, and Brick had Mack Heath with Sue."

Bonnie said to Scott, "Mack is one of the bodybuilding students, and Sue is that nice woman we met at Brick's funeral."

"Our guess is that Sue had Mack out of wedlock, which no doubt put a damper on Brick's and Cheryl's marriage." I lined up my vitamins. "It must also have been the reason why Brick left his ashes to Mack."

"And to the rest of us." Scott helped himself to more gravy.

Noah said, "It also explains why Cheryl was not fond of Mack, and why Sue Heath was at Brick's funeral."

Scott choked up a rice kernel. "It also gives Mack a motive for murder."

I said, "Elementary, my dear Scott. With Brick gone, Mack loses a potential vote for the bodybuilding competition, *but* he no doubt gains more money than a year's worth of tuition at Treemeadow."

"Or maybe Mack got someone else to do the dirty work for him," said Noah.

*I remembered Jimmy's question in my office.*

"Sounds like you need to talk to Mack pronto," said Scott rubbing his overstuffed stomach.

I pulled out my cell phone. "First I want to call Manuello."

With six ears hovered over my phone, I was relieved to

find Manuello in his office. After I filled him in on what Noah and I had uncovered, the detective sounded unimpressed.

"So Brick was Mack's father? Not every kid kills his father, though most of them probably want to. It's pretty flimsy," said Manuello sounding like he couldn't wait to leave for home.

"But don't you think it's a bit of a coincidence?" I asked.

"I've seen lots more surprising 'coincidences,' Nicky. I'm holding to my theory that the two students accidentally killed themselves, and Cheryl killed Brick, Jillian, and herself."

"You're not going to reopen the investigation?" I asked.

Manuello exhaled in resignation. "The college's Board of Trustees is breathing down my neck. I'm making my findings public, and reopening the Physical Education building tomorrow. The bodybuilding competition is back on, Nicky. Go direct it. Get your mind off the deaths." As if a parent telling his kid to "go play," Manuello added, "You and Noah go do what you do…when you aren't meddling in crime solving."

After I hung up the phone, Bonnie (or rather Judy via email) said what we were all thinking, "If you want something done, you have to do it yourself."

The next morning, after breakfast with the family, then teaching our classes, Noah and I headed over to the Physical Education building. After walking past Mary, snoozing on her desk calendar, Noah and I knocked on Van Granite's office door—now laden with a sign reading, "Interim Department Head."

Granite opened the door and welcomed us inside, where we found a disheveled Kim Sim sitting on Granite's sofa.

"Um see you at like rehearsal, Professors." Kim headed for the office door.

"And I will see you tonight," said Granite.

"Um, right," Kim said before excusing himself to put on his Greek god costume for our afternoon dress rehearsal.

Granite sat behind his desk and checked himself out in his wall mirror. "Kim's a good student. He's my pick for the competition. But he's been training so hard, he's fallen a bit behind in a few of his classes. So I'm tutoring him in the evenings."

"I'm sure he's an obedient student," I said with my best snide tone.

"Feeling better, are you, Nicky?"

Noah said, "I want to thank you for training me, Van, and to let you know that when *or if* I resume training, I'll give you call."

"No problem." Granite leaned back in his chair and smiled. "I'll be here."

Using my acting skills, I said, "Yes, congratulations on being named interim department head."

"It's what I've always hoped for," said Granite.

Putting my arm around Noah's shoulders, I said, "We better get to rehearsal. The competition is tomorrow."

Granite rose from his throne. "Hey, speaking of the competition. With Cheryl and Brick gone, we're short two judges. I don't think our new adjunct instructors are up to the task. How would you two guys like to help me out?"

Noah and I looked at one another and shrugged. "Fine with us," we said in unison.

"Great. That makes it a threesome," he added with a wink.

As Granite flexed his shoulders in front of the mirror, Noah and I left for rehearsal.

Once in the main gym, we set up the scenery and equipment, then checked the bodybuilders' costumes. Next, I re-blocked the opening sequence with Rodney Towers, Maria Ruiz, Kim Sim, and Mack Heath. As Noah worked with the bodybuilders for the last time on their individual posing routines, I walked over to Tony's alcove and peeked my head inside.

"Hiya, Professor!" said Tony. "All ready for the competition?"

"As ready as we'll ever be." I entered and stood at his

desk.

He refilled first aid kits with new bandages. "I wish all four of them kids could win. They worked so hard, and they each want it so bad." He lowered his aging voice. "With what's been going on around here, they all deserve it."

"I agree." Gravitating to Robbie's old pictures, I asked, "How's your son doing?"

He waved a brown-spotted hand at me. "Robbie's doing good, Professor. He's moving up in his law firm. Thanks for asking."

I sat at the edge of his desk. "Is Robbie, or anyone in his family, having any problems in Florida?"

Tony laughed. "Nobody has no problems in Florida, unless their air conditioner breaks down."

"This will sound crazy, Tony, but I've had some dreams lately, where Robbie asks me for help."

Tony scratched his gray hair. "It must be your mind playing tricks on you, Professor. Robbie's fine." He looked at me appreciatively. "But thanks for your interest in my son, Professor. You make an old man happy. I hope you get to meet him soon."

"I'd like that." *More than you know.*

We finished our rehearsal and wished the four students good luck at the competition the next day. The young bodybuilders in turn thanked Noah and me for our direction.

After Mack changed into his sweat clothes, I asked Mack and Jimmy to join Noah and me on a bench outside the Physical Education building. It was an unusually tepid fall day, and the bench was surrounded by multicolored leaves swirling in the warm breeze. Squirrels nibbled at acorns as Mack nibbled on a protein bar from Jimmy's book bag.

I looked out at the earth-toned mountains in the distance. "Are you psyched for the competition tomorrow?"

Sharing a smile with Jimmy, Mack replied, "I couldn't be more psyched, Professor, and I'm totally into my Greek god character." He blinked back a tear. "I wish Professor Strong could be at the competition."

I put my hand on Mack's bulging shoulder. "I know

Professor Strong was your father. And I am very sorry for your loss."

Mack rubbed his sneakers against the grass. "You know about that?"

I nodded. "Why did you keep it a secret all this time?"

"At first...for my mom."

"Why?" I asked.

"She's old fashioned. The whole unwed-mother thing." He gazed at the azure sky. "Then I didn't tell anyone so the other bodybuilders wouldn't think I was getting unfair preference."

Noah picked up the rear (so to speak). "We thought that you and Professor Strong were lovers."

"Lovers! That's crazy." Mack put his muscular arms around Jimmy's stick-like shoulders. "There's only one guy for me, Professor."

Jimmy glowed like a jack-o'-lantern under the sun.

"Were you and Strong close?" I asked.

Mack nodded. "My dad is the reason I became a bodybuilder."

"Professor Stryker knew about your relationship?" asked Noah.

"Yes, and she kept throwing it up in my face like lava," answered Mack with a sour look on his handsome face.

"Why?" I asked already knowing the answer to my question.

"Because she wanted her daughter to get all of Dad's attention," said Mack.

*And money.*

"How did Abigail and her father get along?" asked Noah.

Mack shrugged his mountainous shoulders. "Abigail isn't exactly the most fun person to be around."

*Tell me about it.*

"Even though Abigail works at the college, I think Dad avoided her as much as possible," Mack said.

Stretching out my long legs and gazing at the lake in the distance, I said as nonchalantly as possible, "How do you get along with your half-sister, Mack?"

"She's okay, I guess. I've been focused on my training for the competition." Mack squeezed Jimmy's shoulder affectionately and I heard a crack. "And focused on my boyfriend."

Jimmy kissed Mack's thick neck.

Coming in for the kill, I said, "You and Abigail must have spoken recently though. Since your father left you each half of his money."

Mack's face drained of color. "Professor Stryker and Abigail were upset about that. My mom was really happy. I stayed out of it. I mean, it was Dad's money. He had the right to do with it what he wanted, right?"

"Right," I said. "But now you don't need to win the competition to pay for this year's tuition."

"I need to win for *other* reasons," Mack said with the determination of a gladiator going to battle.

Jimmy brushed his red hair away from his face. "The *main* reason is that Mack is the best!"

Mack kissed Jimmy's sunken cheek.

"What are the other reasons?" asked Noah in Watson mode.

After finishing his protein bar, Mack said, "I want to win for Jimmy." Jimmy's brown eyes lit up like sparklers. "For my mother." Mack's voice cracked. "And for my dad."

À la Sherlock Holmes, I asked, "Mack, your father knew gym equipment too well to be the victim of an accident with a barbell. Who do you think killed him?"

Mack took a water bottle from Jimmy and opened it. "Didn't the detective say Professor Stryker killed Jillian, dad, and herself?"

I leaned in face to face with Mack. "But who do *you* think did it?"

Mack's eyes turned to stones. "The same person who killed Jonathan and Tim."

"Who is that?" Noah asked looking like a rabid dog.

Mack took a drink of his water. "Since I don't have any proof, I'd rather not say."

"Just between us," I said like an anti-gay politician at a

gay tea dance.

After looking both ways, Mack said, "It seems to me that the bodybuilding competition has boiled down to three couples: Jimmy and me, Granite and Kim, and Rodney and Maria. Which couple has the most to gain from bumping off Jonathan, Tim, Jillian, Dad, and Stryker? Answer that question, and I think you'll know who did it." Mack rose. "I have to go to my Personal Training class, Professor." He turned to Jimmy. "You want to walk with me?"

Jimmy jumped up like a malaria victim's temperature. Noah stood next to Mack. "I'll walk you back, Mack. Professor Abbondanza wants to talk to Jimmy."

Mack looked concerned.

Noah said, "You know theatre folk. Always planning the next big production." Then he walked Mack to the Physical Education building with Mack straining his head back to watch Jimmy.

Walking to the Theatre building, I asked, "Everything going okay in your classes, Jimmy?"

"Sure, Professor."

As we walked alongside the low stone wall around the campus, I asked, "Have you made a decision yet…about what Mack asked you to do?"

Jimmy's gaunt face drooped. "Not yet, Professor."

I placed my hand on his stark shoulder. "Need any help figuring it out?"

He shook his head and red hair flew in various directions. "Thanks, Professor, but this is something I need to figure out on my own."

After sitting for my office hour (hearing students complain about the high tuition, homework, and class attendance policy), I walked over to the cafeteria.

Since it was between lunch and dinner, the cafeteria was relatively empty. I took a chicken Caesar salad and bottle of water, then headed to check-out. As I paid my bill I asked the ancient cashier if Sue Heath was working today.

The cigarette stench on the cashier's breath nearly knocked me over as she shouted, "Sue!"

Sue Heath appeared from behind the soup section, and I walked over to her.

"Ms. Heath, I hope you remember me from Brick Strong's funeral."

A warm smile lit up Sue Heath's beautiful face. "How are you?"

"At the moment, pretty hungry. Is it possible for you to join me for a late lunch?"

She nodded. "I'm due for a break. I'll meet you at a table."

"Which one?" I asked looking out at the vast dining room.

"Take your pick. There's plenty to choose from at this hour. I'll find you."

A few minutes later Sue and I were seated at a table overlooking the meadows, river, and mountains in the distance. As I chomped away at my salad, Sue sipped her coffee."

"To what do I owe the pleasure of this visit, Professor Abbondanza?"

I speared a piece of chicken. "Please, call me, Nicky."

"Only if you call me, Sue."

"Deal."

We smiled at one another.

I said between bites, "While directing the competition, I've become fond of Mack, but I've noticed he has some...problems. I thought that if I could ask you a few questions, perhaps I could help him."

Her face clouded over as if a storm was brewing. "I know my son carries demons from his past, Professor...Nicky. And it concerns me a great deal." The clouds lifted. "Mack speaks very highly of you, and I appreciate your interest in him. So, please ask away, and I'll do my best."

*I really like Sue Heath.* "Will I see you at the bodybuilding competition tomorrow?"

Sue's violet eyes softened. "I wouldn't miss it. Mack has trained so hard. And you and your partner have helped him a great deal. I've been praying that Mack wins. I've never seen my son want anything so much."

After taking another bite of lettuce, I said, "It's hard to believe Mack was once a skinny kid."

Laugh lines creased her smooth skin. "I used to pray that he wouldn't waste away in his sleep. No matter how much he ate, he never gained a pound. The kids on the block, and at school, used to tease him for that. I cried myself to sleep many nights."

"But then Brick Strong got Mack interested in bodybuilding."

She nodded. "Brick saved Mack's life."

"Which is a good thing, since you and Brick *gave* Mack life."

Sue Heath did a double-take worthy of a vaudeville comedy act. "Mack told you?"

"We discussed it."

She exhaled deeply. "That isn't common knowledge."

After taking a swig of water, I asked, "Why?"

Staring down at her coffee, she replied, "Shortly after Brick and Cheryl Stryker had Abigail, Brick and I met." She raised her delicate hand to present the dining room. "Right in this very room as a matter of fact." She smiled nostalgically. "I was a work-study student at the time. Brick was an assistant professor. He complimented my soup, and I complimented his physique. We shared lunch together each day after that. Eventually we shared a lot more." She ran her thin fingers through her soft red hair. *As they say, men marry their mothers.* "When I became pregnant, I dropped out of school. Luckily, I was able to keep working, except for a few weeks when I was delivering and recuperating. After that, the cafeteria manager was nice enough to hire me full time, and arrange my working hours around the times I could leave Mack in the college daycare center. I appreciated that a great deal, and I've stayed out of loyalty ever since."

"And Brick didn't help you with Mack at all?"

"Brick gave me some money and visited Mack on weekends with the stipulation that we keep Brick's paternity a secret."

I took out my vitamins. "Mack told me *you* were the one

who didn't want anyone to know, because you are 'old fashioned.'"

She laughed. "If I was old fashioned, would I have dated a married man?"

*You have a point there.*

"But why did Brick keep his paternity a secret? Mack is a terrific kid."

She took a sip of cold coffee and pushed it aside. "Brick didn't want Cheryl and Abigail to find out."

"But they eventually *did* find out."

She nodded. "When Mack was eight years old, he woke up in the middle of the night with a high fever, chills, and unable to breathe. It was some kind of virus. While I was waiting for the ambulance to arrive, I panicked and called Brick. Cheryl answered. Cheryl had intuitively figured out something was amiss with Brick, and that cinched her suspicions...and ended their marriage."

I swallowed a mouthful of vitamins. "I'm guessing it also ended your romantic relationship with Brick."

She blushed. "That was over long before that."

"What happened?"

"What happened was that I realized I'm a lesbian."

It was my turn to do a double-take. "And you didn't know until after you had Mack?"

She smiled. "I was always a slow learner."

"No wonder you were so accepting when Mack and Jimmy came out to you as a couple."

"My status had nothing to do with that. No mother who really loves her son would want to deny his happiness." Sue's face glowed like a lantern in a storm. "Jimmy is a sweet, warm, terrific boy. Before Mack met Jimmy, my son was an empty shell incapable of expressing his emotions. I sleep at night now knowing Mack is with someone he loves, and someone who loves him. If anyone tries to hurt my son because of that, they'll have to get past me."

I tried to fill in the blanks. "But if Cheryl knew about you and Brick by the time Mack was eight years old, why continue to hide the fact that Brick was Mack's father?"

"Because Abigail didn't know…until she overheard Brick on the phone with Mack when Mack was much older. By then Mack was the one who wanted to keep it a secret, so the other students in the bodybuilding program wouldn't think Brick was playing favorites."

"But Cheryl Stryker worked in the same department. Didn't it bother you that Cheryl would be Mack's professor?"

Sue's full lips turned downward. "Cheryl Stryker treated my son abominably. As did Abigail. Mack was truly the bastard son to them. It scarred Mack for many years. He was a lonely child who cut off all of his feelings for fear of being hurt and rejected. No matter how much I or his father complimented Mack, his self-esteem was nonexistent. I will never forgive Cheryl and Abigail for that." She added with the same determination I saw in her son's eyes, "But Mack got through it thanks to the sport of bodybuilding, and more recently, thanks to Jimmy. Mack will come out the winner tomorrow."

"And if he doesn't?"

She squeezed my hand. "He has to. He simply *has* to win."

I left Sue and went back to the gym to snoop around. Since none of my suspects were within earshot, I worked out my shoulders and back, did some cardio, then huffed and puffed back to the locker room. Not wanting Martin to have to fumigate his office after our upcoming meeting, I stripped off my sweat clothes, wrapped a towel around my waist, and headed into the shower room. I heard two familiar voices enter the locker room. So I stepped into one of the shower stalls and observed unobtrusively.

"You can't come in here, Maria," said Rodney. "Or are you reverting back to Mario?"

"I am stuck to you like fly paper until we have this out," replied Maria right behind him.

Rodney stopped at the entrance to the shower room. "I'm sweaty after our workout and I need to shower. Can I please do that in peace?"

She pressed her powerful hand on his mountainous

shoulder. "Nobody else is in here. You are not moving until you hear what I have to say."

I pressed my back against the shower wall and breathed as quietly as possible.

Rodney threw his gym bag on the shower room bench, then sat next to it. "All right. What is it?"

Maria plopped down next to him, then took in a few deep breaths in an effort to calm down. "Rodney, after the competition is over tomorrow, we're no longer workout partners."

"Why not?" asked Rodney like a child whose nanny had given notice.

Maria leaned her elbows on her sturdy knees. "Because I don't want to hear any more quotes from that book written thousands of years ago by white, sexist, homophobes. There will be no more telling me I should accept a male identity. The chatter about me being a sinner, going to hell, and needing the Lord ends. I'm done with it. I don't, and I'll repeat, *don't ever* want to hear another syllable about it."

"So that's it? Just like that?"

"That's it, Rodney. Just like that."

Tears welled up in Rodney's dark eyes. "Maria, after all of our training, after everything we've done, with Stryker and Strong gone, one of us has a real chance of winning tomorrow."

"I hope that happens, Rodney. I really do." Maria blinked back her tears. "But whatever happens tomorrow, that's it. You go your way, and I go mine."

"I can't accept that."

"You have to, Rodney. You have no other choice." Maria rose from the bench and started to leave. "I'm sorry."

Rodney held on to her arm. "Don't do this, Maria."

Tears flowed freely down her cheeks. "I have to, Rodney."

She started to leave again, and Rodney pulled her powerful chest into his. As they gazed into one another's eyes, Rodney said, "I don't care if you are a man, woman, or space invader, I want to be with you. You're all that matters to me."

Maria looked at him in a state of confusion. "But what about the Bible?"

"You're more important to me. If you're with me, that's all the heaven I need."

"I want you so much."

Rodney's enormous back muscles contracted as he wrapped his arms around Maria and kissed her passionately. She returned the kiss with even more fervor, as their strong hands massaged one another's massive backs. After they yanked off one another's sweat clothes, Rodney lifted Maria off her feet and placed her inside a shower stall diagonal to mine. Feeling like a patron at a sex-club booth viewing, I watched as Rodney and Maria kissed and caressed each other's bodies as if they had been waiting for this their entire lives. Next, she licked and squeezed his pectoral muscles, and he returned the gesture. He got down on his knees and pleasured her orally, then she did the same to him. Finally, Rodney slipped a condom out of his gym bag, suited up, and entered her. Both of them groaned and growled in ecstasy as their hips thrust back and forth in perfect rhythm.

*Being workout buddies for so long must have paid off!*

After they cried out in rapturous delight, they kissed and hugged, whispering sweetly in each other's ears. As they both dressed, they never lost eye contact. Then Rodney put his arm around his girlfriend, and they left the locker room gazing at one another adoringly.

While thinking about Rodney's comment to Maria, "after all we've done," I turned on the faucets and stood under the shower head. As the water covered my body like soothing rain, I soaped up my hands and rubbed them over my face, neck, arms, chest, back, legs, and feet. As I soaped up my genitals, I felt a presence near me.

"Yowza yowza."

I opened my soap-stained eyes to Van Granite standing next to me with a towel draped around his tiny waist. Like a Mormon staring at a pair of magic underwear, Granite said, "Nicky, you could blacken someone's eye with that pole.

That's the biggest I've ever seen!" He winked. "And I've seen plenty."

Rinsing off, I said, "I get that a lot."

He leaned on the shower room tile with his shoulder muscles bulging. "You know, Nicky, given your... equipment, I could be persuaded to jump into that stall with you."

"Every other stall is empty, Granite. Help yourself to one of them."

He flexed his pectoral muscles. "They say it's better to shower with a bone than shower alone." Leaning into my stall, he added, "I'd even be willing to get down on my knees and give you a little gift."

"No, thanks. I don't have a mirror to put on my stomach." I rubbed shampoo into my hair. "Besides, I'm taken."

"I'm not into Noah, but I'd make an exception for *that*." He looked at my groin and licked his full lips.

Placing my head under the water, I said, "No exception is necessary. Noah and I are happily maxed out at two." I shut off the water. "Doesn't Kim Sim keep you occupied, or have you moved on to another student?"

Granite's face hardened. "Kim is a superior athlete." Unsuccessfully turning on the charm, he added, "I hope you and Noah will give him your vote tomorrow."

Toweling off, I said, "Noah and I will give our vote to the best competitor. Since we aren't *involved* with any of the students, *we* can be fair and unbiased."

As I wrapped the towel around my waist, Granite said, "You don't like me very much, do you? Is this still about me training Noah?"

Our eyes locked, and I replied, "Noah has nothing to do with this. I've never taken to faculty who touch what they teach."

"You wouldn't be thinking about spreading that story about Kim and me to let's say...the Dean, would you?"

"Kim Sim is your concern, Granite. Not mine."

Granite followed me to my locker with a quick glance in

the mirror along the way. "I can't figure it out. You're the only one on campus who doesn't like me."

"Not true." I opened my locker.

"What does *that* mean?"

I slipped on, then buttoned my turquoise shirt. "It means Abigail Strong in Admissions isn't exactly your fan."

He rested his foot on the bench and laughed. "That bitter blowhard bitch." *Try saying that three times fast.* "She came on to me a while back and I turned her down." He looked into a wall mirror and ran his fingers through his gelled hair. "As if I'd ever give that fag hag a second look."

I zipped up my gray slacks. "Abigail didn't mention anything about being attracted to you. Her concern was that you won't hold a candle to her father, or mother, as department head."

"Is *that* what she's spreading all over campus?" Granite's spray-tanned face turned red. "I'm a better department head than old man Strong with his dick up his ass over Jillian Flowers, and butch Cheryl Stryker with her jock twisted over Tim Kim."

"Just like yours is twisted over Tim's twin brother?" I slipped on my black loafers and gray blazer. "See you at the competition tomorrow."

As I closed my locker and walked out of the locker room, I heard Granite say to my back, "If you see Abigail, tell her to shut her whiney mouth, or I'll shut it for her."

After advising the Theatre Club meeting (with a noticeably absent Jimmy Saline), I headed to my department head's office for our meeting. Since it was five o'clock, like every other non-educator on the campus, Shayla raced out of the office as if a bomb had been detected under her desk. As she nearly mowed me down, I pressed my back against the wall. "Have a good night, Shayla."

She sprinted down the hall. "I will as soon as I get home."

I walked into Martin's office, where he and Noah were waiting for me on the tall-backed leather chairs with the fireplace aglow and three china cups filled with hot cocoa. As I sat down and greeted them, Martin adjusted his cherry bowtie and sweater vest and placed a cherry monogrammed cloth napkin over his tiny lap.

Martin said, "Well, the press seems satisfied with Detective Manuello's theory that Jonathan Toner accidentally overdosed on testosterone, Tim Sim took too many bodybuilding herbs, and Cheryl Stryker killed Brick Strong, Jillian Flowers, then herself."

"The press will believe anything, especially if it isn't true," I said. "Gone are the days of investigative reporting."

"Which is why we need you two boys. Tell me, how are things going with the investigation?" asked Martin, sipping his hot cocoa.

I filled Martin and Noah in on the latest events.

Noah said, "I think Mack Heath had it right when he said it all boils down to three couples: Rodney Towers and Maria Ruiz, Van Granite and Kim Sim, and Mack Heath and Jimmy Saline."

"Let's not forget about mama Heath," I said.

"And daughter Strong," Noah à la Marvin Meekbottom added.

Wiping the corner of his mouth with his napkin, Martin stared into the hypnotizing flames. "I have the feeling that everything will come to light at the competition tomorrow."

"Will you be there?" I asked.

"Of course, I've never missed a Nicky Abbondanza production at this college, and I don't intend to start now."

I lifted my china cup in his direction. "Thanks, Martin."

Martin inched to the edge of his seat. "As grand as the bodybuilding competition will be, it won't hold a candle to my fortieth-anniversary tribute." He patted my shoulder. "I can't wait to hear your speech, Nicky."

*Neither can I.*

Noah winked at me. "It should be pretty amazing."

While we were discussing the menu and itinerary for the tribute with Martin dishing (no pun intended) about the personal lives of the caterers, Detective Manuello walked into Martin's office and stood over us like a hawk at a picnic.

"Good, you're all here," said Manuello with a rub of his

wide nose.

"What is it, Detective?" asked Martin with a tense look at Noah and me.

Squeezing his rolls of fat over, then under his belt, Manuello said, "I'm going to cancel the bodybuilding competition tomorrow."

"Whatever for?" asked Martin like a Roman king informed the coliseum was closing.

I stood. "What is it, Manuello?"

He replied, "The investigation is back on."

Rising from his chair, Noah asked, "What's happened?"

Manuello replied, "Abigail Strong was found dead in her home, suffocated with a pillow some time yesterday."

Noah gasped and Martin dropped his cocoa.

"Did anyone see anything?" I asked.

"Yes," Manuello replied. "A neighbor observed a man standing outside of Abigail Strong's window. The man fit your description."

# Chapter Eleven

At dinner (filet of sole in olive oil and lemon, butternut squash, and succotash) in the kitchen nook with the family, Scott proudly displayed the mini trophy he had won playing miniature golf downtown with Bonnie and Noah. Bonnie explained the trophy was a gift from an empathetic seven-year-old girl after Scott's losing streak.

After changing into our gym shorts and T-shirts (our usual night attire), and retiring upstairs to our four-poster, Noah listened in while I phoned Detective Manuello.

"Hello, Detective, this is your favorite college professor," I said tongue firmly in cheek.

"How can I help you?" Manuello asked, obviously concerned about the latest murder.

Leaning back on the carved wooden headboard, I said, "You don't really think I had anything to do with Abigail Strong's murder?"

"I would bring you in for a police lineup with Abigail's neighbor if I didn't think you would break out into a number from *A Chorus Line*."

*He knows me so well!* "As I said in Martin's office, Noah and I were at Abigail's to ask her some questions, and it's a good thing we did! Abigail told Noah, or rather Marvin Meekbottom, that Mack Heath is Brick Strong's son and co-inheritor with Abigail in Brick's will."

"Who's Marvin Meekbottom? On second thought, don't tell me," said Manuello wearily.

"Abigail was fine when we left...except she was crying hysterically on Noah's shoulder."

Manuello groaned like a woman in labor.

"Also, it seems that Abigail has a penchant for gay men. Besides dating the late Jonathan Toner, she evidently made a play for Van Granite."

"How do you know this?" he asked.

"Granite told me in the shower."

Manuello exhaled like a volcanic eruption. "Anything else I can do for you, Nicky?"

"As a matter of fact, there is something. Please allow us to have the bodybuilding competition tomorrow as planned."

"No."

"*Please*, Manuello?"

"Nicky, this may be the only time you ever hear me say this, so please listen closely. You were right. I was wrong. Murder has reared its ugly head again at Treemeadow, at least once, and possibly as many as six times. It's my duty to keep people out of harm's way."

After Noah whispered in my ear (and kissed my sideburn), I said, "Detective, the only way to protect people is to find the killer, and I believe the killer will surface at the competition."

"How do you know this?"

"I need to check out a few things first. But I guarantee, if you let the competition go on, the killer's identity will be revealed."

After promising Manuello everything except our first-born child, Noah and I hung up. Resting my shoulder against his, I said, "There's only one problem with your plan."

"What's that?" Noah asked with his baby blue eyes flashing.

"We don't have a clue as to the identity of the murderer."

Noah moved my laptop from the top of our dresser onto the bed. "We need to figure this out by the end of the competition tomorrow. So, let's compose our list of suspects, motives, and opportunity."

I turned on the laptop.

Noah kissed my head. "I have faith in you." He rested his blond locks on his pillow. "Let me know if you need anything." Then he drifted off to sleep.

After typing "Victims" on the top of the screen, I listed: Brick Strong, Cheryl Stryker, Jillian Flowers, Tim Sim, Jonathan Toner, and Abigail Strong. Next, under "Suspects" I wrote the names of the possible murderers. Realizing each of them had ample opportunity to commit the murders, I moved on to motive and wrote:

Van Granite & Kim Sim: killed Brick and Cheryl (for Granite to become department head, and to remove unsupportive judges for Kim), Tim (to ensure Kim inherits the family fortune), Jonathan and Jillian (to lessen the competition for Kim to win the contest), and Abigail (to stop her rumors about Granite).

Rodney Towers & Maria Ruiz: killed Brick and Cheryl (to remove unsupportive judges), Tim, Jonathan, and Jillian (to lessen the competition for the contest), and Abigail (because she was Brick and Cheryl's privileged daughter).

Mack Heath, Sue Heath & Jimmy Saline: killed Cheryl (revenge for her mistreatment of Mack, and to remove an unsupportive judge for Mack), Tim, Jonathan, Jillian (to lessen the competition for Mack in the contest), and Brick and Abigail (so Mack can receive Brick's entire inheritance).

*Any of the three teams, or any individual in any team, could have committed one or all of the murders. What am I missing? What's the clue that has been there all along that I am not seeing?*

As I closed my laptop, and spooned Noah, my head hit the hypoallergenic pillow and I entered dreamland.

The faces in my dreams were mask-like, grotesque, Greek theatre versions of the murder suspects. Kim fed Granite grapes as Granite chased me with a barbell. Rodney and Maria mud-wrestled, then pulled me into quicksand. Jimmy rubbed oil on my back, which burned like acid, while Mack and Sue Heath twisted my arms and legs into a pretzel.

Thankfully, Robbie rescued me and brought me to his bodybuilding competition eighteen years ago.

The young, flawless bodybuilder posed perfectly in his trunks, then accepted his much-deserved winning cup. Again, I made my way up to the stage through the throngs of fans and congratulators. As my nose was rewarded with Robbie's earthy scent, I wrapped my arms around his stunning, V-shaped back and excitedly awaited his message in my ear, "It's up to you, Nicky. Tomorrow is the day." As Robbie stared into my eyes, I took in his handsome face, puckered my lips, and woke up with my arms around Noah, and a huge stain on my gym shorts.

After cleaning myself up, I went back to bed and Noah cuddled me in his arms.

"I keep having these dreams," I said.

"What kind of dreams?"

*A good relationship needs to be based on honesty.* I sat up, rested my back against the headboard, and told Noah all about Robbie Piccolo.

Noah sat up next to me and rested his head on my shoulder. "I'm not jealous."

"You're a bigger man than I."

He patted my crotch. "No, I'm not."

Nestled in each other's arms, Noah and I thought about young, handsome, muscular Robbie Piccolo, and we drifted off to sleep.

The next morning, over broccoli and cheddar cheese omelets in the breakfast nook, everyone was abuzz about the bodybuilding competition that evening.

"Nicky's going early to set up, so I'll drive us over after dinner," said Noah to his parents.

"Then you'll get there faster than the speed of light," I said.

Noah tweaked my nose. "I've never lost a passenger yet."

"My sonny can drive as fast as he likes," said Bonnie with

a pinch to Noah's scarlet cheek. "We want to get front-row seats so Judy won't complain about heads in my pictures."

Munching on a piece of seven-grain toast, I said, "Judy's a big bodybuilding fan, is she?"

"Judy's a big *anything* fan, as long as she doesn't have to get off the couch," said Scott, reaching for a second omelet.

"Look who's talking," said Bonnie pointing to her husband. "Our sofa back home in Wisconsin has a permanent dent in it the size of your backside."

"And a nice backside it is," said Scott as he wiggled his behind in Bonnie's face.

Bonnie slapped her husband's derrière and laughed. Noah stared at his grapefruit juice.

Pushing a forkful of home fries into her mouth, Bonnie said, "I'm so proud of you two boys for staging the show."

"It's not really a show, Mom," said Noah like a kid whose mother called his school science project a major experiment.

"Every competition is a show, son," said Scott.

"And how many competitions have you been involved in?" asked Scott's wife.

Happy to change the subject, Noah said, "You'll also get to hear Nicky speak at Martin's retirement gala this weekend." He added emphatically, "That's just before you go back to Wisconsin."

Bonnie swallowed her juice. "I'll bet you are a terrific speaker, Nicky. Noah always spoke beautifully too, even as a small child. People in stores used to ask me if he was a midget."

"It's 'little person,' Mom," said Noah like a teenage girl told to be home before two a.m.

"It's so hard to know what people like to be called," said Bonnie. "I bought a book that tells you, but I left it back in Wisconsin."

"Since you boys are such fine orators, I'll bet your wedding vows will be amazing," said Scott, wiping his plate clean.

Noah asked me how the speech for Martin was coming.

"I'll let you know this weekend."

"Is it writer's block?" asked Bonnie. "Judy says that Timmy gets that."

"What does Timmy write?" asked Noah.

Bonnie replied, "He writes a blog about how to get a job."

"Which he doesn't have," said Scott, removing the napkin from his collar.

After swallowing my last vitamin, I said, "Martin has been an institution at Treemeadow College for forty years. He's a terrific Theatre Management professor, and a patient, fair, creative, supportive, and visionary department head. Not to mention he is my, and Noah's, personal mentor and role model."

"So what's the problem?" asked Scott patting his full stomach.

I replied, "The problem is I don't know where to start? I wasn't around forty years ago when Martin was hired, and he doesn't like to talk about 'the old days.'"

Rising and gathering the plates, Bonnie said, "Judy told me that before Timmy writes one of his blogs, he does research on the internet."

Noah answered, "I don't think the web has a lot of information about Treemeadow's past, Mom."

"Doesn't the college keep old scrapbooks?" asked Scott.

It dawned on me. "The Archives Room." I leapt up and kissed Scott's bald head, Bonnie's cheek, and Noah's chin (since he curled up his lips). "See everyone at the competition." And I was out the door.

After my class, office hour, and lunch, I entered the Archives Room in the basement of the college library. I was told by a texting student worker, who never looked up at me, that college yearbooks and college newspaper editions from ten to forty years ago were stored in the Old Archives Room (talk about redundancy) in the lower basement level (and yet again).

After finding my way to the lower basement, I approached the desk, which woke the oldest man I have ever seen in my life sitting behind it. Amidst his hacking, wheezing, and gasping for air, I placed my order. Slower than a priest in an altar boys' dressing room, the withered man set me up in a cubicle with yellowed, bound yearbooks and newspapers from the past.

Feeling as if I had traveled back in time, I flipped through photographs of people wearing formal clothing, old-fashioned hairstyles, and hopeful smiles as they accepted awards, graduated, taught classes, acted in play productions, demonstrated scientific experiments, debated, played sports, and attended parties.

Sidetracked to the sports pictures, I spent a bit of time (okay, an hour) looking at the Physical Education students. Flipping quickly through the years of the young athletes' lives, I glanced at their physiques, their accomplishments, and in some cases their tragedies.

After checking the time, I moved on to the old articles and pictures of the Theatre Department. Martin was in many of the articles (with hair!) dressed in his traditional bowtie and matching sweater vest. I read about Martin's noteworthy lectures, awards, mentored students, and eventual appointment as department head. When my notebook was full of dates, quotes, and quips about Martin, I left the cubicle, thanked the sleeping man, and made a mental note to leave his phone number on Mary's desk in the Bodybuilding Department office.

I stopped for a quick soup and sandwich dinner, and noticed Sue, Mack, and Jimmy huddled together in a corner of the cafeteria. When I approached them, the threesome ended their conversation and said hello. I wished Mack good luck at the competition, then I headed over to the Physical Education building, eating en route.

Once I arrived at the large gym, I was relieved to find Tony Piccolo setting up the chairs for the big event.

"Hiya, Professor. Tonight's the big night, hah."

"Hello, Tony," I replied, swallowing my last vitamin at the water cooler. "It feels like opening night of a new show."

"It's so exciting," said Tony. "I remember when Robbie won. I nearly hit the ceiling." He pointed a wrinkled finger upward. "And as you can see, it's a high ceiling."

We shared a laugh.

Tony said, "I set up the judge's table in the corner."

"Like our box seats," I replied, realizing my theatre lingo was lost on Tony. "Will you help me with the set?"

"Sure thing, Professor."

Tony opened a supply closet and we moved the Styrofoam columns, dry-ice smoke machine, cloud-painted backdrop, and lighting and sound equipment into place. The four stars of the show displayed their white and gold Greek god and goddess costumes to my approval, then took their places behind the backdrop.

Treemeadow faculty, students, friends, and parents entered and noisily filled the gymnasium, along with a few professional bodybuilding talent scouts.

When Noah, Bonnie, and Scott arrived, Scott said, "Maybe you two guys should save some money and have your wedding here."

Noah blushed.

"We'll keep that in mind, Scott," I said with a smile.

Clutching her iPad, Bonnie grabbed Scott's arm and led him to a center front-row seat next to an anticipatory Jimmy Saline.

After wishing me a "good show," Martin, Ruben, and Shayla took chairs in the third row. When Sue Heath entered, Shayla waved her over.

Tucking a stray dark hair into the bun at her neck, Shayla said, "Would you like to sit next to me?"

"I'd like that very much," said Sue.

As Sue sat in the chair, the two women looked at one another and smiled.

Tony took his seat behind the mini lighting and sound board, and Van, Noah, and I settled at the judges' table.

As Tony dimmed the gym lights and faded up the stage lights, Van Granite rose from his seat, walked to the makeshift stage area, and addressed the large crowd.

"Welcome, everyone, to Treemeadow College's twenty-fifth annual bodybuilding competition. And thank you all for coming!" As the audience applauded, Granite took advantage of the break to check himself out in the mirror on the wall. Then he revealed his white laminates and flexed his shoulder muscles under his skintight white shirt and blue blazer. "*I* am Professor Van Granite, Bodybuilding Department Head." Granite waited until the applause finally came, then said as if surprised and touched, "Thank you." He offered a muscular arm in our direction. "Joining me as judges are the theatrical directors of the competition, Professor Nicky Abbondanza and Professor Noah Oliver."

"That's my son and his boyfriend!" Bonnie Oliver stood and started the applause then motioned for the rest of the audience to join her as Noah's face reddened.

Granite flexed his leg muscles under his formfitting gray slacks. "I would also like to introduce our Dean of Physical Education, Dr. Edwin Pyuun."

As the frail, anemic-looking, bespectacled, ancient man struggled to his feet during the light applause, I hoped pictures of Dr. Pyuun were not used in advertising brochures for the physical education programs at Treemeadow. The dean adjusted his wrinkled gray suit and fell back into his seat.

Granite continued. "Ladies and gentlemen, very shortly you will see the talents of the four top seniors in the Bodybuilding Department. One of them will win his or her way to free tuition for this academic year as well as a gold cup for winning the competition." He looked at the talent scouts. "And perhaps entry into the field of professional bodybuilding!"

When the applause subsided, Granite forced his glossed lips into a frown. "This year's competition is dedicated to our two cherished professors and three gifted student athletes who we lost tragically this year: Professor Brick Strong, Professor Cheryl Stryker, Jonathan Toner, Jillian Flowers, and Tim Sim. Please join me in bowing your heads for a moment of silence in their memory."

While the audience members obeyed, Granite took a comb from his back pocket and slid it through his gelled hair. "And now, let the competition begin." Granite took his seat, and said to Noah and me, "I can't wait to see how well Kim performs. What an amazing athlete."

Before we could respond, the gymnasium was filled with the sound of horns and trumpets as the four contestants, bathed in white light, walked through the clouds and formed a heavenly line in front of the white columns. After Tony hit the next lighting cue, the young bodybuilders performed their group poses, embodying their immortal characters. Rodney as Zeus was the largest, displaying smooth, dark muscles packed with power. Next to him was Mack as Ganymede with his perfectly proportioned body and equally chiseled, handsome face. Kim's Adonis was strong and agile. Finally, Maria as Athena was a beautiful, earthy, powerful goddess.

When the group poses ended, the audience cheered in anticipation of the bodybuilder's individual posing routines. Rodney was first, followed by Mack, then Kim, and finally Maria. Clad in only gold briefs, each contestant stood center stage and proudly flexed and displayed each muscle like a valued prize. Moving in time with their selected music, the four students each projected charisma, strength, skill, and fortitude to thunderous applause from the audience.

When the competition ended, the four students lined up on stage anxiously awaiting the verdict. At the judges' table, Granite whispered to Noah and me, "They all did a terrific job."

"Agreed," said Noah and I in unison.

"But—" said Granite, gazing adoringly at Kim "—Kim Sim is a sure bet as winner. Agreed?" He rose to announce the winner.

Noah and I each took a muscle-packed arm and sat Granite back down.

I said, "I know this isn't my field, but I've learned quite a lot by directing the competition. And while each of the four young bodybuilders displayed well-formed muscles, strong stage presence, and amazing physiques, I think Mack Heath had the best definition. So my vote goes to him."

"Mine too," said Noah.

"You have to be kidding me," said Granite. "Two guys from the Theatre Department are telling the Department Head of Bodybuilding who is the best bodybuilder?"

"Van," said Noah, "Mack really did have the best symmetry, and I think you know that."

"Looks like a two-to-one vote, Granite," I said.

Granite sat back in his chair, contemplating his next move. Noah nodded to me, and I moved to the stage area, and said like the host of a beauty pageant, "May I have everyone's attention please? It gives me great pleasure to announce the winner of the Twenty-Fifth Annual Treemeadow Bodybuilding Competition is…Mack Heath!"

As the audience applauded wildly, the other three contestants surrounded Mack with half-hearted back slaps and hugs of congratulations. Noah handed the large gold cup to Mack, and Mack kissed his relieved mother on the cheek and his elated boyfriend on the lips.

Mack posed joyously with the cup as Bonnie took pictures, followed by the college photographer and Sue Heath.

Waving her iPad, Bonnie shouted to me, "Judy says you made the right decision!"

Suddenly a locked door opened in my brain. "Noah, I know who did it."

"Mack did it. Mack won."

"No, I know who killed the six people on campus."

Noah put his arm around me and led me back to the judges' table. "Who?"

I started out of the gym. "I have to make sure I'm right."

"Where are you going?" asked Noah.

"Back to the archives."

Granite followed me out of the gymnasium and pushed me into the hallway. Then he grabbed me by the neck, yanked me into his office, and shut the door. "I heard what you said to Noah."

I reached for the door, but Granite beat me to it. "You aren't going anywhere, Nicky." Granite pushed me down onto the sofa then stood blocking the door. "We need to talk."

# Chapter Twelve

"You had no right to announce the winner, Nicky. *I'm* the Bodybuilding Department Head, not *you*," said Granite unable to stop himself from glancing at his reflection in the mirror.

"Mack won two votes to one vote," I replied straightening my blazer.

Granite said like the King of Siam, "I asked you and Noah to judge the competition because I assumed you would bow to *my* expertise."

"I don't bow to anyone, Granite." I rose from the sofa. "I know all about your fun and games with Kim Sim, and I want no part of it." Heading to the door, I added, "Now if you will excuse me, I have to go to the college's archives."

Granite rested his powerful hand on my shoulder. "I hope you won't tell anyone about my…friendship with Kim."

Looking into his contact lens tinted eyes, I said, "I'll leave that to Kim's friends." I made a dramatic exit out of Granite's office and shut the door behind me. As I walked down the hallway, I felt a sharp pain in my neck, and I blacked out.

I woke feeling like I was strapped to a gurney. I couldn't move my arms or legs, and something was constricting my breathing. *Am I undergoing surgery? Was I abducted by aliens?* I opened my eyes and realized I was in the weight room in the Physical Education building, nestled inside a leg machine with my arms and legs bound to it by ropes, and a thirty-pound weight pressing on my stomach. The door to the room was shut and the window shades were drawn. Though my neck ached and my throat was dry, I used what little air I could summon from my constricted diaphragm and called out weakly for help.

"Nobody will hear you. By now everybody must have left the building, Professor. Besides, I put an 'out of order' sign on the door, before I locked it." Tony Piccolo stepped out from behind a weight rack. "I hope my little hand weight to your neck didn't hurt too much."

After squirming and wiggling, I grunted back onto the machine.

"You won't get out of there, Professor. I tied you in good and tight."

I sucked in air like an overweight celebrity stuffed into a girdle. "Why are you doing this?"

He came closer and looked down at me with a deranged look on his creviced face. "You know why, Professor."

"Noah will find me."

"I don't think so. Before I...invited you in here, I told Professor Oliver you would probably be in the library archives for hours, so he drove his folks home."

Feeling the pressure of the weight on my stomach, I said, "If you let me go, I won't tell anyone about any of this."

He sat on the weight rack. "But you *will* tell about my Robbie." Running a hand through his gray hair, he said, "I wondered why you always stared at Robbie's pictures in my alcove. I'm guessing you were trying to figure it out, and that led you to the library archives." He smiled nostalgically. "That's a nice old article in the archives about Robbie winning Treemeadow's gold cup." His wrinkled face hardened like a prune. "And a not so nice follow-up article about his death the next day." Tony wiped a tear from the bag under his eye. "How did you put it all together, Professor? I thought maybe you caught my mistake in my office when I told you Robbie was defending a case, then later I said Robbie was prosecuting a case." He closed his eyes, deep in thought. "I figure you must have quickly scanned a lot of articles when you was in the archives room. And later after the competition ended when Professor Oliver's mother took a picture of Mack winning the gold cup, you remembered Robbie's picture from the archives' articles. But as you said to Professor Oliver, you wanted to go back to make sure you were right."

I pushed and pulled at the ropes around my arms and legs until my skin bled. Realizing I was getting nowhere, I changed tactics. Speaking in a shallow voice to conserve air, I said in a friendly manner, "Tony, I don't blame you for feeling devastated and enraged by Robbie's death. Your son was an amazing athlete with a captivating presence." *That's for sure.* "He died too young and too tragically."

Tony rested his head in his purple-veined hands. "Robbie had everything going for him. Looks, brains, talent, an amazing physique. He would have won the bodybuilding competition anyway, but Brick Strong wanted his bodybuilders as big and strong as he could get them at any cost...and it cost my Robbie his life." He sat on the edge of my machine and wrapped his frail arms around his bony knees. "At the time, my wife and I didn't know what was wrong. Robbie, the sweetest kid in the world, became irritable and irrational. Acne sprouted up in strange places on his body." His voice choked. "The coroner said the steroids hurt his liver and kidneys. We thought Robbie took it on his own." Tony used his sweatshirt to wipe the tears off his cheeks. "But I found out just recently Strong gave it to him."

My lungs felt ready to collapse. "In Brick Strong's office during our meeting, when Strong finally admitted giving his bodybuilding students steroids years ago, it's no wonder you got enraged. I think any father would have felt the same way."

"Losing Robbie killed my wife, and it nearly killed me."

"How did your wife die?"

"She hung herself in our basement with a picture of Robbie on the floor in front of her." Tony stared straight ahead, as if replaying it in front of him. Then he added like an executioner, "Brick Strong took my family away from me. So I took his family away from him by throwing the barbell on

Brick, hanging Cheryl from the ropes, and putting the pillow over Abigail."

*Thankfully Tony didn't know Mack was Brick's son.* "But why kill Jonathan, Jillian, and Tim?"

Tears gushed through the craters on Tony's face. "I loved those kids like they was my own. When Jonathan started talking about trying steroids, I stored up my testosterone replacement prescriptions and gave them to him. I risked my own health for that boy. You saw the newer prescriptions on my desk, Professor. I thought it would be safe, but he took too much."

*I have to keep him talking until Noah finds me.* "And when Jonathan died, you made sure none of the other students took testosterone."

Tony nodded like a cloth doll on a trampoline. "I wept like a baby when we lost that kid, and I made a promise that it would never happen again. So, when Tim Sim said he was going to try human growth hormones, I remembered an article I read about some herbs, and I went to the health-food store and bought *Tribulus terrestris* and creatine for him instead."

Feeling the weight crushing my stomach, I said, "And you told the saleswoman at the health-food store you were the Department Head of Bodybuilding to set up Brick Strong in case Tim accidentally overdosed, which he did."

"I cried myself to sleep that night. Them kids were the world to me. Each one was a gem. I couldn't believe I lost another one." His ancient face took on a maniacal glare. "Except for Jillian Flowers. She made fun of my Robbie at Brick's funeral."

*Where's Noah?* "So you rinsed Jillian's mouth out with soap to punish her," I said with the little breath I could muster.

Tony wiped his nose on his sweatshirt. "I did it for Robbie." He unleashed a bizarre smile. "I think Robbie smiled down from Heaven that night." Tony seemed to remember I was in the room. "And since you figured it out, I have to kill you too, Professor." He stood over me and placed his coarse hand on my cheek. "But because you had such affection for my Robbie, and you see him in your dreams, I wanted to tell you how and why I did what I did. So you'd understand. So you can explain it all to Robbie when you see him in Heaven."

Gasping for air, I said, "How will killing me help Robbie or his memory?"

"It won't," Tony said. "But it will keep me in my job at the college, so I can be near my memories of my son."

I heard Noah's beautiful voice out in the hallway. "Maybe he decided to work out. Please open the door!"

The door to the weight room was flung open by Van Granite. Noah stepped inside, and said in exasperation, "Nicky, I've been worried sick. We've been looking all over for you." He noticed my prone position. "Is this some new workout technique? If so, I'm glad I stopped training."

I motioned my head toward Tony. As Tony spun around to face him, Noah lifted a ten-pound weight and lobbed it at Tony's head, causing the senior citizen to hit the floor spread eagle like an anti-gay politician at a bathhouse. Just before I blacked out, I heard Noah say, "Like his son, Tony was a knock-out."

# Epilogue

That Saturday evening, I stood in front of our bedroom mirror grateful that my dark blue pinstriped suit covered the bruises on my arms, stomach, and legs. Noah was at the closet still getting dressed. I took in his shapely shoulders, firm chest, and wide back. "I hate to admit this, but I think Granite's training paid off."

Noah handed me his tie. As I did the honors, Noah said, "Maybe I'll join you the next time you go to the gym."

"I thought you didn't like working out."

He lifted his blond locks over his collar. "I don't. I need to protect you."

"Do you want me to strangle you with this tie, Noah?"

He released an adorable dimple. "Based on what you told me, it seems I also need to keep you away from Robbie Piccolo's pictures."

I slapped his backside and he giggled. "And *I* have to keep *you* away from Van Granite," I said.

Looking like a male model in a blue-gray suit that highlighted his stunning blue eyes, Noah wrapped his arms around my neck. "You're the only gym bunny for me."

I kissed his nose. "And Robbie Piccolo, even at twenty-one years old, can't hold a barbell to my handsome lover."

Noah kissed the cleft in my chin. "But just in case, I asked Van to take down Robbie's old pictures and send them to Tony Piccolo in prison."

Expecting to hear spooky music underscoring, I said, "Noah, you know I'm not the most spiritual person in the world, but I really believe Robbie Piccolo was somehow communicating with me, asking me to stop his father from committing the murders."

"And it worked. That's all that matters."

We kissed, and I said, "And *we* work. *That's* all that matters." After we kissed again, I added, "And that's why I think your parents are right and we should talk about—"

Noah looked at his gold watch, "We don't want to be late for Martin's tribute."

I followed Noah down the oak flared staircase, and we met Bonnie and Scott outside on the wraparound porch.

Bonnie modeled her peach dress with matching earrings, and Scott showed off his red shirt and black slacks and blazer.

I said with a surprised choke in my voice, "I'm going to miss you two. Come and visit us again soon."

"We will," answered Bonnie and Scott, equally touched.

Slapping me on the back like a coach with his star quarterback, Scott said, "Maybe the next time we see you two guys, you will be getting married."

I put my arm around Noah and felt his new back muscles stiffen.

"Everybody squish in tight for Judy's picture." Bonnie raised her iPad for a group selfie.

I said, "Since this will be our last group photo for Judy, how about we shock her with a big kiss from each couple."

Scott looked down at his newly shined shoes. "I don't know, Nicky. I'm not big on public displays of affection... especially in front of family."

"That's for sure," said Bonnie with her eyes raised to the puffy white clouds moving through the cobalt sky.

"Wait a minute," Noah said like a referee stopping two hockey players from fighting. "Dad, you don't like to kiss Mom in front of other family members?"

Scott scratched at his newly shaved cheek. "It's kind of an idiosyncrasy."

"He wouldn't even hold my hand at his cousin's wedding," said Bonnie.

Noah's jaw dropped to his blue and gray tie. "Can that be hereditary?"

Bonnie replied, "I guess pretty much everything is genetic." She frowned, and her peach lipstick cracked. "That's why they always blame the mother whenever a murderer is caught, or if a rare disease is discovered. But you never hear them say it is because of the mother when her child wins the Nobel Prize, saves someone's life, or becomes president."

"But in *this* case, it's *Dad's* thing," Noah said.

"I'm not proud of it. It's just how I am," said Scott. "I put on a good front when you lived back at home."

"He's tried all sorts of techniques to overcome it, but it hasn't worked," said Bonnie.

Scott gave his wife a puppy dog smile. "Maybe I can try one more time, honey?"

"Do you really think it's wise, hon?" asked Bonnie with concern filling her face.

"I want to break myself of this horrible thing, Bonnie. It's been eating away at me for so long," Scott said.

Bonnie replied, "I read somewhere that people who suffer from this malady can be cured if they display affection along with others...for support. It's like being afraid to jump out of a helicopter but overcoming your fear if you jump with someone else."

Scott lifted a forearm over his face. "For the health of my marriage, I'll give it one last try." He peeked out from under his arm. "If you two guys will help me?"

"Sure, Dad. What do you need us to do?" asked Noah with his usual big heart.

"Would you guys kiss as Bonnie and I kiss?" asked Scott.

"Sure, Dad," Noah said with compassion in his baby blue eyes.

"Do you mind, Nicky?" asked Scott.

"Of course not, Scott," I replied, taking Noah's hands in mine.

"Thank you, boys."

Bonnie said as if were beginning a relay race, "Everybody ready?"

"Wait!" said Scott fanning himself with his hand. "I think I'm chickening out."

"Come on, Dad. You can do it," said Noah.

"All right," replied Scott weakly. "I'll try to give it a shot. For the field of mental health...and for my future generations."

Bonnie said, "All right, on the count of three." She wrapped her arms around her husband. "One, two, three!"

Bonnie and Scott kissed, and Noah and I kissed as Bonnie took the picture.

After Noah and I came up for air, I noticed Scott and Bonnie giggling together.

"I told you it would work, honey," said Scott. "It's about time we got you two guys to kiss in front of us."

"Wasn't that fun?" asked Bonnie.

"And Noah thinks *he's* the only actor in the family," said Scott, straightening his lapel.

Noah smiled and shook his handsome head as we piled into his car and left for Martin's tribute.

The cafeteria was adorned with banners reading "Forty Years of Service" and framed photographs of Martin Anderson at Treemeadow College over the last forty years. In each picture Martin gained more wrinkles and lost more hair but maintained his puckish style. The snapshots of Martin teaching his classes, making speeches, serving on committees, and advising students were not as captivating as the pictures I had seen of Robbie Piccolo winning Treemeadow's bodybuilding competition, but they were certainly more welcome.

Bonnie, Scott, Noah, and I meandered around the room sipping punch, munching on hors d'oeuvres, and dishing the dirt with other Treemeadow residents. Martin (sporting a gold bowtie and gold sweater vest) and Ruben (decked out in a gold suit) approached us. Martin said to Noah and me, "Congratulations, you two. I knew you would solve the case and once again bring safety and tranquility back to Treemeadow College."

"Until the next time," said Ruben with a wink.

"Our Nicky and Noah can outsmart *any* murderer," said Bonnie proudly.

"And *out-act* him," said Scott. "Noah gets that from his father," he added with a grand bow.

Martin said, "Bonnie, Scott, thank you for coming with Nicky and Noah."

"We couldn't go back to Wisconsin without wishing you well on your anniversary, Martin," said Scott with a pat on Martin's frail back that nearly knocked Martin out.

"Smile, everyone." Bonnie lifted her iPad. Seconds later, Bonnie added, "Judy said it's amazing that you can still work at your age, Martin."

Ruben held his hand over Martin's mouth. "Nicky, is your speech all ready?"

"It sure is," I replied.

"Thanks to the archives at the college," Noah added with a wink.

Noah and I left his parents to relay their high-jinks on getting Noah over his fear of kissing me in front of them to the delighted ears of the thespians in our department.

Then, as Noah and I reached the center of the gymnasium, Mickey Minor offered me an inviting smile and a tight handshake. With the top of his blond head level with my stomach, he said, "Hello, Nicky. When are you coming back to visit me in Human Resources?" He added with a wink, "Where we humans have *various* resources."

I lowered Noah's head down to make eye contact with Mickey. "Mickey, I would like you to meet Noah. He worked out with a trainer at the gym here at Treemeadow. Noah's a terrific lover, except for his uncontrollable temper."

Picking up my cue, Noah flexed his biceps and gritted his teeth.

Mickey backed into a serving tray. "Ah, nice seeing you two. Have a good night." And Mickey was gone.

Noah and I shared a laugh, then made our way to the other side of the gymnasium to greet the members of the Bodybuilding Department.

Passing Mary, the department office assistant sleeping on a chair near the window, we noticed Rodney Towers and Maria Ruiz looking dashing in a matching emerald suit and gown respectively. They gazed into one another's eyes lovingly and held hands like teenagers on a first date.

"Thank you for directing our competition, Professors," said Rodney. "Even though neither of us won, it was a terrific experience."

"And we got to work together." Maria rubbed her large shoulder against Rodney's.

"Actually, we were workout buddies *before* the competition, Maria," explained Rodney like a teacher correcting a student.

She jutted out her large jaw. "We were never *buddies*, Rodney."

He stuck out his mountainous chest. "Yes, we were, Maria."

As they continued their war of the roses, Noah and I moved on to Van Granite and Kim Sim, looking magazine-ready in tight dark suits that accentuated their muscular physiques.

"You never thanked me for unlocking the weight room door when Piccolo had you trapped inside," said Granite while he checked himself out in a mirror on the cafeteria wall.

I replied, "The next time *you* are tied to a leg machine with a weight on your stomach, I'll unlock the door for you."

Kim wrapped his muscular arm around Granite's narrow waist. "Don't like put any um ideas into Van's, you know, head, Professor."

Temporarily looking away from the mirror, Granite said, "Nicky, Noah, Kim may have lost the bodybuilding competition, but he won a bigger prize."

Kim nodded proudly.

Granite announced, "Kim and I are engaged."

Our jaws dropped to our patent leather shoes. Noah's voice cracked. "To be married?"

Granite ran a thick hand through his gelled hair. "That's right. Kim is going to make an honest man out of me." He placed his pumped-up arm on Kim's V-shaped back. "After Kim takes his course equivalency tests and graduates early, that is."

"And um after Van like signs the, you know, prenuptial agreement," said Kim with a kiss to Granite's spray-tanned cheek.

Noah and I wished them well, then joined Jimmy Saline, Mack Heath, and Sue Heath nearby. Sue looked smashing in a form-fitting white velvet dress. Jimmy and Mack seemed like a tree trunk next to a branch in brown suits with green shirts.

Noah said, "Congratulations again on winning the competition, Mack."

"Thank you, Professor." After kissing his intended, Mack said, "A talent scout at the competition offered me a professional contract, but he understood when I postponed it a year until Jimmy graduates."

Jimmy looked like a glow stick. "All my dreams came true." He smiled. "And, Professor, my little problem is solved."

"How's that?" I asked, recalling Jimmy's concern about Mack's secret request.

Mack wrapped his strapping arm around Jimmy's emaciated torso. "Jimmy and I are going to be married! I thought winning the bodybuilding contest was a high, but when Jimmy finally said yes, I hit the ceiling."

Jimmy rested his head on Mack's strong shoulder. "I thought my parents back in the Amish country would be upset, but they were totally cool about it."

"After I had a long phone conversation with them." Sue kissed her son and future son-in-law.

Shayla Johnson (decked out in a silver lamé gown) linked her arm through Sue's. "And after I threatened to tell the neighbors that Jimmy's folks drive around their neighborhood in a Buick after midnight."

We all laughed. "Congratulations, guys," Noah and I said in unison.

"Thanks, Professors," Jimmy and Mack responded in unison.

"Will you and Mom be getting engaged next, Shayla?" asked Mack with a wink at his mother.

Sue and Shayla looked at one another and giggled like sorority sisters with a secret (try saying that three times fast).

I noticed Manuello standing in a corner of the room. I nudged Noah and we excused ourselves to join him.

"Nice of you to come, Detective Manuello," said Noah.

"Martin Anderson is a credit to the college and the community. I wouldn't miss it," he said.

"For once I agree with you, Detective," I said.

Manuello rubbed his wide nose. "It seems that we have even more than that in common, Police Officer *Dick Danghammer*?"

"Time to make my speech." I hurried to the front of the room, stood behind the podium, and called for everyone's attention. Once the audience was seated, I stood behind the microphone and began my speech. The audience members nodded, laughed, and applauded in all the right places as I celebrated Martin's numerous achievements at Treemeadow College over the last forty years, including creating courses, grants, and scholarships, and serving as department head. Closing the speech, I said, "And on a personal note, thank you, Martin, for being my mentor, department head, and best friend. And thank you and Ruben for being role models to me and to Noah. Like Tree and Meadow before you, you both paved the way, and Noah and I humbly follow in your footsteps."

I made my way back to my table, where Martin and I embraced amidst ecstatic cheers from the audience. Then Martin moved to the podium, and tearfully thanked me and all in attendance. It was good for my soul to see someone who has worked so hard for so long finally given his due. I also reveled in the fact that Martin was enjoying the evening so much, and he was able to share it with the longtime love of his life. My eyes filled with moisture, and I excused myself to get a bit of air on the balcony off the cafeteria. Wiping my eyes, I smelled the familiar scent of strawberries, and rested my head on the comforting shoulder of the man I adored.

"Great job on the speech." Noah kissed the top of my head.

Looking out at the gray mountains in the distance, I said, "I meant every word."

"I know."

Our eyes met.

"Looking at Martin and Ruben, Jimmy and Mack, and even Granite and Kim, makes me want to—"

Noah placed his smooth finger over my lips.

Undaunted, I said, "You are my life, my home, my family, I—"

I watched in shock as Noah bent down on one knee. "Nicky, you are the love of my life, the perfect partner I have been longing to meet. Now that I've found you, I want to be with you, forever. Will you consider being my husband?"

My heart sped out of control, like my love for Noah. "But I thought you didn't want to talk about this."

He rose and kissed the tears on my cheeks. "I wanted to wait until we caught the murderer, and until we were alone." Noah added with a kiss to my hand, "And *I* wanted to ask *you*. Do you mind?"

"Do I mind!" I felt as if I could touch the stars shining brightly above us. "I can't believe it. I just can't believe it."

"Are you going to say yes?"

I threw my arms around the man I cherished more than life itself. "Yes, yes. I want to marry you!"

Noah exhaled. "I was worried there for a minute."

"Get over here." I pulled Noah in close to my chest.

"I love you, Nicky Abbondanza."

"I love you, Noah Oliver."

As we looked out at the bronze statues of Tree and his lover Meadow, I held Noah in my welcoming arms, and we kissed under a shooting star.

# About the Author

Bestselling author **Joe Cosentino** was voted Favorite LGBT Mystery, Humorous, and Contemporary Author of the Year by the readers of Divine Magazine for *Drama Queen*. He also wrote the other novels in the Nicky and Noah mystery series: *Drama Muscle, Drama Cruise, Drama Luau, Drama Detective, Drama Fraternity, Drama Castle, Drama Dance*; the Dreamspinner Press novellas: *In My Heart/An Infatuation & A Shooting Star*, the Bobby and Paolo Holiday Stories: *A Home for the Holidays/The Perfect Gift/The First Noel, The Naked Prince and Other Tales from Fairyland*; the Cozzi Cove series: *Cozzi Cove: Bouncing Back, Cozzi Cove: Moving Forward, Cozzi Cove: Stepping Out, Cozzi Cove: New Beginnings, Cozzi Cove: Happy Endings* (NineStar Press); and the Jana Lane mysteries: *Paper Doll, Porcelain Doll, Satin Doll, China Doll, Rag Doll* (The Wild Rose Press). He has appeared in principal acting roles in film, television, and theatre, opposite stars such as Bruce Willis, Rosie O'Donnell, Nathan Lane, Holland Taylor, and Jason Robards. Joe is currently Chair of the Department/Professor at a college in upstate New York and is happily married. Joe was voted 2nd Place Favorite LGBT Author of the Year in Divine Magazine's Readers' Choice Awards, and his books have received numerous Favorite Book of the Month Awards and Rainbow Award Honorable Mentions.

## Connect with this author on social media

**Web site:** http://www.JoeCosentino.weebly.com
**Facebook:** http://www.facebook.com/JoeCosentinoauthor
**Twitter:** https://twitter.com/JoeCosen
**Amazon:** http://Author.to/JoeCosentino
**Goodreads:** https://www.goodreads.com/author/show/4071647.Joe_Cosentino

# And don't miss any of the Nicky and Noah mysteries by Joe Cosentino

## DRAMA QUEEN

It could be curtains for college theatre professor Nicky Abbondanza. With dead bodies popping up all over campus, Nicky must use his drama skills to figure out who is playing the role of murderer before it is lights out for Nicky and his colleagues. Complicating matters is Nicky's huge crush on Noah Oliver, a gorgeous assistant professor in his department, who may or may not be involved with Nicky's cocky graduate assistant and is also the top suspect for the murders! You will be applauding and shouting Bravo for Joe Cosentino's fast-paced, side-splittingly funny, edge-of-your-seat, delightfully entertaining novel. Curtain up!

Winner of *Divine Magazine*'s Readers' Poll Awards as Favorite LGBT Mystery, Crime, Humorous, and Contemporary novel of 2015!

## DRAMA MUSCLE

It could be lights out for college theatre professor Nicky Abbondanza. With dead bodybuilders popping up on campus, Nicky, and his favorite colleague/life partner Noah Oliver, must use their drama skills to figure out who is taking down pumped up musclemen in the Physical Education building before it is curtain down for Nicky and Noah. Complicating matters is a visit from Noah's parents from Wisconsin, and Nicky's suspicion that Noah may be hiding more than a cut, smooth body. You will be applauding and shouting Bravo for Joe Cosentino's fast-paced, side-splittingly funny, edge-of-your-seat entertaining second novel in this delightful series. Curtain up and weights up!

2015-2016 Rainbow Award Honorable Mention

## Drama Cruise

Theatre professors and couple, Nicky Abbondanza and Noah Oliver, are going overboard as usual, but this time on an Alaskan cruise, where dead college theatre professors are popping up everywhere from the swimming pool to the captain's table. Further complicating matters are Nicky's and Noah's parents as surprise cruise passengers, and Nicky's assignment to direct a murder mystery dinner theatre show onboard ship. Nicky and Noah will need to use their drama skills to figure out who is bringing the curtain down on vacationing theatre professors before it is lights out for the handsome couple. You will be applauding and shouting Bravo for Joe Cosentino's fast-paced, side-splittingly funny, edge-of-your-seat entertaining third novel in this delightful series. Curtain up and ship ahoy!

## Drama Detective

Theatre professor Nicky Abbondanza is directing *Sherlock Holmes, the Musical* in a professional summer stock production at Treemeadow College, co-starring his husband and theatre professor colleague, Noah Oliver, as Dr. John Watson. When cast members begin toppling over like hammy actors at a curtain call, Nicky dons Holmes' persona onstage and off. Once again Nicky and Noah will need to use their drama skills to figure out who is lowering the street lamps on the actors before the handsome couple get half-baked on Baker Street. You will be applauding and shouting Bravo for Joe Cosentino's fast-paced, side-splittingly funny, edge-of-your-seat entertaining fifth novel in this delightful series. Curtain up, the game is afoot!

*Coming soon:*

## DRAMA FRATERNITY

Theatre professor Nicky Abbondanza is directing *Tight End Scream Queen*, a slasher movie filmed at Treemeadow College's football fraternity house, co-starring his husband and theatre professor colleague, Noah Oliver. When young hunky cast members begin fading out with their scenes, Nicky and Noah will once again need to use their drama skills to figure out who is sending the quarterback, jammer, wide receiver, and more to the cutting room floor before Nicky and Noah hit the final reel. You will be applauding and shouting Bravo for Joe Cosentino's fast-paced, side-splittingly funny, edge-of-your-seat entertaining sixth novel in this delightful series. Lights, camera, action, frat house murders!

## DRAMA CASTLE

Theatre professor Nicky Abbondanza is directing a historical film at a castle in Scotland, co-starring his spouse, theatre professor Noah Oliver, and their son Taavi. When historical accuracy disappears along with hunky men in kilts, Nicky and Noah will once again need to use their drama skills to figure out who is pitching residents of Conall Castle off the drawbridge and into the moat, before Nicky and Noah land in the dungeon. You will be applauding and shouting Bravo for Joe Cosentino's fast-paced, side-splittingly funny, edge-of-your-seat entertaining seventh novel in this delightful series. Take your seats. The curtain is going up on steep cliffs, ancient turrets, stormy seas, misty moors, malfunctioning kilts, and murder!

## Drama Dance

Theatre professor Nicky Abbondanza is back at Treemeadow College directing their Nutcracker Ballet co-starring his spouse, theatre professor Noah Oliver, their son Taavi, and their best friend and department head, Martin Anderson. With muscular dance students and faculty in the cast, the Christmas tree on stage isn't the only thing rising. When cast members drop faster than their loaded dance belts, Nicky and Noah will once again need to use their drama skills to figure out who is cracking the Nutcracker's nuts, trapping the Mouse King, and being cavalier with the Cavalier, before Nicky and Noah end up stuck in the Land of the Sweets. You will be applauding and shouting Bravo for Joe Cosentino's fast-paced, side-splittingly funny, edge-of-your-seat entertaining eighth novel in this delightful series. Take your seats. The curtain is going up on the Fairy—Sugar Plum that is, clumsy mice, malfunctioning toys, and murder!

Made in the USA
Las Vegas, NV
01 September 2021